POWER AND ATTITUDE

POWER AND ATTITUDE
THE HERO PROPHECY
BOOK ONE

MICHAEL ANDERLE

DON'T MISS OUR NEW RELEASES

Join the LMBPN email list to be notified of new releases and special promotions (which happen often) by following this link:

http://lmbpn.com/email/

This book is a work of fiction. All of the characters, organizations, and events portrayed in this novel are either products of the author's imagination or are used fictitiously. Sometimes both.

Copyright © 2024 LMBPN Publishing
Cover Art by https://fantasybookdesign.com
Cover copyright © LMBPN Publishing
A Michael Anderle Production

LMBPN Publishing supports the right to free expression and the value of copyright. The purpose of copyright is to encourage writers and artists to produce the creative works that enrich our culture.

The distribution of this book without permission is a theft of the author's intellectual property. If you would like permission to use material from the book (other than for review purposes), please contact support@lmbpn.com. Thank you for your support of the author's rights.

LMBPN Publishing
2375 E. Tropicana Avenue, Suite 8-305
Las Vegas, Nevada 89119 USA

Version 1.00, August 2024
eBook ISBN: 979-8-88878-855-4
Print ISBN: 979-8-89354-352-0

THE POWER AND ATTITUDE TEAM

Thanks to the Beta Readers
Kelly O'Donnell, John Ashmore, Rachel Beckford, Mary Morris

Thanks to the JIT Readers
Christopher Gilliard
Veronica Stephan-Miller
Deb Mader
Sean Kesterson
Dorothy Lloyd
Dave Hicks
Diane L. Smith
Peter Manis
Zacc Pelter
Jan Hunnicutt
Paul Westman
Angel LaVey

Editor
SkyFyre Editing Team

CHAPTER ONE

<u>March 5, 2036, Sonoran Baja Hunter-Tourist Rally Bivouac, Sonoran Desert, New Baja Republic</u>

Frontloading the new death threats he received every morning made Trev's day more efficient. He chuckled at the thought as he skimmed the text on the tablet, which awaited his biometric signature via a fingerprint. A frowning official sat at a long plastic table, tapping his fingers on the top.

Trev couldn't blame him for looking annoyed. He felt for the poor guy. The stale air of the enrollment tent and the long lines would have gotten to him too if he had to sit in there all day.

Four small tables held the registration tablets, and four lines of participants snaked out of the tent. Most people stared at their phones as they waited for their turn. Some chatted with other people in line. Rough-looking men and women swept the others with stern looks, ready to start the event with psychological warfare.

This was the main site registration for the 2036

Sonoran Baja Hunter-Tourist Rally. Trev had read about the race for years and wanted to participate, even if it was outside his racing background and skill set.

The logistics of running a three-day rally event paired with monster hunting in the Sonoran Desert must have been staggering. He was happy that he only needed to worry about driving and killing monsters.

"A full waiver for the event organizers for any indemnity," Trev quoted from the tablet, "related to participant death, dismemberment, along with any and all injuries, minor or otherwise." He laughed. "That's redundant, don't you think? If you won't get in trouble for getting us killed, why would you be in trouble for getting us hurt?"

"Hurry up and read and sign. We have a long line." The official sighed. He shared a pained look with the officials at the other tables processing their participants.

"When it is practical and safe for relevant staff, the event organizers," Trev continued, "will make a good-faith effort attempt to rescue participants if they cannot, for whatever reason, continue the race, but the event organizers and onsite staff offer no guarantees of successful retrieval or treatment, especially in incidents occurring in the presence of unculled monsters or armed criminals on the scene.

"Please note that for the purposes of this waiver, any superpower capable of harming a person or damaging equipment and vehicles is equivalent to a conventional weapon for determining if a threat is considered armed. There is no power level required for this clause."

That made sense. Although some people wore them, the organizers didn't require helmets since the injuries would not be their fault under New Baja Republic law. A race involving people fighting monsters inherently carried a risk of getting hurt. Despite that, Trev still planned to wear a helmet. He also had a secret solution that would save people in the event of a crash.

The official grunted. "Congrats, kid. You know how to read. Am I supposed to be impressed? I don't have all day. Can we hurry it up with the signing, please?"

Trev killed the response that he was twenty-one and not a kid and went with his second instinct. "This is so broad that it can mean anything. It's funny, is all. Can't a man have a morning laugh?"

The official shrugged. "This isn't an event for people who like it safe. It's too late to back out now if you want your entry fee refunded. You should have read it all before you signed up for the rally."

"Nah. I'm good." Trev grinned. "I was excited to see it in print just before the race. The threats of death and dismemberment really bring it home. You know what I'm saying?"

The official sighed. "I wish you'd say you'd sign."

Trev put his finger on the fingerprint scanner in the corner of the tablet. "It's been a while since I've been able to cut loose, and in this, I'm getting paid to cut loose against monsters. Damn! This is going to be fun."

"I'm sure you're the fastest driver ever and a real badass," the official offered and rolled his eyes. He picked up a second tablet and handed it to a dangerous-looking man decked out in scars and an impractical number of chains. "Read through it all, please. A biometric signature is required. We can get a retinal scanner if you don't have fingerprints due to injury or baseline mutation. If that's a problem, we'll discuss alternatives. Please be aware that the rally organization staff will not guarantee your ability to participate if your biometrics deviate too much from baseline human standards."

Mr. Chains grunted and took the tablet. He glanced at the card hanging on the lanyard around Trev's neck. "You're a Wave Two driver?" His deep voice matched his image. "You sure that's a good idea, kid? All the fast guys go straight through in Wave One, which means all the monsters go after Wave Two, pissed off because they couldn't catch an easy meal. Rookies should stick to Wave Three and get a feel for things with fewer monsters. It gives you a taste of what the rally can be without getting you killed your first time out."

"The whole point is, there are more monsters in Wave Two." Trev shrugged. "A monster-hunting rally isn't fun if you avoid all the monsters. Otherwise, I would have found a traditional rally to drive in."

"Every year, rookies get killed thinking they're hot shit. They think their weak-ass power will save 'em from the worst monsters out there." Mr. Chains ran his finger over a scar that ran across his forehead. "I got this one my first year. Trust me, kid, throwing a fireball or making plants strangle a man don't mean much out in the Sonoran Desert. The Republic only allows this race because they don't have enough hero teams to keep the monsters in check. Don't kid yourself. It's one step down from war."

"They should be happy I'm here." Trev shot him a merry grin. "I'll clear out any monsters I see. My co-driver and I will cleanse the desert for the Republic."

Two chains peeled off the man and undulated back and forth above him like metal snakes ready to strike. "What's your power, kid?"

"Nothing in the rules says I have to tell anyone."

The official cleared his throat. "Please note that brawling will get you a penalty. Killing will disqualify you and be reported to the Republic authorities for bounty consideration." He delivered the warning with all the enthusiasm of a man who'd rather be elsewhere. He glanced at a uniformed man holding a rifle in the corner of the tent.

"We're not fighting." Trev held up his hands. "Just chatting. All friendly, me and Mr. Snake Chains." He checked Mr. Chain's lanyard. "Sorry, man. I'm driving in the trucks category."

Mr. Chains' face contorted. "What's that got to do with anything? Why are you sorry, kid?"

"You're in the cars category. I'm in trucks. I won't be there to save you when the monsters eat you. Different times, you know?" Trev fingerprinted the last form and handed it to the official before waving at Mr. Chains. "Don't die on me. Next year, race trucks, and we can place real bets against each other."

Mr. Chains chuckled. "It takes more than attitude to survive and a hell of a lot more than attitude to win this race."

"Good!" Trev departed the tent with a wave. "I've got more than attitude, plus this handsome face. It'd be disappointing if it was too easy."

The dimness of the tent gave way to the bright, clear blue of the sky outside and the thick crowds of people walking and talking. The Sonoran Baja Hunter-Tourist Rally bivouac was a temporary tent city that popped up in the desert and moved with the race each day. They even had a field hospital and a food tent. Vendors offered everything a driver might need, like parts and fuel or batteries, depending on a vehicle's power train. Almost every standard caliber and size of small arms ammunition was available for the violently inclined. Trev had spotted one vendor selling grenades and RPGs. A handful sold energy cells, though he hadn't seen anybody carrying laser weapons.

Given the onsite price gouging, experienced and/or budget-conscious participants showed up with their own fuel, weapons, and ammo. That didn't stop the vendors from making a huge profit each year. Not every rookie knew what they were getting into when they drove into the dangerous, less-controlled parts of the New Baja Republic. This territory stretched through what used to be the southwestern United States and parts of northern Mexico before the Big Change tore the world apart and reset human civilization.

Trev hadn't lived in the Republic for long, and mostly in Tucson. He hadn't even made it to the capital of San Diego. He had no sense of whether the new country reflected much of the older culture.

A woman sporting golden wings made of light floated above a pair of bikes, tilting her camera as she tried to get a picture of the two helmeted riders waving from below.

Trev bet her power didn't need the wings. He'd run into many people who tried to make their power seem flashier and more spectacular than it was.

"The sun's glinting too much," she yelled.

One of the riders waved. "Just fly higher."

The woman ascended. Her light wings didn't flap, supporting Trev's theory that they were for show. She turned her phone, took the pictures, and dropped toward the ground. Her movement stopped just before she landed, slowing to a gentle descent for the last few feet.

Moving further through the crowd, Trev spotted a scowling man wearing a bulletproof vest over a skintight black boost suit that covered everything up to his neck. The word SECURITY was emblazoned in bright yellow letters on the front of his vest, with SEGURIDAD written on the back. The man glared at the woman who'd been flying.

Having security with boost suits proved that the race's organizers had deep pockets, which guaranteed the prize money. The expensive boost suits enhanced physical capabilities independent of a person's power.

Trev was unarmed, but many in the crowd carried visible weapons, primarily pistols in belt or shoulder holsters. Sheathed blades were about as rare as water bottles. Rifles strapped over shoulders or backs were also common.

The occasional glow from someone's skin hinted at the nature of their powers. Even unarmed, many of these people would be classified as armed and dangerous, according to the event's rules. Nobody hung out in a monster-infested wilderness without some means of protection, technological or empowered.

A trio of robed, masked people passed him, and a furry tail peeked out from under one of the robes. They must have mutations that left them looking less than what passed for baseline human.

Trev, a fit, handsome young man with brown hair, didn't stand out in any way. That made it easy to wander through the crowd unnoticed toward his truck and the white canvas canopy covering the metal table and chairs that comprised his team's workspace.

He smiled as his truck came into view. The flat-faced old vehicle and its dented, modest trailer didn't look as sexy as many cars or bikes participating in other categories. Still, the ten-ton beast and its massive wheels would get him and his co-driver through the Sonoran Desert without trouble, no matter how many monsters they encountered.

His smile disappeared. A small crowd had gathered on the side of the tent, blocking his view of his co-driver/mechanic, his best friend Jack.

Three scowling men in similar-style leather jackets surrounded Jack. They all wore gun belts, but their weapons remained holstered. That only gave Trev small comfort. One of the thugs poked Jack in the chest. Some people in the gathered crowd laughed.

Trev shook his head and made his way toward Jack. He didn't need to hear what they were saying to understand the problem. Despite the coveralls, the goggles over Jack's eyes, and the gloves concealing his clawlike nails, his outfit didn't hide his green scaly skin or the long tail poking out of the back of his coveralls.

One of the thugs pushed Jack again. "Hey, freak, the race hasn't started yet. You're supposed to be out in the desert threatening us. I don't get any points for killing a monster before the race."

Jack's long tongue flicked out. "Please leave."

"Why should I listen to a freak?" the thug asked. He looked at the crowd with a grin. "This lizard thinks he can boss me around. Isn't that hilarious?"

His buddies laughed. That annoyed Trev far less than the rest of the crowd chuckling. A man near the back of the crowd frowned and looked around for a moment before stepping away.

Trev shoved his way through the crowd, not bothering to offer apologies and meeting every frown with a death glare. That helped him pass through quickly. When the thug tried to shove Jack again, Trev lunged forward and caught his hand.

"That's enough," Trev narrowed his eyes. "You're messing with my co-driver and mechanic. I don't appreciate you trying to sabotage my race."

The thug yanked his arm back. "You should keep your pets leashed if you don't want people worried about them biting 'em and giving 'em rabies."

"The only one here acting like an animal is you." Trev stared at him. "Huh."

"What, asshole?"

"I thought untreated syphilis made you look messed up before it fried your brain."

The crowd laughed. Jack backed away from the table.

The thug silenced the crowd with a glare before scoffing at Trev. "My boss says we've got to keep things quiet until the race is over, so I don't blame you for not knowing your place, boy. That doesn't mean I've got extra patience. Watch what you say if you want to keep your face looking like a human's and not a freak's."

"Nobody told you to come over to our space and be an asshole," Trev shot back. "That's on you."

Wearing an evil grin, the man held his arm out sideways. An ice sword formed hilt-first in his hand.

"There we are." Trev shook his head.

"You want to square up like a big man to protect your pet lizard? Fine, bitch. The rules say as long we don't kill nobody, we're golden."

"You technically get a time penalty," Jack offered in a near-whisper. He shrugged when the ice swordsman glared at him. "Well, you do. If you're going to fight, you should do it with full awareness of what it might cost you."

Trev nodded. "My buddy's right. I'm here to race and kill monsters. If you've got so much energy, you should save it for out there."

"You scared, bitch?"

"I'm only scared of hurting you so badly that they give me too big a time penalty to overcome."

The swordsman sneered. "You got any real powers, or are you just another freak like your friend?" His gaze dipped. "Let me guess. You're all scales and lizard under those clothes. You just have a normal face and hands. That's almost worse than him." He nodded at Jack. "At least that freak doesn't hide what he is."

Trev gritted his jaw. His hands tightened into fists.

"Don't do it, Trev," Jack cautioned. "He's not worth it."

Trev glared at the thug. "Hey, man, I know the mirror can be harsh, but you keep the dream alive. There's somebody out there for everybody, even dumb syphilitic assholes like you." He offered a huge smile. "You almost bring a tear to my eye. You're an inspiration."

The swordsman growled. "If I didn't have to race, I'd gut you where you stand, you cocky little shit. This isn't even about your freak pet anymore. It's about you and me."

Jack put his hand on Trev's shoulder. "We need the money."

"I won't kill him. I promise."

"Oh." Jack nodded. "Feel free to kick him in the balls once for me."

"Gotcha."

One of the other thugs cast a nervous glance at the growing crowd. "It's not worth it, Will. We need to stick to what the boss said. We're not here to make trouble. I think somebody went to get Security."

"I don't care about Security. Don't worry. I know the rules." Will waved his sword. "I won't kill the bitch. I'll just make him look as ugly as his friend."

Trev sighed and shook Jack's hand off his shoulder, then motioned him to the truck. "This is about both of us now." He cracked his knuckles and motioned for Will to attack. That way, he could claim self-defense. "Come on, Mirror Breaker. If you're going to do it, do it. Otherwise, I've got tons to do before the race."

"Yeah. They're right. You're not worth it." Will scoffed and turned around. He lowered his sword before spinning and thrusting it at Trev's face.

CHAPTER TWO

While Trev lacked formal martial arts training, years of beating up assholes who messed with Jack or caused neighborhood trouble in the post-Big Change years had granted Trev a practical street-level education in the fine art of ass-kicking. He'd long since learned that the start was the most critical part of the fight. A predictable enemy was an avoidable enemy, regardless of their powers.

Having expected the asshole swordsman to go for a cheap shot, Trev dodged the stab. He jumped back to avoid the follow-up slash, ending up by the table and a chair.

"What a brave man." Trev clapped. "Acts all tough, then tries a sucker punch." He frowned. "Sucker stab? Sucker sword?"

"Shut your mouth, bitch," Will shouted. He held up the sword. "If you would have kept your mouth shut and apologized to me, this could have gone down differently. Now, you're going to feel the pain because that's the only way people like you learn."

"Funny, that." Trev kept his stance loose and raised his

fists. "'Cause here I was thinking all you had to do was shut your mouth and apologize to my friend. Or, you could have never come here to begin with. I don't need a personal apology. Isn't that generous?"

Using his powers would make things easier, but Trev's opponent had friends. The more they knew about Trev, the more trouble he might be in if they showed up later with reinforcements, looking for trouble. Trev had learned that lesson in brawls back home.

More to the point, a flashy display of his power would go against what he had been trying to do since he'd left NEUS, which was to conceal his actual ability, both because of what his parents had taught him and the harsh reality of the current world.

Mystery could be a person's most potent weapon. Billions of humans on the planet meant there could be billions of different powers, from joke-level to lethal and terrifying. Playing the odds meant the average idiot in the street wouldn't be able to kill a person with their power, but anyone who wanted to live a long time had to remember that they could run into a deadly threat who looked normal until he turned an opponent's bones to jelly with a touch.

Mindful of that, Trev used the table to keep out of Will's reach. The swordsman snarled and lunged again, only to miss.

"Stay where I can nail you, bitch," Will growled.

"Are you seriously telling me to stay still so you can hit me?" Trev asked, laughing. "Does that usually work for you? No wonder you're terrible at this. I bet you're a big hit with chicks, too. 'Go out with me *now!*'"

Will took the bait and ran around the side of the table. Trev grabbed a metal folding chair and swung it at Will to parry the ice sword.

The impact confirmed it was far more than a glorified icicle. The ice blade sliced through a chair leg with ease. However, the appearance of the metal chair caught Will off-guard, and Trev managed to slam the chair into the swordsman's chest.

Will grimaced and jumped back. "You're going to pay for that."

"That sword is sharper than it looks." Trev chuckled and raised the chair pieces like awkward clubs. "You're already trying to cut and stab me, so we're past the cheap threats stage. I'm not going to let you hurt me, even if I have to beat the shit out of you."

Will held his chest with his free hand. Trev never paid attention to the high-level talk by scientists and officials about the potential upper limits of superpowers. The empowered populace continued to defy what scientists thought they understood about the universe and the physics underlying reality. It'd take far more than the one decade since the Big Change for science to catch up with reality.

The bottom line was that Trev didn't care to understand it. He only cared about understanding the immediate tactical reality and threat of a superpower in a fight. He recalled something his mother had told him long ago. *When a hero team goes on a mission, they can never be sure their intel is correct. The first thing they do is establish the limits of an opponent's power.*

How often can it be used? What's the scope and range? Even an AA-ranked threat might be easy to take down if their power only lets them attack and not defend. Everybody has a weakness. It's just a matter of finding and exploiting it.

Will growled and sliced halfway through the table. "You're next. If I cut your arm off, all I have to do is make sure you don't die, and I can still race."

"That's going to be a big penalty," Trev replied. "What's the point of racing if you'll come in last with all the penalties? Are you just here to hunt monsters?" He nodded at the table. "I'm going to be generous and not make you pay for that." He flourished the chair halves in a faux display of skill that earned chuckles from the crowd. "Now I'm going to take you down before you tear up everything I own."

He flung one chair half at Will, then the other. Will, as predicted, sliced back and forth. Trev waited for his chance and charged the man before the backswing. He ducked, smashed his fist into the man's stomach, and introduced his knee to Will's crotch as per Jack's request.

Will groaned and doubled over. Trev yanked his head down and slammed his knee into Will's face, the loud crunch satisfying. Will's nose gushed blood, and he staggered back, waving his sword in front of him. Trev stayed on Will's flank and kidney-punched him before jumping back to avoid his clumsy counterattack swing.

Before the fighting started, Trev had worried about being forced to use his powers in front of a crowd. Will would need to perform much better to make that probable, and his friends hadn't made any moves. That was a good sign.

"You're too dependent on your power." Trev snorted. "You underestimated me."

"I'll kill you."

"Then you'd be disqualified, but don't worry. I'm almost done kicking your ass, so it's not going to be much of a risk soon. Forgetting that, you know what your real problem is?" Trev snagged a chair half from the ground. "Besides being a dumbass who picked a fight he didn't need to and didn't walk away when he had more than one chance?"

Will screamed like a feral animal and lifted his sword. "I don't care anymore. I'm going to gut you. You're dead."

Trev flung the chair half at the charging man. Will swung early, not realizing the chair half was flying toward his abdomen, not his chest. His blade whiffed over the metal, and it nailed him in the stomach.

He stumbled forward again, head down, making him an easy target for Trev to swing the other chair half into the side of his head, knocking out a couple of teeth. Will fell to one knee and gushed blood from his mouth.

Trev wrinkled his nose at the spray of blood. "Damn. Jack's going to make me clean that up. You've been screaming like a rabid coyote. You up to date on your shots, Will? Have you had your mange and heartworm shots lately?"

Will's friends' hands inched toward their guns. Trev needed to finish this before things got out of hand and he was forced to display his power. One of the reasons he didn't carry a gun was to avoid this type of escalation. He sprinted forward to deliver a powerful final kick to Will's face. Will's head snapped back, and he slumped to the ground.

His thug friends narrowed their eyes and exchanged looks, then went for their guns.

"That's enough!" someone shouted.

A high-pitched whine accompanied a distortion in the air that flew through the crowd and nailed one of the thugs. His eyes rolled back in his head and he pitched forward, dropping his gun. The other thug put his hands up. Trev matched him.

The boost suit-wearing security guard stomped through the crowd, his fingers pressed together and his hand held in front of him, rapidly vibrating while producing a soft buzz. Two men with rifles flanked him.

The security guard's hand stopped vibrating. He grabbed the semi-conscious Will by the scruff of his shirt and yanked him up. "I swear I've seen you before, asshole, but where?" He nodded at the still-conscious thug. "Processing more than one of you is too much damned work. Drag your other buddy back to your tent. Don't come back here, or we'll dump all of you numbnuts in the desert and let the monsters have a pre-race snack."

The thug nodded at the guard and hooked his arms under his friend's armpits to drag him away while glaring. Trev kept his arms up the whole time.

He was proud of himself. He'd beaten a man who was using a power without employing his power. That proved his fighting skills had improved since he'd left home and moved to the Republic.

The security guard looked past Trev and stared at Jack lingering by the truck. "Self-defense isn't against the rules, and we appreciate your restraint since I didn't hear anything about you using powers."

Trev lowered his arms. "I *didn't* use my power. Ask anyone here."

The guard looked around the crowd. Most people looked away. A handful nodded their agreement with Trev.

"Those other guys started it," a woman called from the crowd. "The one on the ground tried to stab him after saying he'd leave."

"We've got drones." The guard pointed at a drone hovering high in the sky. "It helps when people are honest." He frowned and nodded at Jack. "Flaunting him is bound to cause trouble. Not everyone likes mutants. That might not be fair, son, but it's true."

"That sounds like a 'them' problem, not an 'us' problem," Trev replied.

The guard grunted. "It becomes my problem when people attack you, and I have to stop them. There better not be more trouble with you two, or next time, we're dragging you in as well, self-defense or not." He flung Will at the feet of the guards with him. "Take him to Medical. I'll talk to him when he wakes up." The guard kept staring at Jack. "You got anything else to say?"

"My friend didn't do anything but stand there," Trev tightened his hands into fists. "Last time I checked, the Republic doesn't have visible mutation laws."

"I don't give two shits about the Republic's laws. I care about keeping order in this camp during the next few days when half you drivers are scum."

"Is there a race organization rule that says he has to stay out of sight?" Trev asked.

The security guard's nostrils flared. "You ever heard of unwritten rules? He's not the only mutant around here. Ask yourself why you're the only one having trouble."

Trev folded his arms, remembering the trio in the robes

and the furry tail. "Everybody's a mutant since the Big Change. Could you throw sonic stuns before, or whatever it is you did to take that dickhead out?"

"Whatever. I don't have time for this. I warned you. Next time, I won't be so nice." The security guard glared at the crowd. "Show's over. Disperse, or I'll make you disperse."

A mix of angry mutters and amused chuckles spread through the crowd. People checked Trev and Jack out one last time before wandering away from their pre-race entertainment.

The security guard waved and walked away. "Last piece of advice. You won't recruit a good tourist for the race with a mutant like that."

"You worry about keeping order, and I'll worry about my tourist," Trev called back.

"Don't say I didn't warn you."

CHAPTER THREE

Jack sighed and stepped away from the truck, his long, rough tongue flicking as he gathered the metal chair's pieces. "I should be able to weld these back together without much trouble. That guy almost did us a favor by using a weapon that made such clean cuts. It would have been way more annoying if you'd knocked somebody onto it, and it bent and broke."

Trev gestured at the table. "It's a good thing we only use metal tables and chairs, isn't it? Or you'd need to up your carpentry game."

Jack's shoulders slumped. "I'm sorry. It's all my fault. This wouldn't have happened if it wasn't for me."

"You've got nothing to be sorry for." Trev glared after the crowd. "You know I'll always have your back, right? You want to put a fist in somebody's face when that happens, I don't care. I could have found that guy in a pool of blood at your feet, and I wouldn't have asked you why. I would help you take down whoever else was out there. It's you and me against the world."

"I know, Trev." Jack lifted his goggles, revealing yellow eyes and vertically slitted pupils. He stared at Trev. "Would you really not stop to even ask if I had a reason to murder someone? What if it was a petty reason?"

Trev laughed. "Let's be real, Jack. Of the two of us, we both know who's more likely to end up with a dead guy at his feet and questions about how he ended up there. I'm far more likely to punch a guy because he looked at me the wrong way."

Jack lowered his goggles and looked away. "You've been talking like that more since we moved to the Republic."

"You've been regressing."

"I'm not regressing. I understand we're in a new environment, and our default assumptions won't always serve us well."

Trev scoffed. "When you let someone push you around, it encourages more people to do so."

"That's easy—" Jack shook his head. "I'm sorry."

"I get it. It's been tougher since we've moved to the Republic. It's not as stable as DC. We don't know many people, but remember who we are." Trev smacked his chest. "We'd both be dead if we were soft. It doesn't matter."

He motioned at the crowd. "I'll back you, no matter what or who it pisses off. I don't care if it's security, ice users with delusions of grandeur, or an asshole from a hero team. This isn't about who we know or who we expect to react well." He frowned. "If anything, we have to be more aggressive now. We don't have anyone to watch our backs anymore."

Jack carried the chair parts to the back of the trailer,

calling, "We both know how things would have turned out if I hit him first. I get where you're coming from, but we have to be practical."

Trev offered him a lopsided grin. "Yeah, we *do* know what would have happened, which is why I goaded him into hitting me." He walked over to Jack. "Self-defense and no punishment for me other than a warning."

Jack set the chair parts by the back of the trailer. "In other words, despite your big speech about standing up for myself, you made a calculated effort to avenge me in a way that would keep us out of trouble."

"That doesn't change anything I said," Trev insisted. "You want to take a bastard down, then do it."

Jack considered for a moment and nodded. "Thanks. Seeing you do that felt good, even if I know it will cause us trouble despite your scheme."

"Hey, what are friends for if not getting you out of trouble by causing more trouble?" Trev grinned. "Don't call it a scheme. That makes it sound like standing up for my friend is sketchy."

Jack headed toward the half-sliced table. "This was more trouble than we planned for. I'm surprised. It wasn't as bad in Tucson."

"Eh, that's a city. This isn't exactly the wasteland, but this hunter race wouldn't exist if this part of the Republic was under real control."

"True."

"We'll be okay." Trev slammed his fist into his palm. "I sent a message today. Everybody will understand what it means to mess with us, so they won't, not openly. It's like they say. When you get to a new place, you go up to the biggest guy and punch him in the face to establish dominance. That saves you trouble down the line."

Jack cocked his head to the side. "That's advice for prisons, Trev."

"It's good life advice in general."

"Punch the biggest man you see on your first day is good life advice?"

"Yep." Trev motioned around. "Most people here are angry and ready to hurt people and only respect a uniformed guy with weapons and authority. It's basically an open-air prison." He clapped his friend on the shoulder. "The important thing is, I got the satisfaction of kicking the guy's ass, and we wiggled out of the situation without any race penalties. I wouldn't have regretted it even if we did get penalties, but as far as I'm concerned, this was a complete and total win."

Jack frowned. He looked over his shoulder before moving closer and lowering his voice. "They were going to shoot you."

"We both know that wouldn't have mattered as long as I saw it coming."

"You said you didn't want to show your power."

Trev shrugged. "That's more for our protection than anything. The point is I had the situation under control from start to finish. I promised I wouldn't kill the bastard, and I didn't kill him." He scoffed. "All I did was break his nose and knock out a couple of teeth. I didn't even break his arm. He got off easy."

Jack nodded. "True. You've done far worse to people."

"He really, really had it coming."

"Also true. That doesn't change him being right about the race tourist. Is there anything in the rules about racing without recruiting one?"

"No." Trev scrubbed a hand down his face. "But just because an asshole says something doesn't mean we have to believe him."

"Judging by the crowd's reaction, he knows how people will respond better than we do," Jack suggested.

"Really?" Trev shook his head. "I don't think so. It was Will the Ice Dick and his buddies who screwed with you, not anybody else. Sure, the crowd's full of bloodthirsty assholes looking for a good fight, but if they all had problems with visible mutations, they would have joined in."

"What about the security guard?"

"He was pissed that he had to do his job. We won't have trouble finding a tourist for the race because of you. I guarantee it."

Jack squinted into the crowd. "I can wear a robe or a hood for the race. It'd make things easier. We need this money to get back to Square One. I don't want to be the reason we don't get it."

"Screw that, and screw that guard," Trev growled. "I'll kick the ass of everybody who participates in this race before I make you hide." He nodded at the truck. "Let's check on our baby. I don't think those guys were smart enough to distract us and do something to our gear, but looks can be deceiving."

Jack unlatched the trailer door and pushed it up. Dust billowed out. Tools hung from reinforced racks above the crates. A long metal gray container filled the bulk of the space. He gathered the chair halves and hopped into the trailer, then set them down against the wall.

"Is the secret weapon okay?" Trev asked, glancing at the regular weapons cases. They all looked untouched.

Jack circled the gray container. "Nobody's opened it." He looked at the chair pieces. "You don't think we made a mistake, do you?"

"By signing up for this race?" Trev shook his head. "Hell, no. Don't let it get to you, even if it's rougher than the races you're used to working support for. I expected other drivers to be rowdy. This is an all-terrain race through a monster-infested part of the Sonoran Desert. You kind of have to be crazy to want to participate. We might have another brawl or two before the end, but nothing serious."

"I meant that we made a mistake by leaving DC." Jack shrugged, then sighed. "I'm sorry."

"Stop saying you're sorry, Jack," Trev growled. "We moved to have a better life. Don't revert because we're in a new place." He slapped his chest. "You know how good it feels to make someone shut the hell up? It's the best feeling in the world, but even if you are telling me to screw off, no, I don't think we made a mistake leaving Washington. We both needed to start over, and flying halfway across the continent was a good way to do that without having to learn a new language. More Spanish might help, but you know what I mean."

"We had more connections back home. Even the people who didn't like us knew enough to leave us alone."

"Not really." Trev frowned. "We knew people here and there, but everyone who counted is gone." He knelt and opened a weapons crate to examine the rifles inside. "Moving to the Republic is better for both of us and signing up for the race was a stroke of genius. We'll win this rally to get the cash we need. It'll help us refine and test things, including improving the secret weapon, while we figure out our next move."

He closed the weapons crate and tapped the gray container with his boot. "By the way, test the roller system before the race starts. We need to make sure the weapon deploys far enough from the truck for this to work out."

"I'll do that later tonight," Jack agreed. "I'm serious about what I said."

Trev smiled at his friend. "Look, the truth is, the money from my parents was only going to go so far, and we had a limited chance to get the hell out of DC before it ran out." He gestured at himself and then at Jack. "We both needed to find a new way to live in an area where a government and 46P1 weren't going to breathe down our necks."

"Moving to the Southwest will do that for us?"

"You heard what people said in Tucson when we asked. The New Baja Republic doesn't like the New Eastern United States, but they're far enough apart that it's not like they will fight. It's the best situation for us."

Jack's tongue flicked. "There is a major 46P1 facility in San Diego. You're not worried about a corporate facility in the Republic's capital?"

Trev shrugged. "If I avoided every place that had ties to 46P1, I'd end up in the middle of nowhere. Like, I don't know, in Australia? I just didn't want them breathing down my neck in DC until we know more about my parents' warning." He wrapped his arm around Jack's shoulders. "Think about it, buddy. Can you think of a cooler way of earning money than clearing out monsters during a rally race? We're helping people while having a great time. We might even impress a pair of gorgeous chicks if we get lucky."

"That security guard wasn't wrong," Jack replied. "It was better in DC, but not by much. Many people won't want to ride with a freak and a mutant, including your imaginary gorgeous chicks."

"They're not imaginary. I've seen tons around here." Trev laughed. "Don't you go saying that crap about being a mutant. Remember…"

"Everybody's a mutant since the Big Change," Jack chanted in unison with Trev.

"Exactly." Trev pulled away.

Jack scoffed. "I'm not a kid anymore. Just because you believe that doesn't mean everybody else does."

"I live with you, so I'm the most important one. The rest of them can go jump on a cactus."

Trev knelt to open a crate and double-check the ammo inside. "If you think about it, the real freaks are people without any powers or changes. I've met far more people who look slightly different than people like that."

"We'll get stuck with a loser tourist," Jack muttered. "We won't get our pick. We'll get someone who'll bitch the entire time or throw up in the truck. Or they'll be gassy."

"It doesn't matter. Screw 'em if they've got a problem. I'll glare at them until they shut up, or we can mess with them and tell them you'll eat their fingers if they aren't quiet."

"Don't you think that'll make things worse?"

"Depends on who we're dealing with." Trev closed the ammo crate. "We'll need to double-check the truck and then some before the race in case Will's friends try to get revenge in a less obvious way. As for the tourists, let me worry about them. We'll get somebody, and even if we get no volunteers, we'll get a rando and bonus time. If it comes down to skipping the race or riding with us, I'm sure I can convince someone not to be an idiot."

"You sure?" Jack asked, his voice quiet. "Can you do that without threatening them?"

Trev shrugged. "I'll convince them…one way or another." He smiled. "I know we're still new to the Republic, but if you think about it, this is one of our first real problems."

"Not counting that monster pack that tried to eat us outside Tucson?"

Trev laughed. "Those don't count. We took them down."

"After they ate a tire," Jack noted. "What about those bikers?"

"I convinced them to back off."

"By shooting their leader in the face."

"It worked." Trev shrugged. "We didn't have to kill them all."

"What about—"

"The point is, we're getting used to a new country, and new situations in this new country require—" Trev hopped out of the trailer.

"You to bash a man's skull in with a metal chair," Jack finished.

"Exactly! I'm glad we're in sync on this." Trev peered into the distance. "I'm going to see about getting us a tourist, but we still have time. As for everything else, don't you worry. It's like I told you years ago. No matter what happens, I'll always have your back."

CHAPTER FOUR

Trev was toastier in his sleeping bag than he anticipated in the desert at night, even a landscape covered with shrubs and grasses rather than sand dunes. Jack snored quietly in his bag, lying on the other fold-down bed in the truck's cab. Despite the trouble earlier in the day, the rest had proceeded without incident, good or bad, including a conspicuous lack of tourists signing on to ride with their team.

A quiet grunt escaped Trev. He refused to believe his team couldn't land their required race passenger over something so petty as Jack looking like a lizard. Half the people filling the camp were so ugly they looked like animals. It wasn't even from mutation.

No reason to worry yet. They had another day before they got a random assignment. Even so, Trev had trouble imagining anything terrible happening because of a random assignment. If anything, they could use the bonus time that came with getting a rando.

Trev could keep anyone who joined them under control. He was confident about that.

He'd read the rules about their tourist passenger carefully more than once. If a tourist attempted to harm the driver or the co-driver, the team could leave them in the desert or kill them in self-defense.

Trev had been very careful not to display his powers in camp. Anyone who signed on with them, even if they'd been paid by Will to kill them, wouldn't do that since they didn't know what they'd be facing.

They had no reason to worry about entanglements from back east following them to the race. Trev didn't even know if there were entanglements that *wanted* to follow them. He yawned and closed his eyes. He needed to rest while he could. Jack had set the alarm on the truck. No thugs would get them in the middle of the night, and no one would be insane enough to blow them up with a missile or RPG and risk the wrath of the twitchy security guards.

Trev taking Will down without his power continued to pay dividends, but the encounter hadn't left him untouched. He drifted off to sleep with his grin twitching into a frown, dark memories poking at the core of his consciousness as his dreams recalled humanity's worst day.

June 12, 2026, Cleveland Park Neighborhood, Washington DC, United States of America

Eleven-year-old Trev groaned at the KO on the television and glared at the boy beside him. "Why are you so good at Street

Fighter VII? It just came out. Didn't you say you wouldn't play it until they added Cammy? Ryu isn't Cammy."

Jack rolled his pale blue eyes. "You're mad because all you can do is spam attacks."

"It's a strategy. It's called 'all attacks, all the time.'"

"It's called being bad at the game."

Trev scoffed. He took pride in his gaming abilities. It'd be one thing if he lost to an adult, but not a boy his age, even his best friend. He refused to accept that Jack was better than him, despite Jack kicking his butt at every fighting game they played.

"Keep talking, Cammy-lover," Trev muttered. "I'll get you."

Jack gave Trev a smug smile. "She's coming with the first Season Pass. I can't help it if I'm the King of Street Fighter and you suck at it. You know what they say…"

"If you say, 'get good,' I'll put you in a headlock until you have to call for your mom."

Jack laughed. "All I wanted to say is 'gg.'"

"Hey!" Trev shouted, waving a fist.

"Good game, bro!"

"Funny." Trev rolled his eyes. "We should be playing League of Legends. That's a real game. It takes strategy and skill."

"My mom won't let me play LoL because of what she saw on the screen that time I played with you. I told her it wasn't you saying it and that it was a queue-assigned rando, but she didn't care. No League, and no more Call of Duty."

"I didn't even know that curse existed before," Trev added reverently. "I haven't said it. You haven't said it." He giggled. "I can't think of it without laughing."

"She says those games are a bad influence."

"I say…"

A bright flash cut through the drapes from outside. Both boys turned toward the window.

"What was that?" Jack asked. "Do you think that kid down the street found more fireworks? You think he'll let us light some?"

Trev hopped up and flung the drapes open. He squinted, unsure of what he was seeing. "I don't think this is fireworks." *He ran to the front door with Jack in pursuit.*

"Mom," Jack shouted up the stairs, looking confused. "We're going outside."

"Stay out of the street," his mother called. "I'm going to finish watching my show."

The boys hurried out of the house, looking around.

"Whoa." *Trev ran to the edge of the lawn and stopped. He craned his neck up and gasped.* "Double whoa."

"Triple whoa," *Jack added.*

The rows of houses and small lawns of the neighborhood weren't any different than usual, but the heavens above offered newfound wonders. Ribbons of light in blues, greens, reds, and yellows filled the sky. The pulsating ribbons stretched from the top of the sky to the horizon like fingers of light from a giant grabbing the Earth.

"Is that the Northern Lights?" Trev asked.

Jack scoffed. "We don't get the Northern Lights here."

Trev glared at him. "That's not true. My dad said it happens once in a while."

"Okay, then." *Jack pointed at the sky.* "I don't think the Northern Lights look like that, and even if they do, you can't see them in the middle of the day. That's just stupid."

"You're stupid." *Trev tried to come up with a counterargument other than appealing to his father, but his school and* social media education hadn't prepared him for the subtle nuances of debating the Northern Lights with his best friend. "Yeah. Whatever. Sounds like something a Cammy-lover would say."

"That doesn't make any sense," Jack replied. "What does Cammy have to do with the Northern Lights?"

"I don't know. If it's not the Northern Lights, what is it?" Trev asked.

Jack shrugged. "I don't know."

A rumble filled the air. The boys looked at the ground to check.

"The ground's not moving," Trev muttered. "I don't think it's an earthquake."

"Have you ever felt an earthquake?"

"Not that I remember. My dad said there was one when I was a baby." Trev knelt and put his hand on the grass. "I feel something. That has to be an earthquake."

Jack nodded in eager agreement. "An earthquake makes more sense than the Northern Lights."

The rumble grew louder. Overlapping booms echoed in the distance.

Jack swallowed. "Do earthquakes sound like that?"

"I don't know."

He turned around and loosed the secret super-profanity he'd learned online. A jetliner flew overhead, smoke pouring from the engines and a hole in the side of the passenger cabin.

Jack screamed and pointed. It took Trev a moment to realize he wasn't screaming about the crash when something tumbled through the smoke from the hole—people. They fell, flailing through the air and dropping toward the ground.

Trev trembled. "W-we have to call 9-1-1." He looked away,

grateful that the plane's former passengers would not land in his neighborhood.

"I'm still not allowed to have a phone." Jack wrapped his arms around his shoulders and fell to his knees, shaking. "This isn't happening."

Terror froze the boys. The plane roared overhead, leaving a trail of smoke before crashing with a ground-shaking boom, the massive fireball from the explosion marking its demise far too close to dismiss. A large plume of smoke ascended, joining others in every direction.

Heart thundering, Trev pulled out his phone. Somebody in charge needed to know about this. He didn't have any signal.

"My phone." Trev's hand shook. "My phone's not working."

Jack's mother rushed out of the front door, wild-eyed and shaking. She jerked her head in the direction of the plane crash. "Come inside, boys. It's not safe."

"Mrs. Senna," Trev called. "A plane just—"

Jack collapsed, clutching his stomach, and screamed. He thrashed and kicked. "It hurts! It hurts!"

Trev gritted his teeth. His head throbbed. Jack had to be hurting more. Trev liked to tease him, but he wasn't a wimp. He wouldn't be acting like that unless he was in more pain than Trev was feeling.

Trev grunted and dropped to his knees beside Jack. He grabbed his friend's shoulders and tried to keep him from moving. "What's wrong?"

Mrs. Senna darted from the porch to the boys. She leaned over before yanking her arm back. "No, no, no. This can't be happening."

Jack's skin shifted from the pale pink of a boy who spent too much time indoors to an inhuman dark green, and his skin thickened into rough scales. His eyes changed, turning yellow, and his pupils stretched. His nails hardened and extended. The tip of a tail popped out of the back of his pants.

"No." Mrs. Senna swallowed. "I didn't give birth to an alien."

"He's not an alien!" Trev shouted. "My head hurts, too. Don't you feel it? There must be something in the air. It's messing with Jack more. We need to help him. We need to get him to a hospital."

Jack's screams and sobs grew louder. His back arched, and his claws tore into the lawn.

"No, no, no," Mrs. Senna repeated, backing away. "I don't deserve this. My son can't be like that. He wouldn't be like that. That's not my son." She held up a hand. "It's an alien. They took my son."

Trev hopped up and grabbed her arm. "What is wrong with you? We need to help him. He's sick. You're his mom. You need to do something."

She pulled her arm away and stared at her son, her face contorted into a grimace. "That's not my son. That's a monster."

"Are you drunk, ma'am?" Trev blurted, stress overriding the parental programming that told him to respect adults. "We need to get him to the hospital. The plane that crashed must have had chemicals in it. I saw it in a movie." He frowned. "In the movie, it turned people into zombies, but that's not real."

Another bone-shaking boom rattled the windows of the houses. Jack's screams got piercing. Scales replaced most of his skin.

Trev groaned and put his fingers to his head. His fear and adrenaline had helped him ignore the headache, but the pain got more distracting. Mrs. Senna acting crazy didn't help.

"We need to help him!" Trev shouted. "They need to send a helicopter for him."

Mrs. Senna backed toward the house. "That's not *my* son." She shook her head. "I won't help a monster."

Trev glared at her. "What is wrong with you?"

Mrs. Senna jumped back. Trev didn't know anything about her athletic background. He'd never seen her do anything but housework, but he doubted she'd ever been able to blind-jump twenty feet back without looking.

He'd never seen anything like that outside of movies, not even in the 2024 Olympics. She smashed the back of her head against the door and slumped to the porch.

Trev looked between his screaming friend and Mrs. Senna. When she moaned and rolled onto her back, confirming she wasn't on the edge of death, he decided Jack needed his help more.

He tried to figure out what to do. His phone didn't work, so he couldn't call 9-1-1. Even if he did, the police and firefighters might be busy with the plane crash or other victims of the chemicals that had to be in the air. Mrs. Senna had knocked herself out and had acted drunk and crazy before that, and his best friend was having a seizure and turning into a lizard.

Trev turned when something flashed in the corner of his eye. A gray Toyota RAV4 sped down the street. He jumped to his feet to wave down the driver. They could take Jack to the hospital.

The car broke apart with a loud pop. Pieces flew everywhere, their shapes and connections irregular. It was as if the vehicle was made of puzzle pieces and had been thrown down. Chunks of the car flew in every direction before dissolving into tiny flecks of light, launching the older man and woman inside through the air.

The woman screamed and wrapped her arms around the man as they hit the ground.

Trev grimaced and was about to look away when he noticed a white translucent orb that surrounded the woman and the man. The orb dug into the ground. The man struggled out of her grasp, and the orb disappeared.

Trev's tally of events he'd never seen outside of movies, starting with the plane crash, was going up rapidly.

Jack's screams had been reduced into whimpering moans. He stopped thrashing. Trev wasn't sure that was a good sign.

Something thudded hard on the ground nearby. Trev spun in that direction and raised his fists. A crow twitched on the lawn, coughing up a thick liquid that burned through the grass and dirt with a hiss like acid. A nearby black cat watched with cautious interest. At least the cat looked normal.

He watched the animal in case it split into four cats or started dancing with a top hat. The feline ran away from the dying acid-vomiting bird.

Trev whipped his head around when he heard new screams that didn't sound like Jack. The former RAV4 passengers hurried away from a fire that had started in the driveway of the house across the street.

The fire moved and waved its arms. Trev gasped. It was a man on fire.

"I can't stop burning!" the man shouted. "Somebody help me. It doesn't hurt, but I don't know how to stop it, and it's getting worse. Please!"

Trev swallowed, unsure of what to do. He glanced at the house, trying to remember where the Sennas kept their fire extinguisher. It would take too long to run to his house and get theirs.

He looked at Jack, whose transformation into a lizard person was finished, complete with a long tail.

"Please!" the burning man screamed. "Somebody—" He blew apart. The blast tore through the front of his house and into the nearby homes, setting them and portions of the lawns on fire. Trev threw himself over Jack and squeezed his eyes shut.

He held his breath until he couldn't anymore. When he opened his eyes on an inhalation, his headache from before was gone.

The explosion had scorched most of the Sennas' lawn and almost reached the porch. The ground around Jack and Trev was burned, though an untouched portion extended a few yards past them as if something in front of Trev and Jack had blocked the blast. Trev counted his blessings.

He frowned and looked at the house. Mrs. Senna wasn't there, and the front door was open. He'd get his parents to yell at her later. The first thing he needed to do was get Jack out of there.

Taking him on his bike might work. The problem was that Trev had no idea where the hospital was or how to get there. That left him with Mrs. Senna as their best option.

"Can you hear me?" Trev asked, shaking Jack's shoulders.

Jack groaned. He'd closed his eyes at some point.

"We need to get out of here." Trev shook him again. "We need to get you to the hospital so they can help you. Your mom can drive us. She's freaking out, so I'm gonna go in there and talk to her. You stay here until we're ready with the car."

As if on cue, the garage door rattled open. Mrs. Senna sat in the driver's seat of the family's blue Malibu. She looked out the front window at Trev and Jack.

"See?" Trev smiled. "She was just getting the car." He waved his arms. "I need help getting him into the car, ma'am."

Mrs. Senna wiped away tears and looked behind her, and the car shot out of the garage onto the street. Her abrupt turn almost spun the car, but she maintained enough control to barrel away.

Trev stared after the departing car, blinking. "No way. Okay. Fine. Your mom... I'll figure something out, Jack. I promise." He grabbed his friend and strained to pull him. "This would be easier if you woke up."

"Do you kids need help?" a familiar voice called from a nearby yard. It was an elderly neighbor, Mr. Ellsworth.

Trev looked that way. Mr. Ellsworth stood at the edge of his yard, but the lower half of his body was missing. He had no injuries, but he was nothing but a floating torso.

"No offense, but do you need help, sir?" Trev asked, his voice shaking and his stomach churning. "Doesn't that hurt?"

Mr. Ellsworth looked down. "Oh, this? Don't worry. It's not as bad as it looks. My legs are still there. They're just invisible. It's more inconvenient than anything, but if it sticks, it'll save me having to buy nice shoes." He walked toward them, eying the lizard boy and clucking his tongue. "Is that Jack Senna?"

Trev nodded. "Yes, sir. You've got to help us, sir. My phone's not working, and Mrs. Senna..." He blinked away the tears that welled up. "Mrs. Senna took off. She left him."

Mr. Ellsworth's expression darkened. "I see. You did the right thing by staying with your friend. A real man never leaves his friends behind." He knelt by Jack and clasped his hands together. "Oh, Lord, please help his child. Please help all of us." He looked at Trev and pointed at Jack's chest, which was rising and falling. "He's still breathing. As long as he's breathing, he's alive. What about you, son? Has anything happened to you?"

Trev checked his arms and legs. *"I had a bad headache, but it went away. Mrs. Senna jumped back like a vampire, and I saw people..."*

"I saw 'em, son. I saw Gary, too." Mr. Ellsworth looked at the scorched lawn that marked the epicenter of the earlier explosion. *"The important thing in an emergency, no matter how strange or dangerous the situation becomes, is to keep calm. You're doing a good job of that."*

Bright rays of light shot from the sky toward the ground in the distance. Trev tensed, expecting explosions, but nothing came. More rays appeared, including one that struck a garden a few hundred yards away.

"W-what?" Jack croaked. A long, thin tongue flicked out, and he opened his eyes. *"What's happening?"*

"I don't know." Trev swallowed and looked at Mr. Ellsworth. *"Is it terrorists?"*

Mr. Ellsworth managed a wry chuckle. *"If terrorists could do this sort of thing, our country would have been a crater a long time ago."* He shook his head. *"My phone lost signal just like yours, but before that, I was talking to an old buddy of mine who lives in the fake Washington."*

"'The fake Washington?'" asked Trev.

He smiled. *"You know, Washington state. Sorry. Thought a joke would lighten the mood. Anyway, my buddy's retired Navy and lives close to a big Navy base there. He saw the same lights a few minutes before we did. Things freaking out and people changing just like here. That means whatever is causing this is spreading from west to east."*

He cupped his chin. *"That makes sense if it started in Asia. Could be the North Koreans. Maybe the Chinese, although I have a hard time believing they could pull off something like this."*

"You just sat in your house after he said that?" Trev asked, confused.

"What do you do when you hear something like that?" Mr. Ellsworth shrugged. "My buddy also swore he saw nukes being launched. He was sure they were from nuclear submarines. Ours. He'd know. He spent years serving on them."

Trev's eyes widened. "Are we all going to die, sir?"

Mr. Ellsworth shook his head. "I figure if this is a foreign weapon and if my friend was right about the nukes, we're taking those bastards with us, so that's something. I don't know. Only the Lord knows now."

"Who else could it be?"

Mr. Ellsworth shrugged. More of his body disappeared, leaving only his upper chest, head, and arms. "It could be anything. Aliens, God, the Devil, or some military experiment gone wrong that's opened a gate to another dimension and changed all reality. Maybe that big science ring in Europe did something awful. I heard they were making black holes with it.

"Right now, I'd bet my whole house that nobody knows. The important thing is we keep our heads and watch over our loved ones until we find out." He nodded at his house. "We should take Jack in. I don't think we're going to get anyone to come help us anytime soon."

"What about his..." Trev sighed. "Okay, sir."

"Is it the end of the world?" Jack whimpered from the ground.

"I just don't know, son," Mr. Ellsworth replied.

"Where's my mom?" Jack moaned.

Trev knelt by Jack and squeezed his hand. "Don't worry about her. Mr. Ellsworth is helping us. I've got your back, no matter what happens."

Dawn light filtering through the truck windows shone on Trev's face, stirring him awake. He draped his arm over his eyes. The dream of the past remained fresh and raw.

Like most people who survived the Big Change, he'd never forget that day. Like most people, he'd done his best not to think about the horror and helplessness he'd felt.

He grunted. He hated thinking about the past. Nobody could do anything about it, or at least not yet.

A silly thought made him chuckle and pushed out some of the fear. For all he knew, some time traveler was constantly changing things. He'd never know.

Trev reached under his shirt and ran a finger over the necklace he always wore. He didn't think much about it day-to-day other than when he put it on. It wasn't the fanciest necklace, three nested gold circles connected by a gold chain. His parents had given it to him a year ago.

"The last thing I have left of you," he whispered. "It doesn't matter. We're going to win our race and start a new life here. I won't let your sacrifice be for nothing."

CHAPTER FIVE

<u>March 6, 2036, Sonoran Baja Hunter-Tourist Rally Bivouac, Sonoran Desert, New Baja Republic</u>

Trev sat at his table, sipping from a bottle of water. A canopy kept out the hot sun, which was not blocked by a single cloud. Jack had welded the table and chairs back together. They weren't perfect, but they held weight, and that was all that mattered.

The welded-and-repaired look fit the desert wasteland vibe. While most people in the Republic lived everyday lives in the cities, Trev liked to imagine that they were living a true wasteland lifestyle for that day. Having a rougher finish added to that.

Trev wasn't clear on what he planned to do after they won the race. It didn't matter until he snagged a tourist to ride along for the rally. That was the only way he'd be eligible for the prize money.

He watched the morning crowds stroll around. Despite his bad dreams and his concerns about Will and his friends, nobody had paid much attention to Trev or Jack since the day before. He chalked up their first day's experience to bad luck. Perhaps his prison theory was correct.

The clock had become their real threat. If they didn't sign a tourist by five, they'd get one from the pool. Despite what he'd told Jack, Trev would prefer someone useful unless he had no choice.

An overdressed woman in a fancy coat that looked more appropriate for a high-society party than walking the tents at a monster-killing race strolled by Trev with a German Shepherd on a leash. Men in sunglasses and suits trailed her. They were subtle about checking the area for trouble.

"Huh." Trev took another sip from the bottle. All the water in the Republic tasted off. He had not gotten sick, but he hadn't lived there long enough to get used to it. "It's weird."

"What's weird?" Jack asked, walking up beside Trev and setting a box filled with fluid-stained parts on the table. "Besides us."

Trev shook his head. "It's dumb. I was thinking aloud."

"I've got nothing better to do than listen to you. I'll decide if it's dumb. Do you have a brilliant scheme to land a tourist by threatening someone until they agree?"

"No." Trev retorted, "And just because I can't rebuild a transmission with a bubblegum wrapper and a rusted-out spring doesn't mean I'm an idiot."

"I didn't say anything about transmissions." Jack shrugged.

Trev gave Jack a playful punch on the shoulder. "Yeah. I know what you're thinking better than you." He nodded at the now-distant dog and frowned, unsure what to say or if he should even say it. "The Big Change. People weren't the only things that changed. Tons of animals did, too. It wasn't like with people. Not all animals changed, but some changed enough that we call them monsters. Some animals didn't change at all. With people, we all thought it was one and done, but now we know everyone's got a power. It's just a matter of whether it will show at five or six or from birth."

"Okay." Jack's tongue flicked a few times. "I'm not following you. Philosophical Trev is rare." He leaned toward his friend. "He's usually scary, and there's usually alcohol involved."

"That dog's just a dog, right?" Trev pointed at the German Shepherd. "Everybody's different from before if they're human, but there's a mix of normal animals and monsters living together. It's not like everybody who buys a German Shepherd puppy has to worry if it's going to change into something way different or start blowing buildings up with its bark, but everybody who has a kid knows they'll gain powers and change at some point. We're still figuring it out."

"Oh. I see what you're getting at." Jack nodded. "People smarter than us are working on that. Does it bother you *that* much? You almost never talk about it."

"It doesn't normally bother me. It's not like I lose sleep thinking about animals versus monsters. However, when I see a normal animal walking around in a desert where we're about to hunt monsters, it's hard *not* to think about it." Trev rubbed his temples. "I hate all this thinking, but I suppose without monsters, we wouldn't be about to make a ton of easy money in three days."

Jack leaned over to stare at Trev. "You look tired. Did you sleep okay?"

"Just bad dreams. Nothing big. Everybody has nightmares."

"You want to talk about them?"

"It was about the day of the Big Change. Do you really want to talk about it? I don't."

Jack's father had died that day. Trev's family took Jack in since his mother never came back. Later, they'd tried and failed to track her down.

Jack had forgiven her, convinced she would come to her senses after the shock had worn off. He even theorized that whatever power she was manifesting had affected her mind. Trev couldn't bring himself to forgive the woman for leaving her son screaming and sobbing while his body changed. After more than a few loud arguments, the boys agreed it was best not to dwell on the subject.

"On second thought, no," Jack replied. "Let's not." He motioned to the box. "You done caring about dogs and monsters? I only care about the monsters we'll get paid to kill."

"I'm done for now." Trev frowned at the box. "Why? You got something more interesting to talk about?"

"Yes." Jack nodded at the truck. "It's a good thing I double-checked, or we would have ended up stranded among the cacti and jackrabbits."

"You found sabotage?" Trev grunted. "If it's that ice-sword asshole or his friends, I'm going to teach him how it feels to have an icicle up his ass." He punched his palm. "I've got a lot of anger and frustration to work off. He's a great target."

"Nah. It was not them." Jack pulled his goggles off and set them on the table. "I found an axle seal fluid leak. It looks like simple parts fatigue."

"You sure?" Trev asked. "They could have someone on their team with the power to screw with car parts, or Will could have frozen something in there to mess with it. You can't rule out sabotage."

"No signs of anything like that," Jack reported. "No unnatural cuts, burns, or anything else. There could always be a guy with the perfect power for sabotage, but I put most of that truck together, so I'd know. Yes, I can rule out sabotage."

His tongue flicked. "I'm going to have to replace the seal. Best to replace all of them. There's no way the truck will survive three days of rough terrain and monsters as is, and I'd rather repair it in a patrolled camp than in the middle of monster country where I'm going to have to stop to shoot something between tightening things."

Trev groaned and scrubbed a hand over his face. "The race starts tomorrow. We don't have the time to do major repairs."

"It won't take that long." Jack smiled. "I can get it done today. It'll be a hard push, but I can do it."

A woman walking nearby gasped and put her hand to her mouth. Trev glared at her, even if he understood. He was used to Jack's fang-filled smile. It could look sinister or downright evil to the uninitiated, especially since it tended to generate extra saliva.

"It doesn't matter anyway." Jack pointed at the truck. "We can't go anywhere without our tourist. You were supposed to find one yesterday. Instead, you're sitting here worrying about dogs turning into monsters. Go to the tourist recruitment tent and put in our profile that you want a philosopher. You can talk to them about it during the race."

"Funny, but I did update our race profile with the officials," Trev replied. "I was hoping someone good would come to us. It's like fishing. Sometimes you just have to sit back, drink beer, and wait."

"You're drinking water, not beer."

"I'm waiting for a person, not a fish. It's a metaphor. Don't overanalyze it."

Jack stared at him. "Did you change the prize share offer?"

"I changed our driver and co-driver descriptions. Updated the photos." Trev shook his head. "I stressed our ability to protect ourselves and our tourist."

"We're not trying to get a date. We're trying to get someone to agree to ride with us as we drive through a monster-infested desert. That's going to take money."

"No," Trev countered. "Tourists come to this race because they want excitement, not the money. They have to pay to participate."

"I think they want both excitement and money. A good prize share could easily be higher than their entrance fee."

"We need the money," Trev insisted. "*All* the money. If we don't get the cash from this, things are going to get really tight really quick. If we finish in the top ten and rack up monster kills, we'll be okay if we don't give it away to somebody else."

Jack took a deep breath. "You said I need to stick up for myself more."

Trev nodded. "You do."

"I'll do that by saying you're being stupid, Trev. Nobody will come with us for free when most other teams offer part of the prize." Jack's tongue flicked out. "Did you put a picture of me on our profile?"

"Of course I did," Trev replied. "We're not going over that again. Anyone who has a problem with you has a problem with me. It's a simple way of cutting down on having to punch people in the middle of the race and getting blood in the truck."

"Okay. That makes sense when you put it that way." Jack glanced at the vehicle. "Other teams brag about their powers, you know. They talk about how they can make their vehicles avoid problems or blow away monsters with their awesome combat power."

"I don't want to do that unless I have no choice," Trev frowned. "Not after my fun little exercise with Will yesterday. They still might come after us, so the less they know about what I can do, the better." He shook his head. "I have my reasons."

"You won't be able to hide it for the entire race," Jack replied. "You realize that, don't you?"

"I might." Trev chuckled. "The average monster isn't that tough, and the average monster isn't bulletproof. Besides, as long as I stick with the secret weapon, people will not figure out my power. You're wrong. I will be able to hide it."

Jack scratched his eyelid. "In other words, our tourist has to tolerate me and join a team without knowing anything about your power, and they have to do it for no cut of the prize money. I think your real power is being able to look straight at reality and pretend it doesn't exist."

Trev threw up his arms. "What's the point if we have to pay other people? Besides, we get a time bonus for every stage if we take a rando. If we play our cards right, we could win this thing, not just place high enough for a payout on top of the monster kills."

He patted his chest. "I'm trying to maximize our money. We blew our savings to move to the Republic, buy that warehouse in Tucson, and get this truck and the secret weapon up and running. If we don't do well in this, we'll be running on fumes. We need to get an injection of cash. That way, we will have options and won't end up owing anybody."

Jack dipped his head. "We're going to end up with someone worthless. Their power will be screaming twice as loud, and they'll spend the entire race shrieking their head off."

"Have you looked at the prize share rates people have posted?" challenged Trev. "We're not talking one or two percent here and there. I could stomach that. Most tourists demand twenty or thirty percent, some even more, and half don't even have useful powers." He hissed. "We're not like a lot of those idiots. We're the complete team package. We have what it takes to get the truck through the stages and kill monsters. I have real racing experience from back east."

"Not in this type of rally."

"Driving skill transfers from discipline to discipline," Trev insisted. "The tourist is just there for the rules.

They're ballast in human form. I'm not paying ballast for existing."

Jack frowned. His frown looked semi-cute on his lizard face compared to his horrific smile. "Did you forget the part where the tourist can use their powers from inside the car? That's a huge advantage if we get attacked."

"I'm saying we don't need that huge advantage if it's going to cost us a bunch of money." Trev shook his head and held up a finger. "Ballast. Say it with me. Ballast. Keep repeating that word, and you'll eventually get the idea."

Jack pointed at a man walking into a tent with a rifle slung over his back. "Just go get someone. I can't do it, so we need to use your happy-go-lucky charm and that stupid face chicks think is handsome. And don't pick up a hot chick just because you like the way her ass looks. A tourist who can help is worth it, even if we have to give them part of the prize."

"Fine." Trev stood. "But I'm not going past five percent. I'd rather have the rando with the loud screams."

"Randos are required to agree to be the team's tourist." Jack picked up the box. "Keep that in mind. You have to be charming." He smiled and pointed at the edges of his mouth. "Charming and respectful."

"Don't worry." Trev grinned and hopped out of his chair. "I've got this. Forget your whining. I'll find somebody perfect for free, and you'll have to bow before my greatness."

Jack headed back to the truck, chuckling. "Nah. You'll come back with a hot chick you've promised fifty percent prize share. I guarantee it."

CHAPTER SIX

Trev flowed through the crowd. He did his best to avoid reflexive harsh eye contact with anyone who looked annoyed with him. He'd found that starting a fight with his eyes could get him into trouble as often as out of it.

Jack was right. This wasn't a prison. The Jack-related fight aside, he needed a favor from someone, so he had to change his strategy. He needed a tourist who wanted to join his team.

Also, Trev needed to convince somebody to do that without demanding an organ and half the prize money. That would require him to approach the situation with more finesse than he'd planned.

The rules were clear. No tourist, no participation in prize money.

After taking a roundabout path around the camp, Trev ended up at the huge tourist recruitment tent. The dangerous-looking drivers and their support staff gave way to more diversity and fewer weapons per square foot.

One group was the dictionary definition of the word:

people who'd traveled from other countries to take part in a dangerous race that let them have all the excitement of the event with none of the skill. Many were unarmed, which was a terrible idea, given the rough environment. Trev couldn't decide if he applauded their bravery or disapproved of their naïveté.

Other race tourists were professional passengers for this type of event, people who weren't interested in driving cars but brought utility to any team willing to split the prize money. It was also an excellent opportunity to demonstrate skills to roving monster hunters and mercs, so those types were well represented.

While the New Baja Republic wasn't the first country that arose from the ashes of the Big Change to develop novel means of monster control, the history of off-road rallies in the pre-Big Change Southwest and northern Mexico had become early acceptance of a combination race and monster-killing event only three years after the Big Change. Like many strange traditions, the tourist-as-ballast quirk from the rally, which had been copied worldwide, originated from a coincidence.

The first winner of the event, Juliana Ortiz, had wanted to bring her cousin along for the race in addition to her co-driver. Her cousin didn't have any navigational or driving skills, but he liked the idea of coming along for the ride, and Juliana didn't mind the weight penalty. Despite bringing another person along, she destroyed her competition. The excitement generated by the idea led to the event organizers requiring tourists in the rules.

The local organizers quickly clamped down on tourists paying the drivers for slots. Instead, the tourists had to pay the race organizers modest entrance fees. Advertisers and other supporters found more value in the drivers competing for tourists who could add unexpected variability to the race, depending on their powers and skills.

Trev surveyed the recruitment tent and the area outside. A person with obvious body mutations might want to be a tourist and have trouble getting a team to accept them, making them a prime candidate for his team. He didn't see anybody like that or who appeared to be trying to hide mutations under clothing.

He grunted in frustration. That would have been an easy pickup. He also would have liked Jack to understand that he didn't have to hide all the time.

A well-dressed man leaned over to whisper to a rugged-looking man. The first nodded Trev's way, and they eyed him with a mixture of amusement and contempt. Other people in the tent stared at him for far too long for it to be a coincidence. They averted their eyes when he stared back.

Trev wasn't surprised. News of his brawl must have spread around the camp. Even if people didn't share Will's prejudice against visible inhuman mutations, they wouldn't want to ride with a hothead driver who picked fights with other teams.

A burly, brown-skinned man in a dark uniform stepped into the tent. He wasn't wearing a gun belt, though he carried a small arsenal of knives on his tactical belt. A sunburst overlapping a half-moon symbol covered the back of his uniform.

The symbol was familiar. For that matter, so was the

man. Trev stared at him, trying to figure out the answer to the mystery.

Trev's brow lifted, and he snapped his fingers. "Aren't you Diego Aguirre?"

The uniformed man turned to Trev and looked him over. His lips curled in amusement. "Do I know you, kid?"

"You're MDL, right? *Mano de Luz*? Head of the Scorching Dawn mercs? You took down those raiders outside Mexicali not long ago."

"Again, do I know you, kid?" Diego shifted his hand subtly until his index finger pointed at Trev. "If you're a fanboy, that's fine, but I don't do autographs. If you're the other kind of fanboy, this isn't the place for that. We can take this out of the camp in that case."

"Other kind of fanboy?" Trev didn't know what Diego was implying.

"The kind that figures they can make a name for themselves by taking down an established big name." Diego offered the explanation in a casual tone as if he discussed death threats every day over breakfast.

Eyeing the finder, Trev chose his next words carefully. Diego's nickname came from a powerful energy beam he emitted from his finger.

"I'm just surprised to see a merc with your rep at this event." Trev smiled. "Are you a race driver now? Did you give up on merc work? It's not like you need to impress anybody around here to get jobs."

Diego shook his head and stared at Trev for a while longer before lowering his hand. "There are good monster bounties this year. Like you said, we just finished that big Mexicali job, so this is a nice place to earn cash and get my name and the company's name out there more without needing to mobilize the whole crew. We had a truck that only needed a few mods to get it qualified for the race. That made it an easy choice." He chuckled. "Kid, a working merc always wants to advertise. People have short memories. It's up to me to keep my name and company in their heads."

Diego was driving a truck. They might be direct competitors.

Trev wasn't worried. He suspected he had more experience than many more dangerous participants in getting cars and trucks from point A to point B fast. He was new to the Republic and this type of hunter-tourist rally, but he wasn't new to racing.

"What wave are you driving?" Trev asked. "If you don't mind telling me."

"Wave Two," Diego answered.

"Wave Two trucks?" Trev whistled. It was time to launch the psychological attack. "It's brave of you to go up against me. You can check out my telemetry later to pick up tips on how to get faster. I don't mind. I understand that everybody wants to learn how to win."

Diego snickered before narrowing his eyes. "I know you. You're Trevor Leon, aren't you?"

Trev laughed. "Nobody calls me Trevor." He stuck his hand out. "You can call me Trev. All my friends do. My enemies mostly call me 'asshole.'"

"Until I have to worry about you taking a shot at me, you're not my enemy." Diego considered before reaching up with the hand he'd aimed and shaking Trev's. He didn't try to overwhelm the driver with strength. He offered a firm, normal shake. "I heard you were causing trouble the other day. By now, I figure everybody involved in this race has heard about you. It turns out the guy you tangled with is dropping out."

Trev shrugged. "I don't go looking for trouble. I also don't run from it when it shows up. In my experience, all that happens when you do is you end up cornered with far more trouble to handle. If you handle it right away, life becomes easier."

Diego grinned. "In this world, there's too much trouble. You're right. If you start running, you'll never stop."

"Yeah. Exactly. You're a merc. You know how it goes."

Diego looked around and nodded. "Good luck, kid. Try not to die out there. This world needs more men who stand up to troublemakers." His gaze cut to a pinched-face man in a business suit to one side. "I've got a meeting. See you later. I'll let you check out *my* telemetry later so you can pick up a few tips and tricks. You know, so you can learn to go faster and be a winner."

"Don't die on me, either." Trev laughed. "We'll see who's ahead after the first day. Then we can decide."

He waved and let Diego depart with his annoyed-looking high-end tourist. Trev wandered farther into the tent to examine a large screen on a table next to the wall. The screen displayed tourist descriptions and assignments, along with requirements. As he'd worried, almost everybody left was demanding a large percentage of the prize and bonus money.

That made sense. The useful people or low-hanging fruit had already been grabbed. His messages had been ignored. Nobody had bothered to initiate a negotiation.

"I hear you're still looking for a tourist," a silky woman's voice called from behind him. "Right, Trevor Leon?"

"Sure I am. Like I told Diego, I go by Trev, and before we start anything, I'm not interested in sharing the prize money."

"That's fine by me."

Trev turned around. "Maybe we can work something out." He couldn't hide his grin.

CHAPTER SEVEN

A gorgeous, pale, raven-haired athletic beauty smiled at Trev. Her leather pants were so tight that they might as well have been painted on her legs. Her combat boots were more practical than sexy, and Trev couldn't complain about a woman who understood when fashion needed to give way to reality. Any tourist in the race had to be able to run for their life if something happened.

She wore her leather jacket well, but the shirt ruined the sexy-but-practical biker chick illusion. A stylized goth cartoon black rabbit with angry eyebrows on her shirt injected a dissonant cuteness into her look, making it hard to get a feel for her vibe. A closer examination noted a necklace with the same character.

He wasn't sure what she was going for, so he was unable to figure out how to best approach her. Conversations were a lot like fights. The opening moves could determine the whole flow of the event. He'd already lost in the initial exchange.

The woman laughed and gestured at her face. "Is this

the part where I say, 'Eyes up here?'" She motioned to her body. "Not that I don't work out hard to maintain this body." She smiled. "Then again, I'm looking for a driver, and you're looking for a tourist. The rest doesn't matter, doesn't it?"

Not caring what she thought, Trev continued staring at her shirt before blurting, "What's the deal with the rabbit? It's just bugging me."

"Come on." The woman scoffed. *"That's* your response? You ask me about my rabbit?"

"Yeah. The rabbit." Trev nodded. "You're the one wearing it."

"He's Rage Rabbit, of course." The woman frowned and glanced down at her shirt. She gestured at the rabbit with indignation. "It's not even an alternate design. I don't get why you're confused."

Trev nodded. "I'm supposed to know who Rage Rabbit is because…"

"He's the defining major character from the Dark Little Brutal Woods collection."

"What does he do?"

"He rages and eats carrots, obviously. I'd mention the other characters, but if you don't know who Rage Rabbit is, you won't know the others." The woman sighed and shook her head. "He's big where I'm from, though he started in Seattle. He must not be that big in the Republic yet but don't worry. He'll get there. You'll see why he's cool."

Trev burst out laughing. When she scowled, he stopped. "You really like your angry cartoon rabbit. Sorry. I find that funny."

"Yes, I do, and it's not funny." She folded her arms and cleared her throat. "Forget him. We've got business to discuss."

"That we do."

She gestured around the tent. "You're looking for a tourist, and I'm interested in being your tourist. That's the only thing that's important right now." She pointed at the assignment board. "Your team doesn't have anyone interested or any special requirements, so I figure this will be an easy agreement for both of us. You're lucky I was here."

"Hey, we're not a charity case," complained Trev.

"I'm not saying you are," the woman replied. "I'm sure you're a great driver, but you can't go anywhere without a tourist. I'm your woman." She smiled again. Something was forced about it, as if she was reminding herself to do so. "It wouldn't hurt to have a hot babe along, right? I'll give you something to rest your eyes between the tough parts of the race."

Trev laughed again. "Do you always talk to men like this?"

She winked. "When you've got it, why pretend otherwise? I take advantage of all the assets I have. Isn't that all anybody can do in this messed-up world?"

"Yeah." Trev chuckled. "The problem is, what counts as an asset depends on the situation. This is a desert monster-hunting rally, not a club."

"What are you getting at?" she asked.

"If we were in a city and I was hanging out looking for fun, that'd be one thing." Trev shrugged. "Sorry."

"Wait. What?" The woman blinked. Her voice filled

with genuine shock. "You're saying no? You won't let me be your tourist?"

Trev couldn't help it. He threw his head back and laughed. "You're not used to hearing that word? Or are you, and that's why you need Ragemaster Rabbit as your symbol. The great rabbit of frustration?"

"He's Rage Rabbit," she corrected. "Not Ragemaster Rabbit."

"Excuse me. So different."

The woman groaned and folded her arms. "Do you want me or not?" She grimaced and face-palmed. "Do you want me as your tourist," she added. She rolled her eyes. "You still need a tourist, and I'm interested in being that tourist, not dating you. Don't mistake light banter to mean I'm going jump in bed with you the first chance I get."

"Now we're back to reality. We can talk. First, what's your power?"

"What does it matter?" Her frown deepened. "You're the driver. I'm just there for the ride. You know, like, uh, human ballast. Just like they say on the website description of the race."

Trev's brows rose. "Human ballast, huh? I'm glad you understand the proper role of a tourist, but it doesn't change my feelings. Our truck is going in Wave Two, so we need people who can look after themselves. We don't need help with the monsters, but we can't spend time guarding you and making sure you won't wander off like an idiot if we stop for a minute." He peered at her. "Do you know how this race works? Or is that something you didn't hear about wherever Rage Rabbit's popular?"

A light blush spread over her face. "I traveled a long

way to get here. I didn't do that without checking it out. I understand what I'm signing up for, and I had to pay for the privilege. Don't be a dick about it, Trev."

He motioned for her to continue. "I need to hear you say it. I need to hear you describe the race. I don't mind people who are willing to take risks. I also can't bring anyone along if they don't understand what they're getting into."

Her brow lifted. "Isn't that the job of the organizational staff?"

"They don't care about anything but their money," Trev replied.

"You're racing for glory. You don't have time to worry about your tourist."

Trev chuckled. "No. I'm racing for money, but I also care about not deceiving people. I won't save anyone from themselves if they understand what they're facing. With that in mind, tell me what I want to hear, or we won't be riding together."

"There are other races like this in the world, but this was the closest. That's why I chose it. The race involves three waves of different categories of vehicles. There are no speed limits in the first wave. The drivers focus on monster avoidance, and their vehicles are allowed to be tuned to go faster than other waves' vehicles. The second wave has big bonuses for killing monsters."

Trev nodded. "So far, so good. How do they know who does what? Honor system?"

"The officials monitor times and kills with vehicle and drone sensors. By the third wave, most of the monsters are taken care of. That wave is for rookies like you. Those teams are there to learn about the environment without worrying about monsters."

"Why do you say I'm a rookie?" Trev demanded.

"This is your first year. You're a rookie by definition."

"You checked me out beyond seeing if I needed a tourist."

"It pays to look around. I heard about a man making noise and earning a bad reputation, and I decided he was the one I wanted to ride with."

"I was defending a friend, not making noise," Trev commented with a frown. "By the way, do you have a problem with people who have nonhuman appearances?"

"No. Do you?"

"My best friend looks like a lizard," Trev replied. "That answer your question?"

"You sounded interesting." The woman shrugged. "That's why I'm here, and that's why I want to be your tourist."

Trev laughed. "You just said something funny. When I told you I was going in Wave Two, you said I should go into Wave Three. That makes me question your listening skills. If we ride in a dangerous race together, I need to make sure you will listen to what I say and not just hear what you want to hear."

The woman looked away. "I heard that rookies race in Wave Three, but that doesn't change anything. I still want to be your tourist. If you're confident enough to race in Wave Two, I'm confident enough to ride with you."

Desperation colored her words. As much as Trev liked her, he wasn't delusional enough to believe his masculine aura was overwhelming a woman as beautiful as the one in front of him. Her ability to distract him despite her questionable taste in cartoon mascots proved her hotness.

She was hiding something, and he was missing it. He could all but smell it. He would have brought Jack along for a second opinion, but they didn't need to get into another fight near the tourists. He didn't blame his friend for that. He blamed the small-minded idiots who thought a woman with golden light wings was okay, but a lizardman was all but a monster.

Trev shook his head. "You can race whatever wave you feel like. I'm not convinced you're a good fit for my team. I need a tourist who won't pass out the first time real trouble starts and won't spend the entire race screaming and distracting us."

He smiled at her. "You won't tell me your power, which means it's something that won't help, and you're trying to steer me into an easier division, which means you're afraid of the monsters. I wouldn't care if you had a useless power. I do care that you're afraid."

"I'm not afraid." She put her hands on her hips.

"Maybe. What's your power?"

"I don't..." She closed her eyes and took a deep breath. When she reopened them, she offered him a smile with perfect teeth. "Come on, Trevor. You want me on your team. You need me."

Her response made him laugh louder. "Remember what I said about listening skills? I was going to comment on your research, but I can't hold it against you since you can only do so much research on a guy in a campsite in the middle of nowhere."

"I don't understand."

"Nobody calls me Trevor. They call me Trev. It was the first thing I told you."

The woman stumbled back as if his words had struck her physically. She grimaced, scrubbed a hand down her face, and whispered something under her breath.

"What was that?" Trev asked.

"Fine. I heard you. I just forgot." She sighed. "Come on, Trev." She blinked. "Oh. Sorry. I'm being super rude." She walked forward and offered her hand. "Cassie Laner. Technically, it's Cassandra Laner. I'm like you that way. Nobody calls me Cassandra."

Trev shook her hand, surprised by the strength and roughness of her grip. Her looks weren't in doubt, yet her hands suggested she spent her days doing something physical. From this close, he could tell her athletic litheness belied functional strength.

That was promising. It wasn't enough to convince him that she should join him for such a dangerous race. He let go of her hand and waved. "I'm going to get something to eat and swing by later. Good luck with finding a team. There are still people in Wave Three looking for tourists. You might have better luck with those drivers."

"You're saying no when you have no other choices?" Cassie asked. "Do you really think that's a good idea?"

"Apparently, you don't know how this works." Trev shrugged. "I'll get a rando if I can't get a tourist to sign on before the deadline. Picking somebody, even for free, isn't always your best choice. I don't know. Something about you is sketchy."

Cassie growled, "Excuse me? Did you call me sketchy?"

Trev squeezed his thumb and index finger together. "A

little, yeah. No offense. Half the people around here are shady or sketchy, if not downright criminal bastards, but I need more to balance the scales if I take a tourist I can't trust aboard. Right now, you're not offering anything other than being hot."

He waved. "You wearing those pants is affecting me, but in the wrong way. I want to focus on the race, not the tourist. Sorry." He turned and walked for a few feet before stopping. He recalled her rough hands. "You don't happen to have a boost suit, do you?"

Cassie smirked. "I'm a tourist, not a hero or Special Forces. Is this about you wanting to see me in a skintight outfit? I would look great in a boost suit. Not going to lie about that."

"Just saying anybody could put up a decent fight in a boost suit. I was hoping you were a rich princess who brought all the best toys. That might have made it worth it."

She laughed. "Don't you get it? You need me. You need me more than you realize."

Trev shook his head. "I just got done explaining that I don't. To be honest, now you're coming off as desperate. That makes you even sketchier."

"You forgot," Cassie countered. "I checked you out."

"You think you have something on me?" Trev asked, hostility creeping into his voice. "Oh, I'd love to hear it."

"You're not paying your tourist." Cassie gestured at the recruitment tent. "And if you don't have a tourist by 5:00 PM, it's a random assignment. You said it yourself. At least I've got these pants and I don't smell. That's something.

There are far worse leftover tourists than me. I've been turning down offers left and right."

Trev nodded. "Hey, after I win, look me up in Tucson, and we can party. For now, I need to win this thing."

Cassie stared at him. "Playful banter is one thing. There's a line, and you've crossed it. You're really turning me down?"

Trev laughed. "Don't worry, Cassie. There's a first time for everything. You'll grow from this experience and become a stronger woman."

"You don't understand. You can't turn me down. It wasn't supposed to go down like this. I practiced and everything." She gasped and slapped a hand over her mouth.

Trev felt sorry for her, but that didn't change his mind. "Yeah, keep telling yourself that. People don't always react the way you expect."

Cassie's jaw tightened. "You don't…" She averted her gaze. "Sorry. I didn't mean to come on so strong. I get why it's off-putting."

"I appreciate that, but it doesn't change anything. I'm bouncing for real this time." He waved. "Good luck. I'm serious. You're hot, and I'd love to take you out on a date, but I'm here for the money, not women."

"Fine," Cassie spat through a clenched jaw. "I'll keep that in mind in the future."

She stormed away, muttering under her breath. Trev kept enough control not to laugh at her. She must have been used to every man doing what she said.

One comment had bothered him. She'd said she'd practiced, which sounded odd. A woman like her didn't need to practice her lines to get men. Maybe she understood on some level that being selected as a tourist would take more than putting on tight pants and batting her eyelashes.

Cassie stuck her hands in her pockets and stomped to the edge of the crowd. She passed a truck on a hydraulic lift surrounded by bickering mechanics. One of the mechanics knelt with a wrench to adjust something on the lift. Another man jumped up and yelped before pointing at a rattlesnake sitting atop a rock under it.

Trev barely had time to think about how and why a rattlesnake was near a lot of humans without freaking out when the yelping mechanic bumped into the side of the lift and waved his hand. The side shot up a few feet, and the rattlesnake flew through the air, shaking its eponymous tail with annoyed fury.

"That's one way to use telekinesis," Trev commented.

He was chuckling when he noticed that the snake was flying toward Cassie. She was staring at the ground, shuffling along with her hands in her pockets, and a hissing, rattling snake turned homicidal by a telekinetic throw about to hit her.

"Rabbit girl, duck!" a man nearby shouted.

Cassie looked up and froze, her face suggesting curiosity more than fear. The snake came toward her. She was a peak example of the wrong place at the wrong time, and her reaction to the warning increased the danger.

"Damn it," Trev muttered and raised his hand.

A thin, all but two-dimensional rectangular patch of purple flashed in the sky. The rattlesnake struck the patch and bounced off to drop to the ground in front of a man waiting with a machete. He cut its head off without hesitation and nodded in satisfaction.

The mechanics shouted at one another, gesticulating at the lift, the dead snake, and Cassie. She stared at the dead snake.

Trev checked out the crowd to see if anyone was watching him before heading in the opposite direction. Nobody could associate a half-second transitory forcefield with a man standing far away. Security might have caught him on a recording, but they had no reason to investigate him further. All he'd done was save a woman's life.

Do I really need to keep it secret? Trev wondered. *I wish I knew, and until I do, it's the best bet.*

"I should have used my power when I was fighting Will the Ice Asshole," Trev muttered, shooting one last pitying look at Cassie.

He frowned, not liking what he saw. She stared at the dead rattlesnake with a huge smirk on her face.

"What the hell?" Trev whispered. "Did she *want* to get bitten?" He grimaced and hurried away. "Great. She's a hot danger junkie with a death wish and no combat powers. No wonder she's so desperate to be my tourist. Everyone must turn her down after they talk to her."

He shook his head. "Yeah, she's the last person I need as my tourist."

CHAPTER EIGHT

Frustrated, Cassie nibbled on a ham sandwich in her tent. She wasn't in the mood to pretend to be friendly, and too many people in the cafeteria tent hit on her, adding to her annoyance.

Everyone who approached her reminded her of her dismal failure with Trev. Most of the men asked her to ride with them as their tourist. Their requests only deepened her confusion.

Her failure with Trev was ridiculous. The other men's reaction was in line with what she expected, but she'd struck out with Trev despite tailoring her persona to what she thought he wanted.

She glanced down at her shirt. That was the one exception. Had her love of Rage Rabbit doomed her mission? "That can't be it," Cassie muttered. "It's like he saw right through me."

The snake incident confirmed she was at the right place. That was comforting. She didn't have many more clues to guide her. Trev *had* to be the target. She didn't know where else she could look if it wasn't him. The resemblance was uncanny.

She tore another bite out of her sandwich, the only thing available to take out her irritation on. The heat in her cheeks wouldn't leave despite the time and distance from her earlier failure.

"It's not my fault," she whispered. "I wasn't trained for this type of operation."

The plan had seemed perfect when she thought it up. She figured playing up her charms would easily convince a man like Trev to let her join his team. She'd found nothing to indicate that he was that cautious and thoughtful. What few scraps of information she'd located suggested a playful and self-indulgent young man who was addicted to enjoying himself. He'd raced in his New Eastern United States home and had a reputation with the female fans there.

Her encounter indicated that her strategy calibration had been off. Good intelligence was hard to come by, especially when it was built on a laughable backbone like this mission.

Cassie set her sandwich in her lap and groaned. She rubbed her temples and tried to remember her training. This wasn't the same kind of problem she encountered at home, but that didn't mean the same planning techniques couldn't be used.

A roadblock in a mission called for a strategy pivot. It was that simple. She'd failed, so it was time to move to a new plan. *Okay, I can do this. Sexy, alluring Cassandra didn't work, but I need to end up in that truck, or traveling to the New*

Baja Republic was pointless. Everything has guided me to Trev and this race.

If I try to find him after the race, he'll think I'm a weird stalker. I'll have even less chance of evaluating him as the target. It might be too late.

Cassie frowned. She'd been convinced that this was the critical time and location to contact Trev Leon. All the evidence and her careful research over the last few months pointed her at the man. She'd never imagined tracking him down just for him to blow her off so easily.

She'd been lucky to find info on Trev on a low-security 46P1 server. According to their records, he was the son of a mere mid-level researcher working for the company, but the file had let her confirm that he was alive and gave her a location to start looking: Washington, DC.

The initial decision was about where to approach him, but just when she'd worked out how to go after him in the NEUS, he'd moved to the New Baja Republic.

It was hard to accept that the cocky man she'd talked to outside the tourist tent could be the man she was looking for. That was the real surprise. Whatever else she might have thought, she hadn't expected her first conversation with the target to go as it had. Their confrontation underscored that she knew far less about Trev than she'd believed. That was the result of doing too much research from a distance while avoiding being noticed by the powerful 46P1 corporation's internal security.

Her intel was unverifiable by anyone but her, and she feared that every minute she spent pursuing the wrong target threatened the world's stability.

Cassie sucked in a breath. Trev *had* to be the right man.

She hadn't confirmed that he wasn't. In either case, she'd need to confirm his identity to move on to the next stage in her mission. The question was, what was the best way to do that?

It wasn't as if there was no local evidence to support Trev. She'd watched him take on the ice sword user without breaking a sweat or getting injured. Was his confidence born of his concealed power, or was he just an arrogant young man overloaded with testosterone?

That encounter offered a hint of the truth. Now, she needed to do her part and follow up.

I can do this, she thought. *I have the training, and he's still not at his maximum potential. This is my chance. I have to get him before it's too late.*

Cassie thought about 46P1's information. The entire Leon family's powers were redacted in the records she'd recovered, but she'd managed to find one interesting note about Trev in a secondary file.

Further testing is recommended. Parental self-reporting of the boy's power might be flawed due to limitations of evaluation techniques. Additional training and refinement could lead to more significant potential. Low-priority tasking consideration is recommended at this time.

Cassie swallowed the last bite of her sandwich. She needed a new plan, one that couldn't fail. Seduction was too dependent on the target, and she'd spent years focused on training, not dating and emotional manipulation techniques.

Computers had no ego. They didn't care about a person's appearance, behavior, or what shirts they wore. She could get into a 46P1 server undetected, and a regional race's system couldn't be as well-protected as a corporate server.

Cassie smiled and clapped once. Winning a fight was about controlling the tactical variables, and Trev didn't even know they were in a fight.

She grabbed her holster and jacket. After slipping them on, she stormed out of the tent. She couldn't risk waiting until it was too late to make her move. It would be harder after the officials made the random assignments. She'd risk exposing herself, and that would risk the mission.

Cassie circled the camp, trying to make her way toward the administrative tents without looking obvious. A man she didn't recognize stepped in front of her.

"Hey, beautiful," he greeted her. "Is heaven missing an angel, or is hell missing a succubus? Either way, it's my lucky day."

"I'm in a hurry," Cassie replied. "Also, that line blows."

"Don't be like that." He licked his lips. "I've seen you around. You're hotter than most of the chicks here. I could show you a good time. You a tourist? I'll kick my tourist off my team for you. I don't care if you have a good power. All you have to do is look good."

"Please get out of my way." Cassie frowned. "I'm really in a hurry. I have something important to do, and it's time-sensitive. I'd appreciate you not interfering."

"Don't be cold." The man shook his head. "I'm offering you a good time and an easy race. You should be grateful."

"I'd be grateful if you'd get out of my way." Cassie pinched the bridge of her nose. "I don't have enough patience to pretend to be nice just now, so get the hell out of my way, or I will hurt you. Is that clear enough for you, asshole?"

The man laughed. "You serious, bitch?" He looked around. "I don't see Security nearby. I was trying to be nice, but don't piss me off if you don't want a broken nose messing up that pretty face."

Cassie backed up. She'd felt bad about being rude, but he'd cleared her conscience. She focused on the man and the future, and a punch flashed in her mind. Knowing what was coming, she whipped her arm up and caught his arm halfway through the swing.

"Hey!" he shouted. "Damn it. Let go."

Cassie pivoted and pulled his arm behind him in a painful lock. "That was a really bad idea. You should have walked away when I told you to."

He grunted and strained. She tightened the lock and leaned in to whisper, "You're hurting from the arm lock."

"Of course I am, you crazy bitch. You're about to break my arm."

"If you're hurting, you don't have a power that lets you block pain or bones strong enough to stop me from snapping them. That means you were stupid to initiate the fight."

"You better let me go if you know what's good for you." The man gritted his teeth. "I'm going to mess that pretty face up until nobody but a freak wants you."

Cassie saw his attempt to twist out of the lock in her mind before he initiated the move. She jumped back, pulling his arm with her, and it gave an audible pop. He screamed, and she shoved him forward.

Arm dangling, the shaking man pulled a knife with his

good hand and charged her. Cassie danced around the blade, leaving only air wherever he swung.

"Stay still, bitch," he growled.

He swung back and forth. She ducked, sidestepped, and pivoted, not letting the knife come near her. Her mind telegraphed every swing and thrust, but an ache built in her head.

The man panted. Sweat drenched his face, and his other arm hung limply at his side.

"I admire your ability to keep fighting with a dislocated shoulder," Cassie offered. "That proves you've got real battle experience. I've had to do that before. It's not easy even when you're on painkillers."

Two security guards rushed toward them with rifles at the ready. The injured man spun toward them, wild-eyed, knife still in his hand.

"On the ground," a guard ordered.

Cassie put her hands behind her head and knelt. The injured man looked between her and the guards before dropping to his knees and sobbing.

"It's not fair." The man grimaced. "That bitch hurt me."

"Come with us, ma'am," a guard ordered. "We got the initial report from a surveillance drone, but we need to hear your side."

"That bitch broke my arm," the man shouted. "I didn't deserve it. I need a painkiller."

"I only dislocated it, and only after you tried to punch me in the face for turning you down." Cassie stood and put her hands behind her back. "Do what you need to do."

"It's okay," the guard replied. "Just come with us. This shouldn't take long."

A wasted half-hour later, Cassie offered a polite nod to the security guard and left the security tent. They told her to be careful, though after they realized she had a gun, they thanked her for trying to deal with the matter non-lethally. They'd even told her she could have made a case for self-defense if she'd shot him, but they'd prefer fewer bodies to process.

They were proud that they'd made it through pre-registration and registration with only thefts and assaults. Murders garnered too much attention. The Republic's authorities turned a blind eye to roughness in much of the country if they felt it was self-correcting. Any event that got out of control might get a visit from a military unit or a hero team.

Free of Security and aggressive suitors, Cassie kept looking over her shoulder to ensure she wasn't being followed before deciding to cut between the tents. She needed to circle back to the administrative tents.

The asshole had messed up her timetable. She didn't have much time before the random assignments. It'd be tight, and she hated working under time constraints.

If only my farther-out visions were as clear and not tied to sleep. Thanks, precognition! You showed me my target would somehow save me from a rattlesnake. Why won't you show me something else useful?

Her trainer had discouraged overreliance on her precog power during fights. She understood why despite how useful it was. Setting aside the unreliability beyond the shortest of time horizons, using her power made an exhausting situation much more tiring.

Cassie wondered if she could have convinced Trev to let her join if she'd told him the truth from the beginning. The problem was that he didn't trust her, and they needed to build trust for her mission. If he knew about her precognition, one failure of her ability during the race would plant the seeds for him to deny what she needed him to believe for everything to work out as it had to. He'd never believe her insane story otherwise. She could hardly believe it herself at times.

She shook her head. That would come later. For now, she'd rely on something more fundamental and controllable: subterfuge and hacking. The day hadn't worked out the way she wanted. That didn't mean it wouldn't end the way she wanted.

"I'm going to be your tourist, Trev, whether you want me or not." She cracked her knuckles. "I might as well make it harder for them to detect you using your power while I'm at it." She smiled. "This is going to work out. I know it."

CHAPTER NINE

Leaning against the side of his truck, Trev checked his phone. "4:55 PM and all is well. All that effort for nothing. I might as well not have bothered and just planned on a rando from the beginning."

Jack stood at the front of the truck, inspecting the exposed engine. "I'm annoyed with you."

"Why? I'm the one who went to the tourist tent and wasted my time."

"You had one real job these last couple of days, which was getting a tourist. More, you were supposed to get us a *good* tourist while I was fixing the truck." Jack wiped his hands on a rag. His long tongue flicked out. "I know you, Trev. I bet you poked your head into the tent and went, 'My gut tells me nobody here is worth my time. I'm going to go to the food tent and eat a fire iguana sandwich.'"

"They're so *tasty*. Perfect natural spiciness." Trev shrugged. "Like I said, we'll get a rando. You're worrying about nothing."

"About nothing? We're talking about someone who could make or break our race."

"Have you checked the assignment board? There are good candidates in the rando pool. If we're lucky, this will work out even better for us. Randos can't demand prize-sharing. We'll have all the power in the negotiation."

"You mean a rando like the hot chick you saved with your power?" Jack asked.

"I should have never told you about that. I knew you'd be stupid about it." Trev scoffed and folded his arms. "The whole point of that story is that despite this gorgeous goddess of angry rabbits all but throwing herself at me like I'm a glass of cool water in the desert, I turned her down for the good of the team."

He gestured at Jack. "I had both of us in mind. If this was just about me, I would have invited her along and told you that you can bunk in the trailer at night while we had fun in the fold-down beds."

Jack shook his head. "I knew I shouldn't have sent you there by yourself. You're not taking this seriously." He walked closer and lowered his voice. "You used your power after making such a big deal about how it should be a last resort."

"How am I not taking this seriously? What did I do that was so wrong?" Trev frowned and looked around, then moved closer to Jack. "It *was* a last resort. You wanted me to let a woman get bitten by a rattlesnake? Come on, man. We both know you would have chewed me out for not saving her if I had done that."

"You're right." Jack stepped back and sighed. "It's just you keep going on about how we need to be careful about showing your power around here. I wouldn't be your friend if I didn't support your more important choices."

"It's because we can't trust any of these assholes. We're still figuring out 46P1."

There's never an advantage to letting someone know your power, his father had told him. *Only tell the people you trust, and only use it when there's no other choice. You could be in danger if the wrong people found out. Your mother and I agree on that.*

Trev's jaw tightened. He'd never understood why his parents were so reluctant for him to train his power, but he assumed they had a reason beyond simple paranoia. The problem was, he didn't have any evidence of that, only hunches and wishes and their hints about not trusting 46P1.

Jack walked over and pulled a socket wrench from his toolbox. He leaned toward the engine. "Don't overthink it. We built the secret weapon so you could do what you needed without being seen and make the best use of your power, even without training. I learned tons doing it, so if you decide you don't need it, I don't mind."

"Do you think it's stupid to hide it?" Trev asked. "Do you think Mom and Dad were wrong this whole time?"

"I don't know. I really don't." Jack's tongue flicked out and lingered in the air. "Remember the kitten in the tree?"

Trev nodded, recalling an incident from four years ago. "I was so proud that I saved it using my power, but when I told my dad, he got angry before telling me he was proud of me. I wish they had been honest with me before the end instead of going all enigmatic."

Jack frowned. "They might not have had a choice if someone with a power was using it to monitor them."

"I know, I know." Trev threw up his hands. "That doesn't make it less frustrating." He shook his head. "None of that matters now. We got away from DC. We'll be safe as long as we're careful, and after we get established and know more people, we can figure out if we really need to hide. My parents might have been overreacting because of their jobs. They were always afraid somebody would come after me to get to them. All of this might have been caused by their misunderstanding of the real threats."

"That could be it." Jack leaned into the front of the truck toward the bottom of the engine until Trev could only see his legs and tail. "I'll do what you want. You always do the right thing in the end. The only problem is, sometimes you take a long time to get around to it."

"Gotcha."

Trev turned and walked away, letting the conversation die. They'd talked about this same issue before, bouncing around endless theories after his parents died. Without more information, they'd never have firm answers, and he didn't believe the universe would be so helpful as to deliver new evidence in a race camp in a Southwestern desert.

Jack popped out of the engine and landed in a crouch. He turned and pulled up his goggles. "Oh. Looks like you made an impression. Are you sure your story was true?"

"What are you talking about?" Trev asked. "Every story I tell is true." He tilted his head. "At least seventy-five percent. Sixty?"

Jack pointed behind him. "Unless there's another gorgeous woman in tight leather pants and a cartoon rabbit shirt in this camp who knows you, that has to be Cassie Laner." He scratched the scales under his eyes. "Admirers are a good thing. Stalkers aren't. Figure out which she is before she stabs you in your sleep and I have to avenge your death."

Groaning, Trev turned to find the woman smiling and waving at him. "You didn't get enough of me?" he asked. "When I mentioned the date, I thought you understood that I meant after the race. I really like to keep my focus before big events. Blowing off steam is one thing. I don't think anything with you would be that minor."

Cassie sashayed over with a smirk. "You think I'm high on my own supply, don't you?"

"I think you're a scorching hot chick who's used to getting what she wants," Trev admitted. "In any other circumstance, I'd be down with that."

She poked him in the chest. "You are a cocky bastard, Trev. I'd say I like that in a man, but I really don't."

"Being cocky and great aren't mutually exclusive. You *are* high on your own supply. Need I remind you how shocked you were that cocky ol' Trev was immune to your feminine wiles?"

"I don't have feminine wiles," Cassie protested. "I don't like the sound of that."

"If you don't have feminine wiles, what do you call the routine you threw at me earlier?" Trev laughed. "You don't strike me as the delusional sort, but I could be wrong."

"You haven't checked your messages, have you?" Cassie asked, folding her arms and looking smug. "I'd hold off on insulting me more until you do. It'll clarify things."

Trev frowned and pulled out his phone. "Why? Is this

where I find out your dad owns this whole race organization, and I'm not going to be allowed to race?" He scrolled through an annoying number of vendor spams before finding a surprising text. "Jack, Cassie Laner is our tourist."

Jack's tongue flicked several times. "I specifically asked you not to grab somebody just because they were hot, and you've been talking to me this whole time when you picked her already? Not cool, Trev." He leaned over to talk past him. "No offense to you, Cassie."

"None taken," she answered. "It's weird to hear you fought about me being too hot. Flattering, but still weird."

Trev shook his head. "I didn't pick her. I sent her packing." He held up his phone. "Check yours, too. She's our randomly assigned tourist. I had nothing to do with it unless you think I've suddenly developed technopath powers."

"That'd be useful." Jack yanked his phone out of a pocket. He frowned and scrolled. "I'd say it's ridiculous, but there weren't many randos left. The statistical chance of landing her was high when you think about it." He looked her over. "You're our tourist?"

Cassie waggled her eyebrows. "Looks that way. You're stuck with me now, boys."

"You want to be our tourist despite having the fight with Trev?"

"It wasn't a fight," Trev interjected. "It was only a spirited conversation."

"I don't mind," Cassie told Jack. "It wasn't a big deal. He's funny in an annoying, cocky bastard way. I'll get used to it."

Jack stared at her in silence, his reptilian eyes pinning

her. He pulled off his gloves and stuffed them in his pockets before running his claws over each other.

Trev stared at him, confused until he realized Jack was testing Cassie in his own way. He waited to see how she would respond. Asking her about tolerating obvious visible mutations wasn't the same as Jack shoving his lizard nature in her face.

"Do I have something on my face?" Cassie asked, running a finger over her cheek. "I had a sandwich earlier, but that was long ago, and nobody has said anything."

"You don't have a problem being on this team?" Jack sounded surprised. "Or any of the team members?"

Cassie lowered her hand. "I wanted to be on the team, but your cocky-ass driver thinks I'm not good enough for him because I can't blow up a car with my spit or crush his balls with my mind." She grinned. "I was randomly selected. Maybe my real power is luck." She bowed over her arm. "I, Miss Lucky Laner, am happy to join your team."

"That's not a thing." Trev scoffed and folded his arms.

"What's not a thing?"

"Luck as a power. It doesn't even make sense. Luck's not real."

"How do you know?" Cassie asked. "You the world's preeminent expert on powers now? There are teleporters out there, and teleportation is weirder than luck when you think about it."

"I would have heard about it," Trev insisted. "There'd be a hero out there, like the Lucky Leprechaun or something like that."

"You hadn't even heard of Rage Rabbit. I'm sure there

are tons of people you haven't heard of." Cassie rolled her eyes and turned back to Jack. "Seriously, why would I have a problem being on this team? Are you guys terrible at driving? Are you super-weak? You both keep trying to push me away, and I don't get why."

Jack blinked and lowered his goggles. "No. We're strong, and we won't have any trouble with the monsters on the route. I guarantee that. We have the equipment and experience to get through any monster in this desert."

"Then this will be easy."

Cassie linked her fingers behind her back, leaned forward, and smiled. She projected a clashing and disarming mix of tones, the overall pose coming off as seductive while the rest of her look and attitude were not. The stance seemed like she'd over-practiced it in front of a mirror.

When she leaned over, she revealed the shoulder holster and gun beneath her jacket. The dissonance made Trev trust her more. He pointed at the gun. "At least you're not naïve. Do you know how to use that thing, or is it just there to smash bugs?"

"I'm good, if I say so myself," Cassie replied. "It's not just point and shoot. I can hit things that aren't sitting there waiting to be hit."

"No offense, but I don't hold you up as a high authority about weapons. Spending time shooting at pests isn't as special as you'd think, especially with this crowd, including tourists."

"I've received formal training." Cassie harrumphed and zipped her jacket. "Ranges and professional trainers with combat experience. Does that help?"

"Sure. You're the modern Annie Oakley and have been trained by the best Spec Ops squads on the continent." Trev waved a hand.

"Who is Annie Oakley?" Cassie asked.

Trev scoffed. "She was real and way more famous than your rabbit."

"I bet more people have heard of Rage Rabbit than Annie Oakley."

Jack cleared his throat. "We need to focus on the race, not fame competitions between rabbits and dead markswomen."

"Okay." Trev shrugged. "I got what I wanted. I've got no complaints."

"You got what you wanted? Me?" Cassie smirked.

"I'm getting a bonus for being assigned a rando tourist," Trev replied. "I was serious earlier. This race will require my total concentration. Most of the time, we're stage driving, and when monsters attack, it'll require twice the concentration." He gestured at Jack. "He'll be busy helping me drive, doing the navigation. If you're thinking of this as a three-day date, don't." He shook his head. "By the end of this, you'll be tired, dirty, and sore. Even if you enjoy it, you'll be exhausted."

Cassie's smirk deepened. "You're the one saying it, not me."

Trev scrubbed a hand down his face. "Be here tomorrow at six. Our official departure time is seven thirty, and we have to be in the starting zone by seven for our last scrutineering checks." He offered a taunting smile. "I double-checked the rules. If we're late because of you, they can fine you and hold you. In the worst-case scenario, they can send you to a Republic court on fraud charges."

"I'll be there on time," Cassie replied, sounding amused. "Don't you get it, Trev? I'm not going to screw you over. The only reason this had to be complicated was because you made it that way. All I wanted to do was sit in the back of your truck and look pretty."

"There's way more to you than looking pretty," Trev countered. "I know that."

"I'm glad you think so."

"If you don't have your own tent, gear, and helmet, buy them from a vendor tonight," Trev ordered.

"I thought you didn't have to wear a helmet?"

"You do in my truck. As for the other stuff, despite what I said earlier, only Jack and I sleep in the truck."

CHAPTER TEN

Bathed in sweat, Cassie jerked awake on the cot in her tent. It wasn't the rowdy shouts and loud music outside that had awakened her. She panted, wanting to ignore the dream vision that had snapped her out of sleep and lingered in her mind, taunting her to confront the reality and stop it from happening.

"If I didn't know better," she whispered, "I'd think someone up there is messing with me. Of course, you had to give me a vision like that."

She slowed her breathing, letting the dream images and sensations linger in her consciousness. Pushing them away was dangerous. This was the best time to lock in the details.

At the same time, thinking too hard might color what she believed she'd seen. A vision of the future other than the milliseconds of a fight couldn't easily be pinned down. Far visions were as much a curse as a blessing.

Her mission depended on her keeping a clear head and understanding the real threats. That began with sorting out how immediately relevant any new evidence was, regardless of the source, including her precognitive power.

Starting with what she knew provided a solid anchor to evaluate the evidence. Jack was in her vision. That much was clear. She doubted another tailed lizardman in coveralls and goggles was hanging around the camp. She'd encountered other people with inhuman mutations, but he was the only lizardman she'd met in her life.

Jack wasn't in the camp in the vision. Shrubs, grass, sand, and huge saguaro cacti stood in the background, their prickly arms up like panicked, multi-limbed people. There wasn't a tent in sight, though she saw the passenger door of Trev's and Jack's truck with its window shattered.

Jack held an odd, bulky rifle. She didn't recognize the weapon. A fist wrapped in fire punched through Jack's torso from behind, killing him and burning his entire chest. The angle denied her a clear view of his killer. The only clue was the diamond pinky ring the killer wore.

The vision ended after that, but she didn't need more details. Unless Jack had a secret regeneration power, he'd die from the brutal wound.

Cassie tried to control her heavy breathing and pounding heart. The latest vision didn't prove her mission was on the right track, but she had a chance to save somebody's life. The question was if he deserved it.

She still knew little about Trev and less about his lizardman friend. For all she knew, the fire fist belonged to a hero stopping Jack from murdering a bus full of orphans. Perspective defined whether a future event would be perceived as good or bad.

Unfortunately, life rarely provided moral hypotheticals

of such high contrast. That didn't mean she couldn't wish for them.

"All these damned weeks after starting this," she whispered, "and that's what I get, other than the stupid snake toss. How about more about the target?"

Cassie draped her arm over her eyes. Sometimes, she hated her power.

Shooting stars flared in the sky. Trev looked up at them. He'd read that people used to wish upon falling stars, thinking they were special. Then they'd found out most were nothing more than bits of rock and cared far less. Even so, a meteor show was a special event, uncommon enough to spark interest.

The average human could look at the sky on any given night and almost always see a similar sight, with the vast majority being burning debris left over from the obliteration of every satellite in orbit during the Big Change.

From what Trev had read, the combination of nukes launched and unidentified power discharges had destroyed enough satellites to create a vast cloud of space trash in Earth's low orbit.

Any satellites that had survived the initial destruction would, if they hadn't already, eventually pass through the debris cloud, making more debris. The cycle was now self-sustaining; his dad had told him it was called the Kessler Syndrome. Mankind had lost their access to space.

When he felt cynical, Trev thought that was just an excuse for people not to reach for the stars. Still, it had meant giving up the military and communication advantages of satellites. That had created a new focus on terrestrial communication networks across the planet—and placed a high value on any power that involved nonlocal communication.

Research and efforts by governments focused on producing specific powers with communication and military applications in mind. So far, all such research projects had failed. The world powers had been forced to adapt to the loss of their satellites. Until someone powerful enough to clear out the debris arrived, humanity was once again a purely terrestrial species.

Trev strolled between tents after watching a few more flares in the sky. He whistled, the spices from a perfect fire iguana sandwich lingering in his mouth. He'd been dubious about eating the monster meat when he'd first moved to the Republic. The idea was anathema in the NEUS, but a few bites had convinced him. Not all monster meat was good, but fire iguana was excellent. It tasted like spicy chicken.

Unfortunately, not enough people had animal control powers to make raising most monsters at commercial exploitation levels practical, even in tolerant countries like the New Baja Republic. That meant hunters could supply communities with luxury monster meat.

One of the perks of participating in the race was getting access to monster meat at non-premium prices. He doubted he'd eat this much exotic game again for a long time. There was also the practical consideration of what he could eat and drink while driving most of the day.

"Nothing but meal bars and water for a while," Trev

complained after a yawn. "Don't you worry, fire iguana meat. I'll eat you at night. I won't forget you."

He slowed when two men moved to block his path. Another man walked up behind him. They all sported leather jackets similar to the ones Will and his buddies had worn, though the jackets, much like the earlier ones, lacked identifiable symbols.

He assumed they were part of a gang or an organization, but he wasn't used to members not shouting their name at every opportunity. The identity didn't matter as much as the implication that they'd come looking for trouble and revenge.

Trev was more concerned by their weapons belts since they had pistols and knives. Being surrounded by three men made it far less likely that he'd be able to resolve this as cleanly as he had with Will the Ice Dick Asshole. His efforts to avoid using his power around others were getting more challenging each day.

"You had any of the fire iguana sandwiches yet?" Trev asked. "Trust me, they're worth the price, and it's a steal compared to what you normally have to pay." He patted his stomach. "I'm all but addicted to the stuff. When the race is over, I'm going to find a hookup. Do you happen to know any fire iguana meat sellers in Tucson?"

Disrupting the flow of hatred could prevent a battle from erupting. That was another hard-earned lesson from years of defending Jack. Sometimes, making a man your friend, even for a second, could stop an unnecessary fight.

Trev didn't mind beating people down. However, he had long since learned that he didn't have to beat everyone down, even the ones who deserved that or worse.

Every fight meant risking his life, so he had to consider the time, place, and possible consequences.

"We're not here to talk about sandwiches." One of the men stepped forward and cracked his knuckles. His nasty, unkempt beard disgusted Trev. "You screwed up our buddy's race. We came to talk about that. He's had to drop out."

"I didn't screw up anyone's race," Trev replied. "The race hasn't even started yet, so it'd be hard for me to mess up somebody's race. I'm not a time traveler."

"He got a huge penalty. It was too much to overcome." The bearded man bared his teeth. He needed to stop at the dentist after his trip to the barber. "He'd have to be a racing god to place in the top ten. He might as well not race, and that's all because of you. He's dropping out."

"I assume you're talking about Will the Ass Sword? Excuse me, I meant 'the Ice Sword.'" Trev scoffed. "You're lucky they didn't kick him out entirely from the beginning. Yes, we fought, but why don't you ask him how that fight started?"

"We talked to him." The bearded man motioned to the others. "We're his friends, and he's got other dangerous friends you don't want to fuck with, you stupid little shit. We came here to make that clear."

Trev loosened his shoulders and bounced on his feet. "Were you there? Did you see what happened?"

"We didn't need to see. He told us what happened."

"Your friend messed with my friend. I tried to get him back off, but he decided to cut me. I defended myself, and Event Security said it was self-defense, so I didn't get any penalties, and he did." Trev shook his head. "Don't you get it? He was wrong on two levels. First, your buddy picked an unnecessary fight. Second, your buddy picked a fight he couldn't win and paid for it. Don't make the same mistake."

The bearded man drew his knife. Trev glanced at the other men. They weren't going for weapons yet. "Messing Will up made things hard for the boss," the bearded man continued. "Somebody's got to take responsibility."

"Wouldn't that be Will since he's the one who screwed up?" Trev shrugged. "Beyond starting an unnecessary fight, he couldn't finish what he started. Speaking of that, you three really don't want to start anything." He pointed up. "Just because it's nighttime doesn't mean the drones can't see you. Three guys jumping one guy won't end with penalties. It will end with you getting disqualified or marked with bounties by Republic authorities."

The bearded man pointed at his ear. "You hear anybody but us, shithead?" He pointed up. "You see any drones? Nobody's using power detectors in the camp since they'd be going off all the time. That means all we need to do is take care of anything watching and any sound, and we're free to do what we want." He shot Trev a manic grin. "You think you're the first guy we've messed up since we came here? Not saying we killed anybody, but we've run other shitheads off."

Trev frowned. Even at night, the camp swarmed with people, partying, talking, eating and drinking. Despite that, he couldn't hear anything but the heavy breathing of three thugs and the scratch of their boots as they scraped the dirt and rocks. "Nice party trick, but that means you don't have combat powers."

"Who needs combat powers when it's three-on-one?"

The bearded man laughed. "You get it now, don't you? Nobody can see us. Nobody can hear us, and they aren't going to hear you screaming and calling for help."

Trev looked around. Whatever powers the thugs were using had a limited range. Disabling the surveillance throughout the camp would have tipped off Security and sent the guards into an uproar. "I'm not going to be the one screaming,"

"Don't worry," the bearded man continued, tossing his knife from hand to hand. "We're not gonna kill you since the boss wants everybody to know what a bitch you are, but you'll be pissing blood for a while. I'm sure they can chopper you to a hospital. I'll even be nice. Are you right-handed or left-handed? I'll only take a finger from your off hand if you come over here right now. If you don't, you'll lose fingers on both hands."

Trev groaned. "I go out of my way not to kill people, and this is the thanks I get." He motioned for them to attack. "Screw it. You want a piece of me? Come get it. I'd rather get to sleep earlier if I'm going to have to sleep off pain."

The bearded man nodded at the other two thugs. Trev tensed when they reached behind them, though they pulled out brass knuckles rather than going for their guns. They slipped on the devices.

Their weapons choices confirmed a basic level of restraint. None of the three men had gone for their guns. Uncontrolled gunfire risked detection and angry Security, including the boost-suited sonic stunner.

Trev shook his head. "I don't believe in honorable fights when I'm dealing with greasy thugs."

"Honor?" The bearded man laughed. "You can whine about honor after we break your face."

Trev glanced at the ground and squatted. "Don't say I didn't warn you."

The bearded man scoffed. "Beat his ass, but don't kill him."

CHAPTER ELEVEN

One of the brass knuckles-wearing thugs charged. Trev grabbed a handful of dirt and flung it into his eyes.

The thug grunted and tripped, then rubbed his eyes. "I can't see. You bastard."

He hissed in pain as he scratched his eyelid with his brass knuckles. He stumbled forward, setting himself up for Trev's follow-up uppercut to his chin. Trev landed a solid hit accompanied by a cracking noise. The thug flew back and crashed into his fellow brass knuckles wearer.

"Get off me!" his friend shouted.

The bearded man gritted his teeth. Trev darted forward and landed a wild hook on the second brass knuckles-wearing thug's head. Both men fell to the ground, trying to push off one another. The teary-eyed first man kept blinking, trying to get the dirt out of his eyes.

Trev nailed one of the thugs in the stomach with his boot. The man groaned and clutched his stomach. Trev's elbow drop ended on the face of the other downed man.

The hard blow smacked the thug's head against the ground, leaving it gushing blood.

"I was worried." Trev jumped to his feet and shook out his throbbing fists. "You'd think I'd get used to how much it hurts to punch somebody. Don't worry, though. I've got plenty left in me." He kicked a thug on the ground in the face. "No matter how this ends, this will hurt you way more than it hurts me."

"*You cocky asshole!*" the bearded man screamed. His two friends lay in a heap on the ground, both bleeding, their faces battered. Trev's first victim whimpered.

Trev shot him a grin. "The true elites of the Sonoran. Are we done here? I think I've made my point, so you guys should quit while nobody needs real medical care."

The bearded man growled. "You're dead!"

He charged Trev, leaping over his fallen friends to thrust his knife. Trev jerked back, avoiding the first slice. The aggressive swings kept pushing him back.

"*Where are your jokes now, asshole?*" the bearded man shouted. "*Let's see if you like talking after I cut out your tongue. You think you're funny.*"

"I'm a little funny," Trev countered. He dodged a quick stab with a sidestep and pivoted to avoid a slash. "That's not funny. If you keep playing with sharp toys, you'll get hurt."

The bearded man spun and tossed his knife into the other hand. The exchange took Trev off-guard, allowing the bearded man to slice his chest and his arm on the backswing.

"Who's laughing now?" The bearded man backed away

and held up the bloody knife. "I'm going to make this last. You're going to hurt."

Trev sucked in a breath. His chest and arm burned, and blood dripped from the shallow wounds. "You're really pissing me off."

"You should have brought a gun."

"If I go for my gun, you'll go for yours." The ache in Trev's chest intensified. "That's why I don't walk around with one in camp. I don't need it. Consider it mercy."

The bearded man lunged forward. "I'm going to cut that smirking mouth."

Trev dodged to avoid the swings. Each movement increased the pain in his arm and chest. His restraint had cost him.

"This is self-defense, right?" The bearded tossed his bloody knife back and forth. "You can kill a man in self-defense. I'm going to gut you and plant a gun on you, bitch."

"I won't let you win," Trev replied, raising his fists. "I'm not going to let you stab me to death, no matter what I have to do. You've misunderstood what's going on."

The bearded man spat at Trev's feet. "You took Will down, so I thought you might be something. You're nothing but a bitch who got lucky and is going to die knowing you should have never messed with us." He rushed forward, holding his knife with both hands.

Trev pivoted and grabbed one wrist, then pulled back. He offered a silent thanks to his mother for showing him the move. "Drop it, asshole, or I'll break your damned wrist."

The bearded man laughed and yanked a second knife out. He shoved it toward Trev's neck. "Surprise, asshole!"

Trev grunted as the blade bounced off the thin purple forcefield protecting his throat. The bearded man lost his grip, and the second knife fell and impaled the ground.

"What the hell is that?" The bearded man yanked out of Trev's grip. His first knife went flying, and he jumped to grab it.

Trev glared at his opponent. "It's a power that's not about blocking sound or blinding drones." He let go of the field. "It's the reason you should not come after me. You dumbasses are so used to messing with ordinary people that you forget that when you're doing your wolf act, every once in a while, you're going to run into a hunting dog who's not going to put up with your shit."

"*Screw you!*" The bearded man slashed at Trev's arm.

A thought summoned a new forcefield over Trev's arm. The knife bounced off.

The bearded man followed up by stabbing at different parts of Trev's body with surprising speed and agility. Trev's forcefield shifted with each blow, deflecting the knife.

"There's got to be a limit," the bearded man insisted, slicing at Trev's side. "I got it. You keep blocking, but you can't attack me while I'm attacking you. That's why you didn't use this power before."

A powerful overhead blow bounced back with enough force to give Trev an opening. A series of lightning face jabs and a final right hook battered the bearded man's face and launched him back toward his friends.

"This has crossed the old insanity line." Trev shook out

his hand. "I don't understand what you think you know, but if you've been in any fights with real powers, you'd know that you're not winning just because you're not losing right away."

The panting attacker growled, blood dripping from his nose and several cuts on his cheeks. "Get up, you lazy pieces of shit. We can take this guy if we work together. We can't go back to the boss like this."

His friends staggered to their feet, their faces bruised and swelling. Neither looked eager to continue the fight. "That was how you beat Will," the bearded man declared, glancing at the knife. "He didn't mention you using your power."

"Nope. I didn't use my power against him. He's not that good, so I didn't bother. Now, are we done here, or do you want to die?"

"Yeah. We're done here."

The bearded man tossed his knife to the ground and drew his gun. Trev sighed, and the man fired.

The bullet bounced off a circular forcefield covering his chest. Heart pounding, Trev watched the man's eyes and the gun and moved the shield up and down in response to the shots. Bullet after bullet ricocheted off the shield until one bounced back and grazed the gunman's side.

He hissed in pain. "You bastard. I'll kill you."

"You were hit by your own bullet." Trev scoffed. "You'll only kill *yourself*, asshole."

Trev dropped to one knee and threw up his hand. His shield vanished, and a thin crescent-shaped blade of purple light shot from his hand, sliced through the gun, and took off the gunman's trigger finger.

The gunman stared at his hand, his eyes widening. Then he fell to his knees and dropped what was left of the gun. The energy blade had flown off at a high angle, barely missing the top of a nearby tent.

Trev grimaced. He doubted that whatever power was hiding the fight extended as far as his energy blade had flown. The outside chatter and din from the rest of the camp returned, reinforcing his concern.

"*You son of a bitch!*" the bearded man screamed, clutching his hand.

"You must be the noise guy." Trev looked at the other men. "You want some of that too? What was it earlier? Oh, yeah, he asked me which hand I wanted to lose fingers from."

They swallowed and backed away, hands in front of them. One stopped, knelt, and collected their friend's missing digit.

"I'm tired of asking this, but are we done here, assholes?" Trev glared. "I've tried really hard not to kill you. I need to race, but you guys are going out of your way to die." He lifted his arm and summoned a buckler of pure energy. "You can't hit me, and I can cut you apart from up close or far away. You should leave this camp tonight because if I see you again, I'll reconsider letting you go. Don't make me come looking for you to take your damned heads off."

He pointed his finger at a small rock outcropping and sliced through it with an energy blade. Demonstrations of power were the best reinforcements for threats.

The bearded man glared at Trev before limping away, his battered friends flanking him.

"*Watch your back, bitch!*" the bearded man shouted after he'd stepped behind a tent. "The boss is going to hear about this."

"If he's as stubborn as you are," Trev replied, "I hope he's got life insurance."

He glanced up and folded his arms. He hadn't been sure they'd been lying about drones, but the man had unloaded half his magazine into Trev, and the sound suppression kept anyone nearby from checking things out.

After a few minutes without Security showing up to accost Trev, he stuck his hands in his pockets and emerged from between the tents with a jaunty whistle. He felt much better, wounds notwithstanding. Fire Iguana meat and ass-kicking made for a relaxing pre-race night.

CHAPTER TWELVE

March 7, 2036, Starting Line, Sonoran Desert, New Baja Republic

Tire tracks of varying widths ran in different directions around the encampment. They marked the transition from the primarily clear patch of sandy dirt into the plentiful shrubs and cacti that defined the Sonoran Desert.

Heavy trucks encircled the camp. Trev's and Jack's truck was near the front but behind another truck as they watched an entrant with an earlier starting time disappear behind a hill.

Day One of the rally was finally here. Dealing with annoying thugs and the drama with tourists was over. Now Trev could focus on what he was good at, which was driving and shooting monsters.

His heart pounded. After adjusting his helmet, he bounced in his seat like an excited little boy at a parade. Nothing was better than those few minutes before the start of a race. All the preparation, effort, and adrenaline had led him to this moment.

This rally was an endurance marathon spread over three days, with occasional monsters to add excitement. It was the most significant challenge he'd faced in his short life. He'd have to push his body and truck to the limit.

Trev revved the engine. Jack sat on the far right of the bench-style seat, watching a custom display on his tablet.

"How are we doing, Jack?" Trev laughed. "I don't know why I asked. We're still going to go, even if you tell me the engine's about to blow."

"Everything's loaded and confirmed," Jack announced. "I'm getting good signal from the regional towers and the tracking drone. Helmet comms are good. Truck telemetry is solid." He snorted. "As if I'd let this truck get to the line in anything but perfect condition."

"We're going to smash this first stage," Trev shouted, slapping the steering wheel. "We're going to destroy the time, the monsters, and anything that gets in our way. Let's go!"

"Calm down," Cassie commented from the back seat with a yawn. "The race hasn't even started. Aren't you getting ahead of yourself?"

Trev turned and stared at her. Focused on the race, he'd barely paid attention when she'd put on her helmet.

"What's wrong?" she asked.

"You have a Rage Rabbit racing helmet?" Trev asked.

"Of course I do. I bought it specifically to be a tourist in this race." Cassie flipped the visor up. "I'd prefer it if you didn't crash, though."

Trev chuckled. "I would, too."

"Forget about my helmet. Focus on the race." Cassie gestured at the window. "How do you know there's not a guy planning to teleport his truck?"

"Teleportation and flying are against the rules," Trev explained. "They spelled it out in that big-ass list all the drivers have to acknowledge they read."

Cassie nodded. "I mostly paid attention to the tourist rules."

"They've got a good range. Even stuff like kinetic manipulation. Doesn't matter since the detectors would pick it up, and the drones are watching."

"If you say so." Cassie's gaze flicked up for a second.

To Trev's pleasure, she'd arrived on time with all her gear, though she looked tired. He didn't care. All she needed to do was sit in the back seat and not distract him after he began driving.

She could sleep the whole time if she wanted. He'd heard about tourists who had done just that.

An official waved a starting flag, and the truck in front zoomed away, kicking up rocks and dust in a billowing cloud.

"Our starting time is coming up," Jack announced.

"I know," Trev replied. "I'm so ready."

Trev drove the truck through the dust cloud to the starting line. An official held up his palm, and Trev stopped.

"This is your last chance to get on my good side by telling me your power, tourist." Trev looked over his shoulder and smiled at Cassie. "It doesn't even have to be combat-useful. Navigational stuff helps, too. I knew a woman back home with a living rangefinder power that was super-accurate. It wasn't useful for her job, but stuff like that would help in this situation, and you tourists are allowed to use your powers in the car."

"Shouldn't you have been looking for a tourist who could teleport your truck?" Cassie asked. "Since we're allowed to use our powers freely?"

"Even tourists aren't allowed to manipulate the vehicle in a way that causes it to perform better than others," Trev replied.

Cassie frowned. "You're driving in an all-terrain rally race without nav aids? Isn't that stupid?"

Trev shook his head. "I didn't say that."

Cassie leaned forward. "Jack has a map and location finder."

"I do," Jack confirmed, holding up the tablet.

"Nav aids aren't always great when you're in the wilderness in rough terrain," Trev explained, "and we only have a few nav aerostats and towers on the course. It's not like the Republic's government is sponsoring this thing. Backups never hurt."

"I'm not a living rangefinder or an automapper," Cassie replied. "I can't fly or teleport. I don't like to talk about my power. How's that for an answer?"

"No shame in having a useless power." Trev grinned. "I won't judge you for it."

"What about your powers?" Cassie glanced at Jack. "That was a bitch thing to ask. I'm sorry."

Jack shook his head. "I stopped being ashamed of how I look long ago." He smiled at Trev. "The Leons and others accepted me for who I am."

"Is that your power?"

"I'm more agile than most people, plus tougher and stronger. I can also jump farther." Jack's tongue flicked out. "I don't know why, but when I was a kid, I was good with mechanical stuff, and I got better after the Big Change. I can visualize parts and three-dimensional connections better than most people. I've been told it might be due to my brain being reorganized, but I've tried to avoid doctors or scientists. You can guess the reason."

"I don't blame you." Cassie's voice was sympathetic. "Good for you, Jack. That's more useful than most people's powers, even the so-called heroes." She turned to Trev. "What's *your* power, summoning quips on command? Or is it looking smug regardless of the situation? Class-AA immovable smugness and a smirk that threatens cities."

"No." Trev shook his head. "I was blessed with those talents from birth."

"From birth?" Cassie grinned. "You came out of the womb smug?"

Trev shrugged. "Well, birth plus eight years or so."

He looked at the rearview mirror. He couldn't deny the woman had a sultry, witchlike allure, but he thought she was holding something important back. There was no reason not to respond in kind. "You'll see my Big Change power when the time comes. *If* it comes. That depends on what monsters show up to kill us."

"Oh." Cassie's brows rose. "You're admitting it's useful in combat."

"You could say that."

"Can't you show me now? Give me a preview? Call me curious. I don't like to wait until Christmas morning to open my presents."

Trev wagged a finger. "Haven't you heard that greedy kids get fewer presents?" He pointed at the roof. "Did you see the weird little x-shaped antenna on top of the truck?"

Cassie nodded. "Sure. What about it?"

"It's a short-range MQI wave detector," Trev replied. "Fancy one, made by the 46P1 corporation. Every vehicle in the race gets one installed by the organization's staff. They did it on our arrival before I finished reading and signing all the forms."

"A what?" Cassie batted her eyelashes.

Trev frowned. He doubted a woman who'd come to be a tourist in a race like this one would be that ignorant, especially after she'd demonstrated extensive knowledge of the race procedures. Then again, not everyone had ended up in a good place in life or education after the Big Change. Jack had been lucky that Mr. Ellsworth and Trev were there.

"You don't know what an MQI wave detector is?" Trev asked. "You're kidding, right?"

Cassie opened her mouth and shut it. She nibbled on her lip and looked away. "Why don't you tell me?"

"You seriously don't know?" Trev pressed. "You're making me think less of you, just when I was beginning to think there was something there other than an angry cartoon rabbit fan."

"Do *you* understand the detector?" Cassie's tone was mocking. "I've been told that if somebody understands something, they should be able to explain it to someone who doesn't."

Was it a test? At the minimum, it was a challenge. It wouldn't hurt to show that he wasn't ignorant. "It's a metaphysical qualia interface wave detector," Trev quoted. "I don't understand the physics and a good chunk of the science behind it."

"Most of the world doesn't," Jack interjected. "Even the people who invented it."

"It's basically a power detector," Trev explained. "It senses the waves everybody puts out when they use their power. The gadgets up there are mixed with other sensors and linked to cab cameras, though they are only visual feeds, so we can curse the organizers all we want in here. The cameras are only active during the race stages."

He kept his gaze on the starting line, though he pointed at her. "Basically, if anybody but your cute little tourist ass uses their powers within two meters of the truck during this race, we'll earn a time penalty."

"What's the logic?" Cassie asked. "I think I understand, but I want to hear what you have to say."

"The logic is, we have to get out of our truck and risk our vehicle and ourselves to fight monsters. It's a calculated risk-versus-reward scenario. That makes people choose different options depending on the situation." Trev shrugged. "This is half about excitement and half about being useful by culling monsters. The organizers want to slow people down to engage the monsters, making them choose between the monster bounty and time and the theoretical bigger payoff by finishing higher since, in the end, it *is* a race. Nobody would care about finishing fast if they didn't bother, and you'd lose the rally flavor."

"I hope everybody's detectors are working, then," Cassie replied with a faint smile. "I'd hate for somebody to be able to use a power against the rules."

"Yeah." Trev frowned, wondering if she was getting at something. He let it go.

Cassie's gaze shifted to Jack. "I don't know how to say

this delicately, but your power is always on. Why isn't it tripping the detector?"

"They call it a permanent phenotype modification," Jack explained.

Cassie nodded. "Oh, yeah. I've heard about that, but I didn't connect it."

"Technically, my powers are always on, but I've been fundamentally altered. I don't use MQI waves anymore because I'm not actively using a power." His tongue flicked. "I might have the day I changed. That's the theory, anyway. There have been a few cases where kids' powers are just manifesting. They visibly mutate and put out MQI waves until the process finishes."

"Isn't that a major advantage?" Cassie asked. "According to what you told me, part of your power makes you a better mechanic. The visualization and whatnot."

"That only helps me when I make repairs," Jack said. "As for the rest, it depends on who you ask." He looked away. He nodded at a bloody bandage that was revealed when Trev shifted and his shirt sleeve rode up.

"Are you okay?" Cassie frowned. "You weren't all cut up the last time I saw you."

"It's a scratch." Trev scoffed. "I've had way worse. I should tell you about this girl I dated once. Angelica…"

"He got that because some assholes don't like mutants," Jack interrupted. "Some guys jumped him last night because he defended me from a friend of theirs. I don't know where you're from, but that's what it can mean to look like me in a place like this."

"Everyone's a mutant at this point." Cassie lifted her hand and stared at her palm. "Wouldn't the real freaks be people without any changes? It's weird to be stuck on looking different rather than if they can fly or breathe underwater or turn rocks into glass."

Trev laughed. "Sometimes, you say smart things."

"I say smart things all the time. You're just not listening." She gestured at the front window. "By the way, I don't get this race. We're lining up, and people are starting at different times. Isn't the whole point of the race to beat the other guys?"

"It's a time attack rally raid based on vehicle class." Trev shook his head, wondering why a woman would participate in a race she didn't understand. "The drones, the sensors, and our camera feeds verify monster attacks. We get a few minutes to handle that, but if we take too long, too bad for us. We'll take a minimal time penalty. Otherwise, it's all about navigating the prescribed routes and getting to the next rally point faster than other trucks in our wave and division."

"Why not just avoid them?" Cassie asked. "The monsters, that is. You get a big prize for finishing higher, right?"

"I thought you checked this out." Trev scoffed. "You already described the wave system."

Cassie sighed and folded her arms. "I know the rules, but I want to know what *you* think about them."

Trev blinked. "Really?"

"Yes, really. It's called making conversation. I'm asking to get your perspective and get to know you better. We're going to be driving together for three days. I'd like to know more now that I'm committed. Is that okay, asshole? I'm not planning to bother you while you're barreling through a forest of cacti at a hundred miles an hour."

Trev glanced at Jack. His co-driver shrugged. The plaintive, vulnerable tone in Cassie's voice took Trev off-guard. He'd assumed the questions were a gambit to manipulate him, not to get to know him better and learn more about him.

"Because we get major bonus money for killing monsters," Trev answered. "This is half-race, half-public service, and if we do things right, we can place in the top five and score major cash while also getting a bonus for the monster kills."

"That's what it's about for you?" Cassie sounded disappointed. "Money? You don't care about helping people?"

"We're not training for a hero team," Trev answered. "We need the money. The glory from winning is nice, too. It'll prove we're the best."

Jack jerked his head toward the windshield. "It's almost time."

"Keep it quiet for the start," Trev ordered. "It's not like you'll have to shut up the entire time, but I'll need to concentrate until I get into a groove."

Trev revved his engine and stared at the official and the flag. The seconds ticked away, but finally, the official waved the pennant. Trev floored it, and the truck burst away from the starting line and rumbled onto the shrub-covered track.

Jack stared at his nav display. "Go forward four hundred yards following the middle tracks, then hard left ninety degrees. Otherwise, we'll go through an outcrop and a bunch of saguaros. I don't want to test our windows against full-grown saguaros."

Trev grinned. Shrubs and cacti zoomed by the truck as he accelerated and pushed the truck into a stomach-churning turn that threatened to topple it. He spotted a lone tree in the distance and maneuvered into a natural tunnel between two patches of cacti interspersed among stony mounds.

He spared a glance at the rearview camera and the rearview mirror. The latter didn't do much more than give him a view of the backseat because of the trailer.

Cassie wasn't looking out the windows or closing her eyes in fear. She was staring at him with an annoyed look, probably due to the order to keep quiet.

He didn't care. He didn't have time to impress the tourist, no matter how hot she was. He had a race to win and monsters to kill.

CHAPTER THIRTEEN

Their truck cleared a low dirt mound faster than necessary, briefly taking to the air. Everyone grunted when the vehicle landed with a soft bounce and rattled the passengers.

Trev shouted with joy and slapped the steering wheel. "It's not a rally if you don't jump at least once."

"Please don't break the truck," Jack pleaded. "This isn't a UTV or a bike, Trev. If you kill the transmission out here, they'll have to come get us. They won't tow our truck back, and I won't let you hear the end of it. By the time we get back to recover our truck, it'll be a monster nest."

"Don't worry so much." Trev laughed. "We're good. I know exactly what I'm doing, so I can push it here and there."

"Like you knew what you were doing like that exhibition race in Tucson?"

Trev scoffed. "Totally different type of racing, different car, and the track was slick. That wasn't my fault."

"It hadn't rained in two months."

"Oil, then. It still wasn't my fault."

"You almost died."

"That's like being almost pregnant," Trev challenged. "You're either dead, or you're not."

Jack frowned but fell silent. Trev understood. He'd survived that crash due to a precise application of his power. That wasn't a conversation either wanted to have in front of Cassie.

Trev slipped into a good driving rhythm, with Cassie keeping quiet for the most part so Jack could perform his co-driver role by offering Trev navigational updates. In theory, not being the first vehicle to start in the wave meant having visible tracks to follow. However, they had no guarantee that the vehicles that hit the stage before them would follow the optimal route, and the UTVs, bikes, and cars that started before the trucks would take slightly different routes. Trev and Jack had to be careful.

Even with the addition of monster hunting, this rally raid wasn't that different from conventional events. Navigation was part of the challenge and one of the reasons every driver who could use a co-driver did. Only the bikers rode solo. Trev admired their concentration and physicality.

The navigational checkpoints throughout the stage required the truck to come within ten yards to register on the tracking systems. Simply driving as fast as they could from the starting line to the stage's endpoint would incur penalties that would put them behind the rest of the pack.

The presence of monsters made placing physical checkpoints in the uncontrolled portions of the course impractical, so they had to rely on the race organizers' drones and nav aerosats to confirm their positions, along with a backup comparison of the installed sensor systems.

That worried Trev. He didn't like relying on equipment Jack didn't maintain, but as far as he knew, there'd never been a confirmed case where a navigational failure was on the race organizer's side. He frowned, remembering Cassie's comment about hoping nobody's detector failed. Had she heard something about trouble? She'd been wandering around the camp. Some half-drunk race staff member might have opened up in exchange for her having a drink with him.

Trev pushed the thought away. He wasn't going to worry about equipment failure. He liked to think he wasn't superstitious, but it was hard to race and not worry about jinxes. That was why Cassie's comment about luck had set him off.

Jack swiped on the tablet. "Stay on the tracks, but sweep forty-five degrees to the right after the second outcrop. You can follow that for a few miles without much trouble."

"Roger," Trev replied. "We're making good time, and we're way ahead of my goal so far." He took a deep breath. "If we keep this up, we'll be in the top ten."

Cassie stared out the window. "In a so-called desert, I expected fewer plants. I even see trees on occasion." She frowned. "Sure, there are tons of cacti, but it's like…I don't know. Where is the sand?" She lifted her visor and squinted. "Half these plants are in bloom. A cactus with flowers? I didn't even know that was a thing. Now I feel stupid. It makes sense that a big plant like that has flowers."

"It's sandy soil out here, and it's a desert because it doesn't get much rain. Technically, Antarctica is a desert."

"It's a desert because it doesn't get much precipitation," Jack added. "It doesn't have to be rain."

"Oh, sorry." Trev laughed. *"Precipitation,"* he added in an exaggerated English accent.

Cassie looked between the men. "Are you climatologists?"

"I get where you're coming from," Trev replied. "The whole desert thing confused me when we first moved here. They say the Sonoran is a living desert, so it's different from the sand dune version. It's also the only place in the world that has saguaro cacti, even though they are iconic and show up in many depictions of what people expect when they think desert. In a way, it's the ultimate desert because of that."

Cassie chuckled. "Forget scientists. You sound like a tourism brochure."

"Not far off. I got that speech from a visitor center display in Tucson, but it's true. You're not from the New Baja Republic, are you?"

"No, just visiting," Cassie replied. "A tourist in the common meaning of the word. Is that so weird? I'd be willing to bet that tons of people participating in this race aren't from the Republic."

"A gradual left turn up a mild slope in four hundred yards," Jack directed. "Right after that, either slow down and turn right within five hundred yards or hard turn to avoid the remains of several crashed airliners." He frowned.

Trev grunted. "Roger that."

Everybody was quiet as the truck lumbered through the desert toward the unexpected symbol of mass death. Their first turn took them past a low hill surrounded by piles of rusted, blackened metal.

Trev gave the obstacle a wide berth. He didn't speak for a few minutes after they'd passed the planes. He wasn't sure why they bothered him so much. It wasn't his first time seeing reminders of mass death while traveling. Maybe it was because he'd had a dream about the Big Change not long ago.

Civilization hadn't collapsed, though many countries had splintered. The civilizations that arose from the ashes of the old world had focused on the survivors.

Horrors had played out all over the globe. The remains of thousands of planes that had fallen that day were strewn all over. The lucky ones got a burial at sea.

"Where are you from, Cassie?" Trev asked to push the gloom away. "We got interrupted earlier."

"I'm from the Northern Confederation. Believe it or not, I'm an Iowa girl. Des Moines. It was a nice place to grow up. Although the Change hit us hard, it wasn't as bad as it was in some places."

"Isn't Des Moines close to Chicago?" Trev asked, hands tightening on the wheel. So much for pushing away the gloom.

Cassie shook her head. "Not that close. Over three hundred miles."

"Just saying," Trev muttered.

"Just saying what?" Anger leaked into Cassie's tone. "Spit it out while we can still talk."

"All those nukes, you know?" Trev shrugged. "Everybody launched their nukes into space for whatever reason during the Big Change, and the other half vaporized in their silos without harming anybody. I mean, that's got to be a greater miracle than the Big Change itself."

"I suppose."

"Everyone panicked," Trev continued. "People thought it was the end of the world and set the nukes off. I figure the survivors in the governments lied about not launching them because they didn't want to get executed when people realized they almost destroyed the world in their panic."

Cassie nodded. "Yeah, so? You going somewhere with this, or are you practicing rambling for when you're an old man?"

"Every nuke disappeared or blew up in space," Trev commented, his voice distant and hollow. "If the governments aren't lying, they can't make new nukes work."

"That is a great thing," Cassie replied. "I don't know why that upsets you. One less threat isn't a bad thing in a world still recovering from something as crazy as the Big Change."

"We're going into a cactus maze," Jack reported.

"Give me a few, Cassie," Trev snapped. "I've got to concentrate now."

"Take your time." She folded her arms.

Jack barked out distances and turns with machinelike precision. Trev took advantage of his friend's efforts to achieve maximum safe speed before every turn. Their huge truck danced through the narrow paths between the tall cacti with only the occasional scrape.

Theoretically, a ten-ton truck versus a cactus wasn't a threat. The problem was that saguaros could reach the height of four-story buildings and weigh thousands of pounds. Running into one at high speed was an excellent way to end their race, if not their lives.

Trev blew out a breath he hadn't known he'd been holding after he pulled out of the last cluster of saguaros into a rough but less dense portion of the stage. "It's a good thing the Big Change only messed up animals." He shivered. "Imagine this race with walking cacti who could shoot their needles at you or fly and drop needles on you."

"I'd rather not," Jack replied. "For all we know, there *are* plants out there that changed."

"No known plants were altered by the Big Change," Cassie offered.

"If we're climatologists, are you a botanist?" Trev asked.

"46P1 has been taking biological samples for years and sharing research with other companies and governments," Cassie replied. "They've been researching everything. According to them, only animals were altered by the Big Change. No plants. No microbes. No fungi. Humans are the only species where every individual member changed. Even the rare people with no apparent powers have mutations in their DNA."

"Huh." Trev nodded. "I hadn't thought that much about it until now."

"And it's later now." Cassie's voice was tight.

"Huh? What do you mean, it's later? Isn't any time after another time later by definition?" Trev didn't turn around. He couldn't risk it at their current speed.

"You were talking about nuclear bombs," Cassie noted. "You were making some meandering point. I want to hear it."

"Oh." Trev nodded. "That. I just thought it was weird

that the entire planet basically vomited up its nukes, yet only Chicago got nuked. Talk about bad luck."

Cassie hissed. "That wasn't a nuclear weapon. That was a nuclear man."

Trev laughed.

"What's so funny?" Cassie lowered her visor. "You think the first Class-AA villain threat was funny? Do you think Ground Zero killing all those people was funny? That's messed up, Trev. I didn't think you were that twisted."

"No, not at all. I don't find any of that funny." Trev sighed and shook his head. "I wish the bastard had blown himself up in the middle of a lake or somewhere else harmless."

"Then what are you laughing about?"

"You."

"Huh?" Cassie replied.

Trev drove the truck around a fallen cactus. "I just find it interesting that you acted like you didn't know what an MQI detector is, but you know about Ground Zero. If I take you at your word, education's all over the place in the Northern Confederation."

"So, you're an expert on everything except racing and living deserts?" Cassie scoffed.

"No." Trev shook his head. "When the Big Change happened, we thought it was a nuclear war." He nodded at Jack. "We had a friendly neighbor who helped us out that first day. He'd talked to people who saw some things and were convinced it was, and there were all those communications and GPS problems at first."

He shook his head. "Our country—every country, really—fell apart. People died, lots of them, but after that first couple of months, everyone thought they understood what had happened. There was even a chance that the United States would stay together through tons of rebuilding. Many other countries weren't in such good shape."

"Then Chicago disappeared in a mushroom cloud, and the panic returned. Everyone thought they were going to die in a nuclear war." Cassie mused.

"Exactly." Trev licked his lips and shivered. "The old worries about the nukes came back. That's the ironic thing. I don't know if that would have been better or worse than what really happened. The truth just freaked people out more. I remember my parents looking at the images from Chicago on the internet." He inhaled sharply. "They were terrible."

"Of course," Cassie replied. "It was a horrific sight."

"No, I meant the quality. The fuzziness and blurriness made it worse because you knew it was real and not a trick." Trev slowed to avoid jumping a small hill. "I read about it. I know they were taken from far away by amateur photographers trying to document post-Big Change Chicago."

He concentrated as they crested the hill. "For me, after everything that had happened, that was the real Big Change. Before that, it hadn't sunk in. My parents were okay. My best friend had trouble, but he was living with me, and then I saw the pictures showing Ground Zero and the detonation. I saw the city going up in a mushroom cloud, and I thought, *The world really is going to end.*"

"I know what you mean," Cassie replied. "We'd all heard about nasty powers that were really dangerous, but I think we were all thinking about jerks with superstrength robbing a bank or a guy poisoning people with his touch, not about someone blowing up an entire city. Nobody had a real understanding of the true scope of the new powers."

"Ground Zero, the first empowered villain of the new empowered era," Trev quoted, remembering a retrospective on the incident. "He killed Chicago and what was left of American unity along with it."

"Canada had already fallen apart," Jack commented. "We were doing well by that standard."

"All the chaos and collapsed governments." Cassie sighed. "People still hadn't accounted for the bodies. Then 46P1 comes along, good little conglomerate that they are, saying they'll save us all from people like Ground Zero. They formed the first hero team in Seattle."

Trev knew the story, but he wanted to take a page from Cassie and hear her tell it. What she chose to relate would help him learn how she viewed the world.

"You sound angry when you describe it." Trev's heart pounded. The conversation had taken an odd turn, and it was his fault, so he couldn't complain. "You hate the Pacific Shield? Did they not save somebody you know?"

"I don't have a problem with them." Cassie shook her head. "They calmed things down a bunch in the Pacific Northwest. However, that probably contributed to the collapse of the US. I doubt the Pacific Alliance and their subsequent government-sponsored hero team would have formed without the Pacific Shield as an example. It's weird to think the first real team of superheroes came from a multinational corporation. It all led back to the nuclear man, but I wonder if hero teams are just as bad."

"How can a hero team be as bad as Ground Zero?" Trev

asked. "Oh, I get what you're saying. It was a while before every government admitted the truth about what happened to their nukes, right? Years before they admitted they couldn't make new ones. Are hero teams the new nukes? An AA-ranked hero or a team of A-ranked heroes can trash a city without killing themselves. Is that what you're getting at?"

"Most people aren't anywhere near that," Jack interjected. "Many people's powers are F or E strength." He narrowed his eyes at the nav display. "We've got a rough patch coming. A really rough patch."

"Back to quiet time."

Trev fell into a near trance, hands moving as if they responded directly to Jack's instructions. Despite his concentration, the earlier conversation and the unsolved mysteries of the Big Change lingered in his thoughts.

An AA-ranked villain could threaten a city. Not yet assigned, though officially an option, according to most governments and corporations, an AAA threat rating was powerful enough to threaten the entire planet.

Trev had always wondered if a secret AAA-level hero had manifested during the Big Change and used their power to destroy the nuclear weapons. The contradictory statements after the Big Change about the launch of nuclear weapons and the subsequent inability of any government to produce a new one left him and many other people wondering. For all he knew, a mystery AAA person could have been out there, both cursing and saving the world.

Tense minutes of concentration flowed together until the truck hit a long, conveniently flat patch of ground that offered twenty minutes of driving in a relatively straight direction, threatened only by sparse vegetation and rock outcrops on the edges.

"Do you ever think about why it started?" Trev asked, breaking the silence in the cab.

"The Big Change?" Jack glanced his way. "You always said it didn't matter. We couldn't alter the past, so worrying about it was a waste of time."

"Sure, but if we know why it happened, we could keep something worse from happening in the future." Trev frowned. "It rubs me the wrong way that we don't understand."

Jack shrugged. "There are all sorts of rumors about something that happened in Antarctica right before the change. I'm sure somebody went down there to check things out. We just didn't hear about it."

Cassie cleared her throat. "They know there was an energy spike in Antarctica, but that might not have been the cause, just the first recorded appearance of the energy. We might never know the answer."

"The woman who didn't know about MQI detectors knows that." Trev snickered. "Talk about an inconsistent education."

Cassie harrumphed. "You don't know what I know."

"Which is why you should be honest," Trev challenged.

"I'm honest enough."

"Somebody has to know the truth," Jack interjected. "The world doesn't change overnight without somebody knowing the reason, even if it takes them a while to figure it out."

"I'm just glad we're all still here." Trev grunted as the

truck rattled. He slowed before accelerating down a mild slope. "In a weird way, the Big Change gave me faith in humanity."

"Even though you're constantly fighting people, and you say we can't trust anyone and your preferred problem-solving strategy is punching people in the face?" Jack asked, chuckling.

"Countries fell apart," Trev noted. "And too many people died, but civilization didn't completely fall apart. Humanity didn't die out." He smiled. "The countries are different. People have powers now, and we can't go into space anymore, but it's not like this world is so weird compared to the past."

Cassie laughed. "A world where everyone has powers isn't weird compared to one where they didn't?"

Jack's head slumped forward. He groaned.

"What's wrong?" Trev asked, risking a look that way.

"I hadn't thought about it for a while. I just realized we'll never get *Street Fighter VIII*."

Trev smiled. "You'll just have to create it, you old Cammy-lover."

He slowed and peered to his left. They would be making a turn past a good-sized hill. He'd thought about trying to power over it, but it was steep, and he couldn't risk rolling.

The truck cleared the hill, but Trev slammed on the brakes.

Cassie hissed, "What the hell are you doing, Trev?"

Trev pointed out the window. "Did you forget what's special about this race?"

A truck lay on its side, missing a tire, with smoke

pouring from the engine. Shredded rubber lay in a wide arc to the side. Four fire iguanas surrounded the truck, each the size of a small car. One of the monsters breathed a stream of fire at the back of the vehicle. Another clawed at the trailer, tearing long, jagged holes. Shadows moved in the cab.

Trev narrowed his eyes. "I see people in there. Time to hunt and save lives."

CHAPTER FOURTEEN

Trev reached into the glove box and pulled out a .50 caliber Revenger, which, in his opinion, was the finest product of the San Diego Arms company. He'd been dubious about the weapon when he arrived in the Republic, but then he took one from a dead bandit and used it on other soon-to-be-dead bandits. He didn't want to flaunt it in the camp and risk unnecessary escalations, but taking down monsters required a big punch.

Dumb monsters like fire iguanas didn't require his secret weapon in the back. He'd run into fire iguanas before as a result of taking a less-traveled path to Tucson. He had a good idea of how to handle them.

Jack reached under the front seat and pulled out a long, bulky black rifle. "Ready."

"What's that?" Cassie asked, gesturing at Jack's weapon.

"My custom coilgun," Jack explained, voice filled with pride.

"What is that? I've heard of railguns, but I don't know what a coilgun is."

Jack pulled out a rectangular energy cell and slapped it into a slot in the weapon. "It uses magnetic fields to move the ammo. Powerful and way quieter than you'd suspect. Custom flechette ammo. I make it myself. Armor-piercing." He patted the barrel. "Really good for going through bandit cars."

"It uses magnetic fields? Isn't that a railgun?"

Indignation filled Jack's voice. "No, the designs are different. The principles of projectile acceleration are different. First—"

"Not now, you two." Trev opened his door. "We can discuss the technical details later. Let's kill some monsters before the people in that truck are roasted to death. Remember, we're also on the clock to avoid a penalty." He turned to Cassie. "Stay in here. Those cornstalks in Iowa don't breathe fire."

"We have monsters in Iowa, too." Cassie pulled her jacket back. "I have a gun."

"You're still staying in the truck."

"Your funeral."

Trev rolled out and hit the ground in a crouch, raising his gun. Jack ran around the front to join his partner, lowering the visor on his helmet against the sun.

The fire iguanas continued scorching the back of the trailer and the truck, the concentrated flame turning the metal red-hot. None of the monsters reacted to the new truck or the appearance of two armed men.

That was why Trev liked fighting the bigger monsters. They were rarely smart. It was like they'd traded brain cells for more power. "I'm insulted that they don't view us as a threat."

"What's the plan?" Jack asked. "I'm assuming there is one, or hoping so. Please tell me there's a plan."

"We'll split up and distance ourselves from our truck before getting their attention," Trev called as he jogged toward the monsters. "That counts as a plan!"

Jack shook his head and sprinted toward the monsters and the overturned truck at a different angle to put distance between Trev and him while they moved in the general direction of the iguanas.

Trev wasn't worried. He and Jack weren't mercenaries, but they'd been in their share of scraps. Jack had learned to follow Trev's lead, even if he didn't like it, and his speed made it easy for him to adapt to formation changes. They just had to apply what they'd learned from their last fire iguana showdown.

The most important was getting the monsters' attention. The passengers had only survived because the fire iguanas were focused on the trailer. When they started roasting the front, the passengers would die. Even if an individual passenger could protect himself from the heat and flames, not everybody could.

Three people was the minimum team size. It wasn't every day that Trev could do something that would feel good and help him earn money.

"We'll just do this like before," Trev murmured. "It'll work out."

He lifted his Revenger and lined up the sights on the closest fire iguana, then fired. The bullet left the weapon with a resounding crack and bounced off the thick hide.

The crushed bullet hit the ground. He hadn't expected

to take a monster that big down easily, not that he would have minded. His goal was different.

"Come on, look at me, you big bastard," Trev shouted. *"Toast me if you can."*

The fire iguanas stopped torching the trailer and rounded on the prey that had dared sting one of them.

Trev smiled at his successful distraction. *"I don't care how big something is. You can always win when it's stupid."* He waved the gun. *"Come on, you stupid wannabe dragon dinosaurs. You think you're the top of the animal kingdom in the desert. Don't you dare look down on humans."*

Jack aimed his coilgun at the fire iguanas, and with a barely audible click and pop, a dart-like flechette whizzed out and exploded a fire iguana's eye in a shower of blood.

The wounded monster scampered back, hissing. The other three froze, confused about how their fellow iguana had been hit. Whatever experience they had with conventional firearms wasn't applicable to the coilgun.

Trev swung his Revenger toward the fleeing iguana and put three rounds through the wounded eye, finishing off what was left of the head. The body tumbled to the ground and kicked up dust.

"Too easy!" Trev yelled. *"Good setup, Jack. We've got this."*

The surviving fire iguanas spewed fire at Trev and Jack, but the flames didn't reach either man. The nearby undergrowth and cacti caught fire, however, and smoke rose from the burning plants.

Trev couldn't line up his next eye-shot because of the wavering heat, smoke, and flames, so two bullets bounced off a fire iguana's head. *"Don't tell me you overgrown bastards did that on purpose. I'll never live it down if I'm outwitted by something I eat on a sandwich."*

Jack didn't do any better with his next attack. A cheek scale deflected a flechette and sent it spinning into the air above the flames.

"Just keep distracting them, Jack." Trev jogged around the flames. "Annoy them with shots, and I'll finish them off."

"Roger!" Jack sprinted toward the burning vegetation and leaped, clearing the flames with ease. His speed and jumping distance put the average human to shame. He was more than capable of protecting himself without Trev's help, although he'd learned to put up with idiots throughout the years.

Trev was determined to cure that, though Jack had no problem taking down monsters or bandits with him in the lead.

At the height of Jack's jump, he swept his coilgun in an arc and fired more flechettes. They ripped into two of the fire iguana's eyes, but the armored hide of the third deflected the final flechette. Jack landed in a crouch and instantly darted away, thus escaping the converging jets of flame from the barking and hissing fire iguanas.

"Or you can show off." Trev chuckled as he ran behind the flames.

Jack ran toward their truck. "I need to reload. I hurt them, but I didn't finish them."

"What have I told you about bringing extra ammo? Screw all that 'fights are over in seconds' nonsense."

Charging to the right of the enraged fire iguanas, Trev kept his gun level. The monsters wove their heads back and forth, toasting more of the local plants. He didn't shoot until he'd closed to about ten yards. The monsters realized their mistake at the last moment and pivoted to face the immediate threat.

A fire iguana opened its mouth, and flames formed at the back of its throat. The other two shuffled forward. Three bullets struck their wounded eyes, and the monsters collapsed, twitching.

"That's what you get for forgetting your place." Trev spun his gun before holstering the smoking weapon. "You're supposed to be in my stomach, not trying to roast my best friend. You weren't even worthy of my power." He sighed and jogged toward the overturned truck. "I hope the organizers grab these guys and grill this meat."

CHAPTER FIFTEEN

When the fight was over, Cassie grabbed a fire extinguisher and hopped out of the truck. She ran toward the smoke to kill the worst of the flames while Jack and Trev pulled the passengers out of the overturned truck. Given the hand-shaking and laughter, she assumed nobody was seriously hurt.

She had to give it to Trev and Jack. They had faced dangerous monsters without hesitating and knew how to use their weapons. They had obviously been in similar situations. For the first time, she felt like she was getting to see the real Trev Leon.

Despite that, Cassie didn't know if the fight helped her figure out anything of importance. Trev was a good shot and brave, but so were many people, including Jack. Taking down an oversized reptile with incendiary breath offered evidence of bravery and a reckless disdain for personal injury. For all she knew, he'd gone out of his way to take the monsters down to impress her, but it did not confirm that he was her target.

She'd all but abandoned the seduction plan. While Trev's comments proved his attraction to her, she couldn't manipulate him using, as he'd put it, her feminine wiles.

"They should have trained me for that," Cassie muttered. She kicked dirt onto a smoldering shrub while coating a burning cactus with the fire extinguisher. "There are many ways to approach a target."

Trev walked her way and waved. "You didn't have to put that fire out. It's been cool lately, and that'll stop it from spreading too far." He gestured at the extinguisher. "Remind me to fill that at the camp. We have others in the back, but those are for different types of fires."

"That explains why this area hasn't burned to the ground with monsters like that around," Cassie mused. "At least I learned something from watching the fight."

"That I'm awesome?"

"Now I know that you can't control fires. I was half-convinced that you would walk over to those iguanas and push their flames back inside."

"Yeah." Trev spread his arms. "You got me. I have zero fire control." He grinned. "By the way, process of elimination's not going to work. I might have a power you've never heard of."

Cassie shook a finger. "I bet it *is* super-luck."

"That's not a thing." Trev shook his head.

"Why does super-luck bother you more than other powers?" Cassie asked. "They all defy logic, and most of them defy what we thought we knew about science. It's not impossible that someone could have super-luck or control luck."

"Because controllable luck means something like fate might be real."

Cassie frowned. "You don't believe in fate? It bothers you?"

"Hell, yeah, it bothers me. I want to believe *I* control my destiny. No grand prophecy or plan is pushing me around. Free will." Trev shrugged. "Or something like that. Luck leads to fate, and fate leads to me being a puppet. I'm nobody's puppet."

Cassie stared at him, digesting what he'd said. Depending on how firm he was in those beliefs, if he was her target, proceeding further could be complicated.

"Is the other team all right?" she asked, not wanting to dwell on something she didn't need to deal with immediately. "It looked like it from the truck, but I wasn't sure."

Trev jerked his thumb over his shoulder. "They got surprised, is all. If you walk over to the truck, you will see a rock patch where the fire iguanas wouldn't be visible, depending on the angle. The monsters charged them from the side and knocked them over. The fire scorched the heck out of their trailer, but they're not hurt, so we did our part. Let's get back in our truck."

"But—" Cassie began.

"Back in the truck," Trev barked. "I wasted time talking to them, so we're too close to our penalty window."

He jogged toward the cab. Jack sprinted that way, with a final ten-foot jump to the passenger-side door. He opened it and motioned for her to climb inside.

Cassie ran back and jumped into the truck, throwing the empty extinguisher on the floor in the back seat. Trev hopped into the driver's seat and accelerated before securing his seatbelt, tires shooting up dirt behind the truck to add to the dust and smoke in the area. He didn't even wait for Cassie to finish settling into the back.

"*Hey!*" Cassie's elbow slammed into the back seat. "Careful. You just admitted you're the one who wasted time. Don't take it out on me."

"Sorry." Trev chuckled. "Those fire iguanas went down fast. Hurrying saved us from a penalty even though we had to check on the other drivers. The rules count the hunting encounter as ending when you get back in your vehicle and are moving at least fifty miles an hour. I'm just restarting the clock. I'll slow down so we can get our belts on."

"Next time, don't spend so much time congratulating yourself." Cassie shifted and shimmied until she got her seatbelt fastened. "Have you fought fire iguanas before? You seemed to know what you were doing. Or it could just be the super-luck."

Trev nodded. "Technically, that was our third time taking them on, though we haven't fought four at once."

"Pairs and singles only," Jack added. "It's easy when it's a singleton."

"They're not bad if you have good aim," Trev explained. "If we had to get near them, it would be rough." He slowed and took a moment to buckle his seatbelt. "I don't know how closely you were watching, but they bounced my .50 caliber rounds off like they had tank armor. I don't know if faster or bigger rounds would get through. Those scales also have good blast resistance."

He shook his head. "Nothing less satisfying than hitting a monster's body dead-on with a grenade and the monster shrugging it off. It's like the monster version of an opponent calling you a weak loser."

Jack grabbed the nav tablet. "You need to head northeast, and you did okay our first time against fire iguanas."

Trev laughed. "That's not how I remember it."

"You had the right idea," Jack countered. "You couldn't have known what would happen."

"You have to be careful. In my first battle, I just figured I'd put bullets down a fire iguana's throat. Even monsters are softer on the inside."

She nodded. "That makes biological sense. I'm guessing it didn't work out.'"

Trev turned the wheel and straightened out after they curved onto old tire tracks. "It turns out that knowledge of monster anatomy is useful. Fire iguanas have these little sacs where they store their fuel at the back of their throat."

Cassie frowned. "I don't understand. Are they armored? Did your shots not work?"

Trev shook his head. "No armor on those sacs. I bet a kid throwing a rock hard enough could rip 'em open. My bullet did the job. They blew up and roasted the fire iguana from the inside out. The problem is the fire iguanas use tiny amounts of fuel when they do their dragon impression. Release that all at once, and things get interesting." He grunted and turned to Jack. "How did you describe it? I remember you having a great description."

"Biological napalm spewed everywhere," Jack offered with a nod.

"Yeah, that was it. Not one of my finer hours."

Cassie grinned. "Jack, I was impressed. That was badass."

He shrugged. "I did okay. Trev finished them off."

"Only because you set him up. You two are a good team."

"We are." Jack smiled. "We're brothers in all but name."

Cassie leaned back in the seat. Trev had proven he was brave and could adapt in dangerous situations. Her mission might not be pointless, despite his earlier questionable statements.

A flash of her vision about Jack's death turned her stomach. She didn't know him well yet, but the poor guy's power forced him to grow up looking like a lizard. She didn't need to know his life story to understand that he'd suffered in the paranoid and chaotic post-Change world. She had a hard time believing Jack deserved to be killed.

Cassie took a deep breath. She wouldn't pretend her emotions didn't play a part in her mission, but she couldn't let them distract her. She had to focus on pulling more intelligence out of Trev. She couldn't move forward without confirming the intelligence that had brought her to the Republic.

She'd screwed up too many times already. Her strategy to play pretty and ignorant arm candy had failed. Trev had seen through her from the beginning, and she sensed his antipathy when she tried to influence him using that strategy.

That didn't bode well. Her investigation in Tucson before the race had led her astray, and she still didn't understand how she'd gotten it so wrong. What she'd expected and what had confronted her were far apart.

Cassie cleared her throat. "You didn't confirm there

weren't more monsters in the area before taking off. Isn't that dangerous?"

Trev laughed. "I'm sure there are."

"What about the other team?"

"They'll be fine. Nobody was seriously injured. They were surprised and got knocked over by the fire iguanas. If that hadn't happened, they would have defeated them. They had nice weapons, and I'm sure they have at least one helpful power."

"You have space in the back of your trailer," Cassie offered. "They could have ridden with us. That would have assured they were safe."

"Riding in a trailer without seatbelts in this race will end in broken bones. I'd be bouncing them off metal for hours."

"The monsters could kill them."

Trev shook his head. "Now that we've cleared the big ones, the organizers will send a helicopter for the team. We're already riding heavy, even before considering how unsafe it'd be for them."

"Excuse me?" Cassie frowned. "'Heavy?'"

"Not because of you, Princess Rage Rabbit." Trev laughed. "We have tons of gear in the trailer. If Jack hadn't tuned this beast as well as he did, we'd be in big trouble."

"Why are you running so heavy?" Cassie asked, glancing behind her.

"We've got toys that might help if things get out of hand."

"Like what?"

"Nothing you have to worry about."

Cassie groaned. "You're frustrating. You know that?"

"Jack tells me that all the time," Trev replied.

Jack nodded. "I do. I really do. It doesn't help."

"What if you're wrong about the other team? What's to stop other monsters from getting them if their weapons don't work? Won't rescue helicopters refuse to land if monsters are present?"

"I shouldn't have overplayed their weapons when I mentioned them earlier." Trev glanced her way. "Their real advantage is a quirk of Sonoran monsters. It's not unique to them, but it's more common in this area than in other places. Most monsters around here stay away from an area when they smell the blood of their kind or that of their known predators, and fire iguanas are high on the food chain here. It's not like the race organizers are trying to get people killed. I figure that's one of the reasons this weird hunter-style race started here before spreading to other places. The ecology is uniquely suited for this kind of race."

Cassie took in the information with a frown. "That's not a guarantee of their safety."

"It works, for the most part." He clucked his tongue. "Too bad the effect only lasts, like, a day. It'd be much easier to drive off monsters. On the other hand, people like us wouldn't make money if we could clear all the monsters out of places like this easily."

Cassie frowned. Every time he advanced in her estimation, he said something to send him back down.

"The rules weren't clear," she protested. "Do you get money for killing monsters that attacked other people, or was that pure altruism?"

"We do for the monsters, but not to rescue other teams."

"Would you have helped them if you didn't get a reward?"

"I don't know," Trev answered. "I don't think the average driver deserves to get roasted alive, but the money helps. I'm not complaining about getting paid to save them."

Cassie shook her head. "They make it sound like it's some great civic race. Kill monsters and earn money, but anyone who gets in trouble can be left to die since the organizers care more about security at their camp than individual teams surviving."

"They don't want amateurs who can't hack it driving in the race," Trev replied. "They reserve the right to reject teams if the officials think they have no realistic chance of surviving or finishing the race."

"That's more reasonable than I thought."

"More than a few tourists want to participate in the race but can't convince the organizers they have what it takes, so instead, they ride along. I'm sure you signed the same forms we did, with all the warnings about how many different ways we could die or be horribly wounded."

"I—"

Jack hissed and pointed at the windshield. "Why are you going toward those hills? Shouldn't you go around?"

"Small jumps won't hurt the truck," Trev argued. He turned the wheel and headed for a slope.

"That's not always true," Jack insisted.

"Live a little."

"That's what I'm trying to do by stopping you."

"You can't be…" Cassie began.

The truck did its best heavy-glider-skimming-the-ground imitation before hitting the dirt with a loud rattle that challenged the passengers' seatbelts. Cassie's stomach flipped, and Jack's tongue flicked out. Trev whooped and hollered, though he kept a firm grip on the wheel.

Engine roaring and cab rattling, the truck shot forward, leaving a dusty wake behind as it charged a hill that was more of a mound. The second jump and landing made bile rise in the back of Cassie's throat. Trev would get them all killed by amusing himself with stupid truck tricks.

Forget it, Cassie thought. *This guy* can't *be who I'm looking for. He's immature and insane. He likes and protects his friend, but I'm not sure he would have stopped and helped those people if there were no monsters there to earn him money. Nobody this undisciplined and frivolous could be my target.*

I was wrong. I didn't see what I thought I saw.

Trev threw his head back. "Four monsters down for a bonus, and we're making great time. Let's go!"

CHAPTER SIXTEEN

Trev yawned. Driving in any bastion of humanity that passed for part of civilization was more autopilot than skill. The roads facilitated control of wheeled vehicles. Concepts like evenness and grip were fundamental considerations.

A rally-raid stage offered nature's unbridled antivehicle fury. Keeping control of a ten-ton truck rattling over rough terrain and avoiding the holes and obstacles threatening to impair them required intense focus and concentration. It was exhausting, and as much fun as Trev was having, he was looking forward to the end of the first day.

"How do we look, Jack?" Trev glanced at the dashboard clock. "Is that time right? We have to be getting close to the end."

"We should hit the first-day endpoint in about an hour, based on our average speed," Jack reported. "We're good for another twenty minutes in this direction. Not seeing any reported obstacles of concern."

"I think the organizers wanted to show mercy the first

day." Trev smiled. "I'm not going to complain." He pumped his fist. "Damn, we're good. We're almost too good for this race."

"Shouldn't you win before you say that?" Cassie asked.

"Nothing wrong with stating the obvious," Trev replied. "It's inevitable that we'll take first."

Cassie's brows went up. "Inevitable? How do you figure?"

"Because of average speeds and how well we've been doing," Trev replied. "Think of it like this. If I drop a rock, it's going to fall, right? Inevitable."

Cassie smirked and shook her head. "Someone could catch it. The wind could push it. A bird could grab and carry it away. The inevitable can become the never."

"Talk about killing the vibe." Trev laughed. "Whatever. You should be happy, my hot tourist friend. Your team is winning, which means you're winning by extension." He slapped the steering wheel. "We could have used more monsters, but who cares when we're making such good time."

Cassie leaned forward. "Why are you sure nobody else is moving as fast as we are? Is Jack getting real-time updates on positions and times?" She peered at the tablet. "I only see your location on the map."

Jack shook his head. "No. This nav data shows stage waypoints and reported obstacles relative to our position. Those obstacles are based on course evaluation before the race starts. It's not real-time."

"How can your friend over there be so certain, then?" Cassie nodded at Trev.

Trev patted his stomach. "I feel it in my gut. This isn't

my first race. After a while, you get a sense for this type of thing. It's hard to explain. It's almost like having a power."

"Is that your power? Relative locational awareness?" Cassie asked.

"Nice try, but no."

Trev gestured out the side window at another truck with two flat tires. The drivers stood on the roof of their trailer holding rifles. They nodded at Trev and company as they passed.

"I also know because stuff like that," he continued. "When you break it down, the rules ensure that all the trucks perform roughly the same. It will come down to how often you stop for monsters, how good a driver you are, and how reliable your truck is more than speed. Same thing with the other vehicles, whatever your division.

"Reliability is by far the biggest threat to success in this rally. Three days of Sonoran Desert driving can take out even the most well-prepared vehicle. I'm way more worried about the truck breaking down than monsters."

Jack scoffed. "Which is why you keep jumping it. You're obviously worried."

"I know how far I can push it."

"A greater lie was never spoken."

"You're a great truck driver, Trev?" Cassie asked with a hint of derision. "So much so that you don't have to worry about being outdriven, only an unexpected breakdown?"

"I spent years practicing all types of driving in sims before I got into my first vehicle," Trev explained. "After the Big Change, my parents were happy I had a hobby that kept me close to home and distracted. That led to a minor career in racing in different disciplines in the NEUS, even if this is my first hunter-tourist rally and only my second race outside the NEUS. The important difference is Jack."

"What about him? He's not driving."

"He's made sure this baby's reliable." Trev's grin grew. "My biggest fear is the least likely to happen. If you were paying attention, you'd know that's not the only truck we've passed that broke down, and we were far up the order. Get it?"

"You think more breakdowns are coming," Cassie concluded.

"Definitely. I wouldn't be surprised if a quarter of our competition won't complete the first day. Add in the carnage from days two and three, and it's a truck massacre." Trev chuckled. "Think about it. Has this been a smooth ride? Would you recommend someone ride along in a truck like this across the Sonoran Desert if they want to enjoy the terrain?"

The truck rattled with every foot, the wheels occasionally rising and falling even without jumps. Trev had watched Cassie in the rearview mirror, so he'd known she was annoyed. He hoped she'd understand this wasn't just him being delusional. Cassie didn't need to accept his analysis. Nothing in the rules said tourists had to like or believe their drivers. Still, he couldn't let it go. She had to understand.

"It's been rough," she admitted. "This isn't anyone's idea of a comfortable drive."

"That's after Jack's suspension adjustment," Trev replied. "I guarantee it's worse in most of our competitors' trucks." He slowed to drive over a mound. "We don't do as many big dune jumps and river crossings as you see in other big open-terrain rally-raid races, but going through the Sonoran offers challenges even without the monsters."

He gestured at the windshield. "This isn't a sprint. This is a marathon." The truck shook when he accelerated. "This isn't about speed. It's about endurance, so let's go!" He hit the steering wheel again. "It feels great to be so good, and it will feel great to win."

Cassie laughed. "Confidence isn't a problem for you, is it? I get it. You're not just talking out your ass. That was a clear and good explanation, if I'm honest. You've impressed me in more than one way today."

Trev glanced at the rearview mirror. She didn't look like she wanted to shoot him in the back of the head, which was a nice change. He hadn't minded her over-the-top flirting at the pre-race bivouac, but he couldn't get over how forced and unnatural it had felt, as if she'd thought she had to act that way to be picked as his tourist. That diminished the spirit of the event. Every driver, male or female, was there to prove his or her skills, both driving and fighting.

He wanted her to learn about him, and he wanted to know more about her. "Hey, how old are you?"

"What?" Cassie winced. "That's rude. Didn't your mom tell you not to ask a girl her age?"

"She did tell me that. So, how old are you?"

Jack chuckled. "You'll never get anywhere with Trev by telling him he's rude. He takes it as a sign that he's on the right path."

Cassie folded her arms. "Twenty-five. Why do you care? Am I ready for retirement in Trev Land?"

"Huh?" Trev scrunched his forehead. "Nothing like that.

Sure, your fashion sense is messed up, but I'd have to be blind not to admit you're the hottest woman I've ever seen. That won't change just because of a number."

"Why are you asking about my age?"

"I was wondering if, when the Big Change went down, being older would make it better or worse for you," Trev replied. "Jack and I were just kids, and…" He frowned and looked at Jack, who'd returned to ignoring the conversation and focusing on his tablet. "We were little kids who thought the world had ended, but we still trusted and believed in adults. It was hard at first, but it got easier. We always had someone to follow, people we trusted."

"I don't know if being older helped." Cassie looked down at her hands. "I mean, I was a moody teenager."

"Was that when you discovered Rage Rabbit?"

"Rage Rabbit wasn't created until 2028."

Trev chuckled. "Sorry. Keep going."

Cassie frowned. Trev worried that he'd messed with her too much. His tendency toward humorous defusing could backfire. This wouldn't be the first time. "Even after things were calmer, I spent a lot of time scared, convinced I was going to die or worse," Cassie continued. "Then, one day, I just accepted it."

"Accepted you were going to die?" Trev asked. "That's messed up."

She shook her head. "No. I accepted the opposite. I accepted that life goes on, no matter what terrible thing has occurred. Sure, people developed strange powers, and corporations and governments started sending hero squads out to deal with criminals with powers, but life went on."

"Huh." Trev nodded. "I never thought of it that way. To me, the new world was totally disconnected from what happened before. I wasn't pining for the old world. Life did go on."

"Funny how that works," Cassie replied. "Like you, I adapted to the new normal despite all the people who'd died and all the changes."

"Why do you think it was like that for you?"

"I believe that's what it's like for most people. I think that's human nature." Cassie shrugged. "We're still here, aren't we? Humanity didn't die out. As a species, we adapt and overcome. You trusted adults, huh? That means you had people who cared about you and survived to help. That's good."

Trev glanced at Jack. "My parents wanted me to be safe. My dad worked for the government before the country broke apart. We were living in DC, so it was an easy transition to work for the NEUS government."

"Did your mom make it, too?"

"Yeah. Mom worked for the DC branch of the 46P1 Corporation. You know how they went from zero to everywhere overnight, especially after the Big Change? The established branches got even more attention and resources. The little biotech company became a world-striding conglomerate." He snickered. "There's always opportunity if you know where to look for it, I guess."

Cassie's expression darkened. "Your mom worked for 46P1? What did you think about that?"

"There was good and bad with them, especially back then," Jack interjected, not looking up from his device. "There were rumors about them doing shady things in the

NEUS and other countries, but the NEUS would have been conquered without them. We would have all been slaves to the Dark Empress of Bangor."

"Really?" Cassie smirked. "How do you figure? I think I know what you'll say, but I want to hear the spin you bought into."

"You can understand propaganda and still get that it's not *all* lies." Jack shrugged. "Once they formed the Pacific Shield, 46P1 started talking about forming teams everywhere they had facilities, but different governments weren't always aboard. Things were rough in many places in the NEUS, even before the Dark Empress of Bangor declared the formation of her new empire and her goal of unifying all of North America under her control."

Cassie shivered. "She could control minds even when she wasn't nearby. That freaks me out to think about."

"You believe she was a legitimate threat?" Jack asked.

"People where I was from did," Cassie replied. "They talked about what would happen if she conquered the NEUS. I remember people debating if she'd go west, south, or north first. At the time, I was wrapping my mind around the fact that this woman could control people's minds and make them do horrible things against their will."

"Yeah." Trev narrowed his eyes. "People focus on the flashier powers and how they're a big threat. A huge guy throwing a car. Somebody can be weak and small, yet take out the strongest heroes, depending on their power."

"Anyway, the first NEUS hero team, the Sword of Liberty, joined the newly founded Atlantic Shield of 46P1," Jack continued. "I don't know what they teach in the Northern Confederation, and I don't like 46P1 that much, but I have it on good authority that without the Atlantic Shield's help, the Sword of Liberty couldn't have stopped the empress' armies. The entire eastern seaboard would have fallen."

"That is what I thought you'd say," Cassie replied. "I've also heard people claim the Sword of Liberty would have been enough."

Jack shook his head. "That's not true. The Atlantic Shield had the heroine Neith. Without her psychic power to protect the hero teams, the empress wouldn't have been taken down by the Sword of Liberty-Atlantic Shield team-up. We all got lucky that Neith had the right power, and she happened to work for 46P1."

"He's right, you know," Trev added. "I knew people who…" He stopped for a second before nodding. "I've heard about those battles. The Atlantic Shield and the Sword of Liberty were strong, but they always had to restrain themselves. Most of the empress' army were mind-controlled minions. The heroes couldn't just kill people who couldn't control themselves. They were always fighting with one arm tied behind their backs."

A patch of rocks and a field full of animals' holes grabbed Trev's attention. Quick wheel work saved the truck, though the swerving challenged their seatbelts and killed the conversation. Even after the terrain got more reasonable, nobody spoke until Trev laughed at a stray thought.

"What's so funny?" Cassie asked. "Have you finally lost it?"

"I was thinking about our previous conversation. I still find it hilarious that a team would call themselves the

Sword of Liberty. It's really on the nose, though over the top."

"That's half the point of hero teams," Cassie suggested. "To be flashy and over-the-top symbols. I'm surprised that you're surprised."

"I'm not surprised. I just..." Trev's mouth twitched, and dark memories floated up. Maybe it was a mistake to talk about this. "That's all in the past. Jack needed my family and me after the Big Change, and I needed adults I could trust. We all got what we needed. He's my lizard brother from another mother."

Jack looked away and groaned. "I hate it when you say that."

"Yeah." He frowned. "That bitch doesn't deserve to be called your mother. Anyone who left their... Sorry. I've been all nostalgic these last few days. It's embarrassing. I'm turning into an old man."

Cassie nodded. Trev hated the knowing look on her face.

"You moved out to the Republic," she said. "Aren't you worried about staying in touch with your parents? I get that war isn't practical with the Confederation and Greater Texas in the way, but the Republic and the NEUS don't always get along. They could cut communication lines."

Trev locked his gaze on the road and avoided his reflexive check of the rearview mirror. He didn't want to see the pity in her eyes when he told her the truth. "My parents are dead."

"I'm sorry." Cassie sighed. "Plenty of parents didn't make it out of the Big Change." She blinked. "I'm confused. I thought you said you had adults you could trust, and Jack needed your family. It sounded like you were saying your parents were alive."

"They did survive," Trev replied. "Both of them, but they died last year. That was one of the big reasons I moved to the Republic. I needed a change. Jack was kind enough to come with me."

Jack just shrugged.

Cassie winced. "Still, I'm sorry. I should have known that."

"There's no reason you should," Trev replied, confused by what she'd said. "I didn't make it clear. I'm sorry for asking your age, even if you are a cougar."

Cassie's eyes widened. "C-cougar?"

"Going after a boy of twenty-one like me." Trev clucked his tongue. "Sounds like a classic cougar move to me."

"You're twenty-one, idiot. I'm twenty-five. I'm not a cougar." Cassie face-palmed. "Ugh. I walked right into that. Have you been messing with me this entire time with the maudlin talk of the past? Was it all to set me up for the joke?"

"Maybe," Trev lied, forcing a smile. "Hey, I changed my mind." He looked at Jack. "If it's okay with Jack, you don't have to sleep in your tent when we get to the bivouac. We've got fold-out beds for the seats. You can sleep in one of the beds in the truck, and Jack can sleep in the other. The truck is alarmed, so it's safer. Can't do anything about technopaths, but how often do you run into one of those?"

"What about you?" Cassie asked, concern on her face.

"I can sleep on a cot in the trailer," Trev explained. "I'm good at sleeping anywhere."

Cassie looked down and shook her head. "I appreciate

the offer, but my tent will be fine." She lifted her head. "Maybe this is just paranoia, but a number of expensive trucks, many of which will get stranded, sound like an excellent target for the two-legged type of monsters. You ever worry about bandits?"

"Yeah." Trev nodded. "Remember, each truck has a dedicated drone watching it, along with the telemetry and feeds from the sensors. Sure, they separate us by a few minutes, but there are lots of people coming through, and bandits know that anyone in those trucks is armed and likely to have a power that helps them kill monsters. Hunter-tourist rally teams aren't great targets unless you're really crazy. Bandits have never taken anybody out during this race."

Cassie frowned. "Are you saying they've never attacked?"

"Nah. They've tried, like, every other year, and they attacked last year, so we'll be okay."

"That's not how patterns... Well, it is how..." Cassie scrubbed a hand over her face. "That doesn't prove anything, or rather, it doesn't prove what you think it does."

"It doesn't matter." Trev snorted. "Those bandits got their asses handed to them. Remember, teams and their combat powers."

"Like yours?"

"You haven't even seen my power."

"Which has me oh-so-curious." Cassie's smile turned feline. "Is it the power to hide your truck from people's minds? Mental invisibility?"

"Nope," Trev replied.

"Would you tell me the truth if I guessed right?"

"Sure, but you get a maximum guess of one per hour from now on, and you at least have to buy me dinner first. I don't just whip out my powers for anybody." He nodded at Jack. "We can't all be that easy."

"Funny, and by funny, I mean not funny." Jack rolled his eyes.

"I try."

"And often fail."

Trev offered the rearview mirror a tight smile before checking the more useful rearview camera and not seeing anything troubling. "If I use my power, Cassie, things have gotten tougher than we planned. It'd be better for a tourist like you not to worry about that."

"If you say so."

"I do." Trev returned his attention to the front. "I sure hope they're not wasting those fire iguanas."

CHAPTER SEVENTEEN

Cassie leaned forward. Hours and endless hours of shrubs, pitiful excuses for trees, and giant cacti had recalibrated what she expected to see out here. "What's all that off in the distance? Is that a monster horde?"

Trev smiled. "That's the race bivouac. The vendors have to drive there themselves, but they go when the organizers travel, so it's a huge, well-defended convoy, including at least one angry guy with a boost suit. They also take the safest, fastest route instead of wandering off to weird waypoints in the middle of nowhere. They arrive even before the earliest Wave One participants."

"That sounds exhausting for the organizers," Cassie replied.

"I'm sure it is. Nobody involved in a race like this gets off easy."

Cassie pointed out the side window at two men trying to change the enormous tire on a stopped truck. "Another victim of reliability. I see what you were talking about."

"The true nature of rally raids." Trev pushed the accelerator down. "We've got our mechanic, so let's do this last stretch in style!"

Near sunset, Trev munched on a fire iguana sandwich, savoring the spicy flavor, while he and Cassie sat at the repaired table under their canopy. Desert breezes wafted delicious smells from the nearby food tent. He might need to supplement his diet with additional food choices. His stomach rumbled.

He patted it. "Give me time, my friend. Give me time. I'll make sure you're full."

Trev had been so focused driving that he had not bothered to eat much, so they had more meal bars and snacks for the next few days. That allowed him to justify buying iguana sandwiches and other luxury foods. His tongue and stomach would thank him.

A well-rested, well-fed driver was a superior driver. He liked to think of his meal choices as an investment.

Cassie was looking at something on her phone. Surrounded by tools, Jack lay under the truck inspecting the damage from Trev's courageous driving, which Jack insisted on calling insane and reckless.

"It was a hard day," Trev began. He finished his sandwich and dropped his feet to the ground. "That makes it all the more satisfying when you finish. Now I wish I'd been rally-raid-focused from the beginning. There's just something about this style of race."

"I'm surprised you're not topping that sandwich off with a beer," Cassie commented, still looking at her phone.

"Why?" Trev asked.

"You seem the type."

"I never drink when I'm racing," Trev explained. "That includes the days leading up to a race and the nights between."

"Is that part of being a winner?" Cassie asked.

"It's an easy way to give myself an edge over drivers with less discipline. Every advantage adds up, including equipment, mechanics, co-driving, and experience."

Cassie laughed. "Trev and discipline don't fit together in my mind."

Trev smiled. "I take care of myself and do the right thing at the right time to get what I want. I'd say I'm disciplined."

"Then stop jumping the truck!" Jack shouted. *"You're driving me crazy."*

Trev laughed. "I didn't say I was completely disciplined."

Cassie set her phone down and smiled at the yellow-pink sky. She tucked a strand of dark hair behind her ear. Despite their long day, she looked less tired than when she'd climbed into the truck that morning. She looked fresher and more alive, as if she'd set down a burden she'd been carrying.

She hadn't tried the dumb eye candy act again. That might explain the change in her attitude.

"The bandits and fire-breathing giant lizards are annoying," Cassie began, "but you can't beat a desert sunset." She smirked. "Excuse me, a living desert sunset."

"You're becoming a Sonoran Desert lover. I'm sure there's cute cartoon scorpion merch you can buy. I bet

Sadistic Scorpion can kill Rage Rabbit." Trev's phone buzzed. He pulled it out of his pocket and read the message, then jumped out of his chair and threw up his arms. "Yes! I *am* the greatest!"

People walking nearby stopped to watch him. A couple took pictures with their phones.

"*Get your mementos while you can, people,*" Trev shouted. "*I'll sign autographs if you want.*"

A woman flipped him off as she walked past.

He waved back. "Hey, your choice."

"Good news?" Cassie quirked a brow. "Or did you rattle your brain with all the jumps?"

"I told you I could feel it. I knew my gut wasn't lying." Trev slapped his stomach. "We're officially first place in our wave and division. They confirmed no penalty for our monster hunt, and we've got a twelve-minute lead."

"Is that good?" Cassie asked. "I'm not trying to be cute. I honestly don't know."

"It's damned good, though one breakdown or a couple of too-long fights, and we lose our lead," Trev replied. "These multi-day rallies can swing leads big-time, so we can't let our guard down. Don't plan on tomorrow being any easier or slower." He pumped his fist. "I knew my years of east-coast experience and sim time would pay off. I'm going to win big my first time out here!"

"As a certain man told me about thirty seconds ago, don't let your guard down," Cassie suggested, grinning. "Congratulations, though. I'm impressed."

Trev gave her a huge smile before spinning at movement in the corner of his eye. A haggard-looking woman approached the table with STAFF printed on her shirt. Her

ID card identified her as Lana Garcia, a member of the scrutineering staff. She held up a tablet connected to a small box.

"What can I do for you?" Trev asked warmly. Nothing could bring him down. Will could show up again and try to kill him, and he'd still be happy.

"Mr. Leon, I need to do a direct download of your telemetry," Lana began.

Trev motioned toward the truck. "My co-driver's working on things, but just tell him to get out of the way if needed."

"I shouldn't need to," Lana replied.

"Good to hear."

Cassie eyed the woman, suspicion coloring her face. "Don't they download the information via the drones? Why do they need another download?"

Trev laughed. "You *did* pay attention when you signed up."

"I mean, why do they need more data? I want to know."

She sounded aggressive. Perhaps she was worried that Lana was a spy for another team.

Lana sighed and rolled her eyes. "This is your tourist, right?" She lifted her tablet and swiped. "Cassandra Laner?"

"That's me," Cassie replied, then waved.

"Well, Miss Laner, all it takes is one or two people with powers who can disrupt or alter signals." She swept her arm around the camp. "We've already had a couple of incidents with people sabotaging equipment, including an obvious fight that was concealed. We can't allow anyone to cheat."

Cassie swallowed. "I see."

Trev chuckled nervously. He hadn't been the one who messed with the drones when Will's buddies showed up. All he did was defend himself, which would be his argument if they confirmed his involvement in the incident.

"We do our best to run a fair and balanced race," Lana continued, cutting the air with her hand, her voice rising and her eyes bulging. "All people do is bitch and moan about us bothering them. Do you have any idea how hard it is to keep everything balanced when everyone's powers are unique? The race stewards and the director have to decide if someone's cheating."

She pinched the bridge of her nose. "A rider in Wave One bikes can produce localized tailwinds. We only figured that out because his telemetry said he was faster than his bike's top speed. He argues that the rules say weather phenomena, positive or negative, are part of the experience. Is he cheating? Is he not? Is it a weather phenomenon when it's artificially created?"

Trev waved his hands. "Forgive her, ma'am. She's only a tourist. She doesn't know about the complexities of the race. I know you're doing your best. I am just a dumb driver who needs someone else to tell me where to go and occasionally shoots a monster. We appreciate everything you're doing, and we understand that you're trying to ensure a fair and balanced race."

Lana scoffed. "At least *someone* understands." She glared at Cassandra. "People like you ruin the race."

"Sorry I asked a simple question." Cassie rolled her eyes. "Next time, I'll drown myself before I do."

Lana walked toward the truck and stopped after a few feet. She turned back to Trev and lowered her voice. "They will issue a formal warning in the morning. Not to alarm you, but we've had a handful of unusual sightings of other vehicles along the route from Wave One drivers. The vehicles were keeping their distance. We've yet to confirm them with our staff drones or any drivers in Waves Two and Three."

"Unusual sightings of other vehicles?" Trev shook his head. "I don't follow."

"We can't confirm anything, but we're concerned that they might be bandit scouts," Lana explained. "That might also explain why we're having trouble getting video or direct sensor detection from these vehicles. There are a handful of bandit gangs in this area known to use technopathy and other powers that mess with drones and cameras."

"I'm sure it said something about bandits in those waivers." Trev shrugged. "I'd be surprised if it didn't."

Lana turned away, her expression pained. She leaned over Trev and spoke quietly. "The race director and the senior staff are going to cover their asses by offering a one-time chance to withdraw from the race and recover a portion of your entry fee. Since you seem like a nice guy, I'll tell you that's rare. In my experience, it means they think there's a greater danger than normal. I'm on the scrutineering team, so I don't hear everything. They might have more info they're keeping to themselves."

"If it was really dangerous, wouldn't they cancel the race?" Trev asked.

"No," Lana answered. "The race director made that clear from Day One. He said, 'Unless we have a second Big Change, this race won't be canceled.' He'd be fine with everyone dropping out, though. Then he can blame it on their fear."

Trev nodded. "Fair enough. Are there any bounties for bandits?"

Lana shrugged. "You don't get any rewards from the race organizers. It's all wasted time. The Republic might have bounties, but there are many restrictions on claiming those, including licensing. If you aren't licensed, you won't get the full bounty on anyone you take down. Keep that in mind if you want to be a hero."

"That's a damned rip-off," Trev complained.

"The government doesn't want amateurs messing with bandits or other bounties." Lana frowned. "Stay away from them. Fighting bandits isn't like fighting monsters. It's very dangerous. That's one reason the organizers don't pay bounties for bandits. They don't want teams getting in over their heads."

Trev almost laughed at the idea that fighting a giant fire-breathing monster or another mutated desert creature was safer than facing off against humans. However, if pressed, he would admit that an intelligent enemy could surprise him in a way an animal or monster could not.

"We could get bounties from the government," Trev noted. "That's what you're saying. They're just not going to be full value. It might still be worth it."

Lana sighed and clutched her tablet to her chest. "It's not. Trust me." She swallowed. "The major regional bandit gangs are dangerous. There's been trouble in this part of the Republic these last few months with a bandit leader who calls himself Burning End."

Trev couldn't help the snort that came out. "Burning

End? Doesn't he know he can get surgery for that? Or he can start with medicine."

"I'm serious," Lana scolded. "He's a dangerous man. The Republic wants him dead or alive, and they'd prefer dead. He's murdered countless people. He has no concept of mercy. Men, women, children. He's more of a monster than the mutants." She shook her head. "I heard whispers about canceling the race, despite what the race director said, but the last sighting of Burning End put him far from here. That doesn't guarantee he won't show up, though."

"I've dealt with bandits before." Trev patted the holster under his jacket. "I'm not scared of a guy whose name makes him sound like he needs a proctologist."

She backed away. "It's your call, but listen to me, please. If you see Burning End, don't stop and fight. Just run. He'll only kill you if you're lucky. He'll torture you first if you're not. He's a monster, and if he attacks your truck, it might be over before we even know what's going on. Our security staff will not engage bandits who aren't attacking either the bivouac or the convoy during transit. You're on your own."

"Thanks for the warning. I'll keep that in mind."

"Just keep what I said in mind." She shivered and jogged away.

Trev turned to Cassie to laugh about the paranoid official. He stopped and stared instead. Her face had paled, and she was trembling.

"You should consider quitting," Cassie suggested.

"Because of Burning End?" Trev scoffed. "A guy with that stupid a villain name doesn't deserve my respect or fear. Before you say anything, I get that he's supposed to end you with fire or whatever. I don't care. He's a dumbass, and I'm not worried about him."

Cassie frowned. "These bandits are bad enough that the Republic wants them, and the organizers are scared. You don't know anything about him other than his name. You can't be sure you can beat him."

"I know he's a bitch who hides in the desert and attacks people when they're least expecting him," Trev replied. "That makes him weak. He's not a real villain. He's a thug playing at being one."

"Don't you get it, Trev?" Cassie narrowed her eyes. "She didn't tell you all that because he's someone you can scare off with a big handgun." She grabbed her phone and typed. "Based on eyewitness reports, he's at least a Class-B threat, if not a Class-A. There's also talk of recruitment and him absorbing other local bandit gang members."

"Hey, he's not an AA." Trev nodded at the passersby. "It's good that he's so scary. That means a bunch of people will quit tomorrow. I'm not too proud to win by default when I know I would have won an honest race anyway."

Cassie shot up and leaned over to the table to glare at Trev. "If I quit, your race is over, right? You can't race without a tourist."

"Oh, come on." Trev shook his head. "You saw Jack and me in action today. We kicked monster ass like a well-oiled machine. A race official spins you a story about the bandit boogeyman, and you're ready to run back to the corn stalks of the Confederation and suck your thumb? I thought you were tougher than that, Cassie. I'm disappointed in you."

Cassie ground her teeth and looked away. When she

looked back at Trev, there was no determination on her face, only fear. "You need me to keep racing."

"That's true."

"I want part of your prize because of the danger. This was never supposed to be about bandits."

Trev stared her down and offered a cold smile. "It's been dangerous from the beginning. If anything, it's less dangerous."

"What drug-addled logic led you to that conclusion?" Cassie asked. "Let me know so I can understand how you operate with so much brain damage."

"I can prepare for a known enemy," Trev explained. "I don't think you really want my money. Even if you did, I won't give it to you."

"*I'll quit*," Cassie yelled. "*I will.*"

"This might be the only real adventure you'll ever have, Des Moines. Something you can look back on with pride and not fear like the Big Change." Trev's expression softened. "If you have it with me, I guarantee you'll be safe. I guarantee you'll return home alive. I guarantee I can take out Burning End if he dares show his face."

Cassie swallowed and backed away. "What about Jack?"

"I'll kill every last person on this planet before I let Jack die, and I'll trade my life to protect my friend." Trev scoffed. "If you know anything about me, know that. No matter what happens, that'll never change."

"I... Sorry."

"Don't be sorry." Trev spun and stomped over to the truck. "Just don't quit because you've let rumors spook you."

CHAPTER EIGHTEEN

That night, Cassie tossed on her cot, afraid to go to sleep and risk dark visions of Jack being murdered. The most direct way to get Trev to back off would be to tell him the truth about her precognition powers, but she couldn't guarantee that he'd believe her. That held her back. They were developing a mutual respect that she hoped to build on for her mission.

Trev saw Burning End as nothing more than a rumor or a convenient bounty to kill if he showed up. He didn't know about her vision of a man with a flaming fist killing Jack. The bandit warning, combined with the vision of Jack's death, had changed everything. She was running out of time.

I'll kill every last person on this planet before I let Jack die.

Cassie didn't doubt Trev's sincerity, but she had more insight into the future than he did. Harsh life experiences had taught her that intentions didn't always triumph.

Trev believed he could beat whoever was before him, but the bond of friendship was no substitute for more weapons and powers. For all she knew, Jack had died in her vision as a sacrifice to protect Trev and Cassie.

That limited her options. Most of them involved offering Trev a piece of the truth to get him to quit the race. Traveling with him and Jack to a more heavily patrolled area closer to a town or city would reduce the danger.

The problem was that Trev would ask questions she wasn't ready to answer. That would lead to him insisting he could protect his friend in all cases. Thus far, all she'd seen from him was bravery and good shots.

A man like Burning End wouldn't fear guns. The reports were unclear on his exact capabilities other than noting he could punch through metal with his burning fist.

Trev's mysterious secret weapon was still hidden. She didn't want to lose the trust she'd built up by sneaking in to check on it. Unless he had a portable nuke in there, she didn't see how it'd help. A bigger gun wouldn't be enough to stop Burning End.

"Is this my fault? Is my being here screwing things up? Is Jack supposed to die?" She got up. After taking a deep breath, she slapped herself hard on the cheek.

Being precognitive didn't mean she was a goddess of fate. She couldn't just tell herself that people had to die for a desired future to arrive. The minute she accepted that thinking, she'd be no better than villains like the Altruist or the Dark Empress of Bangor, claiming they would build peace and stability on mountains of dead innocents.

The point of her mission was to stop unnecessary suffering and sacrifice. That had to start with saving Jack.

Cassie's power meant she had gotten a genuine warning. Even if Trev was her target, telling him directly wouldn't work. She'd spent enough time with him to understand that he wasn't ready to hear what she had to say.

Walking away and forcing him out of the race was the obvious play. However, she couldn't complete her mission if she didn't spend more time around him. She needed to save Jack without sabotaging the mission.

Cassie frowned, remembering Trev's bloody bandage. That wound ruled out regeneration, protective skin, and various other powers. His power might involve hand-eye coordination or driving, or it might include empowering his bullets. For all she knew, fire iguanas were tougher than they looked, and a subtle enhancement of his weapon hid his true power from a suspicious woman watching from the truck.

Cassie rubbed her stinging cheek. "Think, think. There's got to be something."

One hazy set of distance visions combined with hacked 46P1 data implied that Trev might be more than a cocky young man interested only in winning races and talking trash. That combination of evidence had led to her seeking him out, even with all the difficulties and risks involved in leaving the Confederation and traveling to the New Baja Republic after her abrupt resignation from 46P1.

Now, she was in the field and in contact with her target. She'd achieved her initial mission objectives with ease. Despite their paranoia, there was no indication that the race staff had detected her hacking the tourist assignment records or the MQI detector's operating system.

She scoffed. Everyone spent so much time worrying

about empowered threats they often overlooked the harsh reality that conventional threats were the most common and effective.

That brought her back to what to do about Trev and Jack. Her evidence suggested that Trev was just a loyal, handsome young man who was too cocky for his own good. His fighting abilities were above average, but he had not displayed a significant power.

She moaned and rubbed her temples. Trev didn't have to win the race. Her quitting would force him out and save Jack. Her breath caught. She couldn't be sure that quitting would save Jack. This was the problem when she dealt with anything but immediate precognitive visions. The flow of time and reality wasn't easy to understand or manipulate.

She spent a lot of time second-guessing herself. Making Trev quit might lead to a sequence of events that ended with Jack being killed. Not making Trev quit could also be the problem. "I wonder if this would be easier if I changed my name," she muttered.

Cassie could easily devise a scenario ending with Jack being killed following her forcing Trev out of the race. Without the prize money, Trev might scour the Sonoran Desert for Burning End to earn his bounty and the money he craved, and that confrontation could end with Jack being killed.

Without better control of her ability, she didn't *know* the right choice. She could only guess. There was no way she could master her precognition overnight in the Sonoran Desert in a tent city filled with rowdy racers and mercs. That left few options and insufficient time to figure out how to save a man's life without endangering others.

The key was focusing on what she could control. She could spend all day thinking through conditional scenarios. How could she cut down the number of variables?

Cassie nodded. As long as she was with Trev and Jack, she could alter the future she saw. She couldn't guarantee Trev or Jack would listen to her, but she had to stay with them to help them.

Whatever she felt about Trev and if he was her target, Jack didn't deserve to die at the hands of a brutal killer. However, she couldn't escape the fear that her involvement with Trev and his lizard brother from another mother had pushed them onto a path that ended with their deaths.

Cassie took slow, deep breaths. When might it happen? She thought back to the vision. The truck, no tents, and the surrounding wilderness all pointed to it happening on the second or third day or after the race.

I can't figure out if Trev is the target without taking risks. All I have to do is survive two more days in rough monster- and bandit-infested terrain to pull that off and make sure his best friend isn't murdered by a villain-level bandit. Perfect. Easy.

She reached under her pillow for her gun. She'd complete her mission and save Jack. Trev wasn't the only person who would risk his life to save people.

CHAPTER NINETEEN

<u>March 8, 2036, Sonoran Desert, New Baja Republic</u>

Trev drummed his fingers on the wheel in time with the rhythmic thump of the wheels on the ground beneath them. He could almost hear the music, and it relaxed him.

That music had defined this drive so far. The terrain hadn't always been fun, but he'd sunk into an almost zenlike state during the process. Jack's navigational directions registered in his mind, and he reacted. Hours had passed in what felt like minutes.

Late on the morning of the second day, they were crossing a flat section with rocks dense enough to form a natural cobblestone road, their first stretch in this stage that didn't involve constant turns to avoid cacti, rocks, or animals.

The reduced difficulty pulled Trev out of his driving trance. He smiled, satisfied with their progress. They hadn't spotted any monsters yet, to his disappointment. The largest beast he'd seen was a javelina, which was a normal animal, not a monster. The Goddess of Racing might not be on his side regarding monster hunting.

It helped that whatever miracles Jack had worked the night before had smoothed their ride despite the harsher terrain. He'd almost forgotten he was in a race.

In their third hour, they'd reached the natural cobblestone road. The rough earlier terrain had slowed them, even with Trev's heroic, focused driving, but the number of cacti and outcrops forming mazes had dropped. That had let them make up time as long as Trev was careful.

He continued drumming as a subtle unease wormed its way into his previously satisfied mind. He didn't understand the source, and that worried him. Despite what Cassie might think, his confidence stemmed from anticipating threats rather than ignoring them. That was why his growing current discomfort bothered him.

He glanced into the rearview mirror to see Cassie chewing her lip. He wouldn't let that beautiful but distracting face drag him down further. Looking at her confirmed that she was the source of his discomfort. He'd been so focused on driving that he had not dealt with his thoughts on their conversation the night before.

Was it as simple as her threatening to quit over the bandits? Maybe, but he sensed something more in play for them both.

Seeing him looking, Cassie's expression hardened. "We haven't run across any monsters yet. I'm surprised. I anticipated an action-packed day of hunting." She dropped her eyes. "You might not believe this, but I genuinely want to see you take on a monster scorpion."

"Because you hate me, and you want to see me stung to death?" Trev asked.

Cassie shook her head. "I've never seen a scorpion, so I might as well see a big one. That'll give me the true desert experience."

"They're easy to kill," Trev replied. "Monster scorpions are slow. You'd think they'd be as well-armored as fire iguanas, but they're not, and they're far slower than regular scorpions." He shrugged. "I've heard they're dying out. Don't worry. Still plenty of regular scorpions around." He grinned. "You didn't read the suggested safety procedures for scorpions, did you?"

"What?" Cassie frowned. "If they're so slow, why should I worry?"

"I'm talking about the little ones." Trev gestured at his feet. "When you're camping in the desert, always take your boots out of your tent in the morning. Hold them upside down and smack them to make sure there are no scorpions inside. Hate for you to get stung."

Cassie grimaced. "Oh. Good idea. I'll start doing that, but ignoring the little scorpions, why aren't there more monsters?"

Trev nodded. "The Day Two starting time is chosen by the top finisher. We were number one, so I picked a later timeslot, and that's before taking into account that the cars and bikes go first. Trucks will always have fewer monsters, and trucks that start later are guaranteed to run into even fewer monsters. We're practically Wave Three."

"I thought it was weird that I got to sleep in. Why did you pick a later slot? Why not go first? I thought you wanted to hunt monsters."

Trev motioned to Jack. "Because he was up half the night repairing and improving the truck. Not needing sleep isn't one of his powers."

Jack looked his way. "I didn't ask, but I appreciate it."

Trev grinned. "You don't have to ask. I know you better than you know yourself."

"Another interesting delusion you carry, but it got me more sleep this time. I won't complain."

Cassie's brow lifted. "You were improving the truck?"

"Suspension, quick engine tune, and a few other things here and there," Jack explained. "We had completed a day of racing, so I had more experience with what to expect. That made it easy to figure out how to improve. I will do anything I can do to help us win."

Cassie looked out the side window. "I didn't mind not having to rush out. I was just surprised because, after the way you carried on yesterday, I assumed you'd want ten monster packs to appear so you could kill them and brag about being King of All Monster Hunters."

"It's all about balance," Trev replied. "If I had known I would do this well, I would have competed in Wave One and not worried about the monsters. The race is going better than I ever imagined."

"You mean you didn't think you would get first place from the beginning?" Cassie scoffed. "The way you were acting, I assumed you believed that."

"I planned to do well, but I also knew I'd be competing with drivers with more experience in this rally," Trev answered. "Now I know I'm awesome on these stages. Racing is governed by a fickle goddess. She can snatch your victory in ways you can't anticipate. I always visualize victory, but I don't assume I'll win until we cross the finish line."

Cassie smiled. "That's strangely mature. You aren't Mr. Inevitable after all."

"Strangely mature?" Trev chuckled. "You always have to stick the knife in, huh?"

"That was a compliment."

"Don't add 'strangely' next time. Then it'll be a compliment, not an insult."

Cassie laughed. "I'll keep that in mind."

"Glad you can learn. Let me concentrate for a sec."

Trev frowned before shifting to get up a steep hill. The truck lurched over the top and bounced as it sped toward a narrow path between two of the largest cacti they'd encountered since starting the race. The gargantuan desert plants would take out a house if they fell on one.

The truck waggled through the path under Trev's careful control. The back slid, forcing an overcorrection that led to a few seconds of grinding metal and the truck tilting. It dropped back to the ground, and Trev emerged from the danger zone.

"There we go." He smiled. "Even without monsters and moderate speed, there are ways to make good money on this race. Jack and I didn't come here to leave empty-handed. We'll do fine."

"You're not planning on hunting Burning End, are you?" Cassie's question came out as a venomous accusation.

"Nope," Trev replied, keeping his merry smile and not

taking the bait. He'd worried the night before that she'd quit, so he didn't want to turn this into a debate rather than presenting a confirmed plan. "If he comes at us, he'll get his ass kicked. However, with people dropping out because of monsters, mechanical failures, and a few who were scared because of the bandit warning, and given our existing lead, we're a shoo-in for the top three. The prize money from that alone is worth it without a single monster bonus or bandit bounty, and we have the fire iguanas from yesterday."

Cassie put her hand over her heart and sighed in relief. "A win through attrition is still a win. I can get behind that strategy."

"Hey, it's not like only three trucks are left in our category." Trev grunted. "My driving set up for this. I'm playing the numbers, but I have to execute throughout the rest of today and tomorrow to pull this off."

"Sure, sure." Cassie bowed, arms outstretched. "You are the grandmaster of all racing drivers. I worship your skill and will burn a fire iguana sacrifice to the Goddess of Racing." She smirked. "Is that your power? Pathfinding? Hand-eye coordination? Improved reactions?"

"I said I'd only answer if you asked one per hour, and you already asked about variations on those earlier," Trev noted.

"I haven't asked for the last three hours, and I wanted to make sure I was wording them in a specific way."

"Okay, fine." The driver laughed. "Nope. None of those are my power. You're just dying to know, aren't you?" He glanced at Jack. "Should I tell her and put her out of her misery?"

To Trev's frustration, Jack just shrugged. "It's your power and your call."

"Oh, come on, man. You're making me the bad guy. That's not fair."

"Life rarely is."

Jack looked at his side mirror and frowned. He tapped his tablet, and a rear aerial display appeared on a dashboard screen above the rearview camera. A small black cloud with flashes of orange and red followed the truck.

Trev frowned. "You weren't kidding when you said life wasn't fair."

Cassie's breath caught. "What are those? Should we be concerned?"

"It's a swarm of emperor wasps," Trev explained. "Yes. That's bad luck. I think the Goddess of Racing decided she's had enough of me winning."

"So, they aren't tasty?" Cassie asked.

Trev jerked his head around with a confused look. "Who the hell knows?"

"What do you know about them?"

"They're foot-long wasps that can chew through metal and have venomous stingers. I'm sure they have antivenin at the camp, but emperor wasp stings kill people long before they can get medical help." Trev's jaw tightened. "Unless you have a secret healing or antivenin power."

"Sorry, nope." Cassie rested her hand on her gun. "When I was in middle school biology before the Big Change, they always said there was a hard limit on the size of many insects because of how they breathed." She shook her head. "I'm really starting to miss Iowa. We had some wild beasts and a few scary monsters there, but these Sonoran creatures are next-level messed-up."

Trev shifted gears and accelerated. The truck shook harder. He redlined the engine before shifting again and weaving between cacti and dangerous outcroppings.

His skill meant nothing. He could have thrown off a land-based monster with clever driving, but the wasps didn't care. The terrain didn't affect them. He needed to figure something out, or they would come to a bad end on their second day.

"We slam into something at this speed, and I can't fix it out here," Jack shouted.

"Just give me a few minutes of playing around," Trev replied, his grip tightening. "There are too many of those things. If I outpace them, they might get tired or bored and peel off."

Jack set his tablet in the center of the front bench seat. He reached under the seat and pulled out a grenade launcher instead of the coilgun.

Trev nodded. "Yeah. Good idea. Cassie, it's a—"

"Grenade launcher," she observed. "I know."

Jack pulled a full box of grenade cartridges out from beneath his feet and loaded the five-shot launcher before rolling down the window.

He unbuckled his seatbelt and turned to Cassie in the back. "I need you to stabilize me for my shots."

"Meaning what?" Cassie asked. "You want me to hold your feet?"

"Not exactly." Jack averted his gaze. "Hold onto my tail while I lean out of the car. I'm going to hook my feet on the door."

"Is that even possible?"

"For me, it is. My ankles bend farther than most people's."

Cassie shook her head. "That's still crazy. One big bump, and you'll fall out and get killed. Trev's driving like a maniac, and it's not like this is flat city streets."

"Just do it," Trev snapped. "Jack knows what he's doing, and I know what I'm doing."

"Have you fought emperor wasps before?" Cassie asked.

"No, but we have a strategy. Now, hurry up and do what he says."

Cassie groaned. "Okay. If this doesn't work, we'll be dead anyway, so I won't be around to complain."

Holding the grenade launcher, Jack wiggled out the window and bent his feet to catch the door. "Go ahead, please."

Cassie grabbed Jack's tail and locked her hands around it. "Please don't fall. You seem like a good guy."

"I won't. Thank you for the compliment."

Jack twisted his body and fired rapidly. The grenades exploded in the swarm. The blasts created bright flashes in the rearview camera and side mirrors.

Smoking dark bits rained down from the sky with each shot, but after Jack emptied his grenade launcher, most of the swarm remained. The emperor wasps reacted to the holes in the swarm by filling them with surviving wasps.

Jack threw himself back into the truck. Cassie let go of his tail.

"I'm sorry." He shook his head. "I thought that'd thin them out more than it did."

"You know what I said about the S word," Trev replied,

pushing the truck into a screeching turn. "It wasn't like you didn't kill any of them."

Jack cradled the grenade launcher in his arms. "I'm not killing enough of the wasps with each grenade."

"*Use them all*," Cassie shouted. "Fumigate those damned bugs with any explosives you have."

"It won't work." Jack shook his head. "Enough of the swarm would be left to kill us."

Trev sucked in a breath. "We don't have a choice. Time to use the secret weapon."

"How are we going to do that?" Jack asked, pushing the grenade launcher back under the seat. "Especially without blowing the race." He glanced into the backseat. "It's my fault. I should have built a door from the cab to the trailer."

"Saying it's your fault is the same as saying you're sorry. Cut it out. I'll kick your ass after we die, not before. We're not dying here today, and there's no way in hell I'll get killed by a bunch of bugs. My pride won't allow it."

"Do you have a viable plan?" Jack sounded hopeful.

Trev squinted and yanked the truck to the left. The right wheels bounced over chunks of dried wood as they passed a collapsed Palo Verde tree. "See that hill over there? It looks like there might be a cave. You'll just have to keep them busy while I deploy the secret weapon, and it will do the rest."

"I can help," Cassie said. "If you have another grenade launcher, I can shoot it. I've trained with and fired grenade launchers."

Trev considered. It wasn't impossible. She might have gone through a crash course in weapons before deciding to come down to a crazy Baja race.

"You're going to get out and run as far into the cave as you can." Trev's tone was curt despite the manic grin he used to hide his concern. "Jack, if you need to, you run into the cave, too. The emperor wasps will concentrate on the truck and me."

"That isn't a good plan," Jack protested.

"It's *a* plan."

Jack shook his head. "Why waste time using the secret weapon inste—"

"It's more reliable," Trev insisted, shaking his head. "That's half the reason we built the damned thing, not just for secrets."

Cassie frowned and looked at the two of them. "If you have anything that will save our lives, now's the time to use it."

Trev swerved to avoid a small squadron of javelinas that burst out from behind an outcrop where they'd been resting in the shadows. The animals scattered, but the emperor wasps didn't go after the softer prey.

Trev's initial annoyance was replaced by relief. He didn't want to escape his enemies by inflicting them on others.

"You want human flesh and metal, huh?" Trev yelled. *"Bring it on, you glorified maggots. You don't know who you're messing with. Let's fucking go!"*

Cassie sighed. "You do know you can't taunt bugs, right?"

"Fighting's all about mindset," Trev countered. He swung the truck back toward the cave. "Trust me. Those emperor wasps will feel my contempt, and it'll slow them down."

"This secret weapon better work, or we're all dead."

"What did I tell you last night?" Trev asked. "No matter what, you and Jack will get out of this alive."

Cassie just grimaced.

CHAPTER TWENTY

Cassie's frustration with the limitations of her power left her nails digging into her palms until she drew blood. She could use her precognition to fight but lacked the necessary control to advise Trev on the best course of action. That, combined with her reluctance to admit the nature of her power, gave her nothing to do except what he ordered.

She didn't have time to come up with clever strategies and plans. Her only chance of surviving was helping Jack and Trev deploy their mysterious secret weapon, which was presumably more powerful than a .50 caliber handgun, a coilgun, or a grenade launcher.

Trev was convinced that whatever it was, it would work against a swarm of giant flying insects. That had to be more than desperation talking.

The cave loomed before the truck, which was shaking and bouncing. She'd expected Trev to brake far earlier.

Her heart thundered as much from the impending collision as the swarm of monster insects following them.

For the first time since coming to the Republic, Cassie feared for her life.

Where was the damned vision of the wasps? She thought.

Trev slammed on the brakes and turned the truck, sliding over the sandy soil and ripping through brush without tipping the massive vehicle over. The huge tires tore up the ground, spewing rock and dirt into the air yet surviving without punctures. By the time the truck came to a stop right inside the mouth of the cave, Trev had produced a good-sized dust cloud that obscured their position.

Cassie gasped. Had he planned that, or was it luck? She'd take it in either case.

Trev didn't bother reaching for his gun before throwing open the door and darting toward the back of the truck. Jack pulled out the box of grenade cartridges and the launcher before hopping out the passenger side. Cassie registered their departure just before she heard the first pop of the grenade launcher and the boom of an explosion.

Whatever else she could say about Trev and Jack, they were brave. They reacted quickly to fight for survival and took on monsters with unflinching tenacity. She could understand how they had traveled from the NEUS to a new country and believed they could prosper.

The thick dust cloud rendered the grenade blasts nothing more than bright flashes of light on the rearview camera. Dark dots approached, the distortion from their rapidly flapping wings marking the shapes as the emperor wasps. The enemy was wounded but not defeated.

"Okay, think," Cassie whispered. "What can I do to help?"

She grunted in frustration. Trev had been right in his earlier rant. She'd not come to the Sonoran Desert to die from the stings of giant wasps. She crawled forward and out the passenger-side door.

Cassie stood beside Jack and pulled out her pistol. "Are they bulletproof?"

"No," Jack answered. "You shouldn't be over here. You should be heading for the cave." He fired another grenade into the dust cloud. "It's not safe, and it's not your responsibility."

Metal rattled in the back of the truck. Trev's secret weapon was coming. The truck shook again.

Cassie aimed her gun at the swarm. "Emperor wasps eat metal. That means hiding in the truck will only delay my death. If I'm going to die either way, I'd rather die on my feet, and if they're not bulletproof…"

She pulled the trigger, aiming for the swarm rather than any individual wasp. Her bullet tore through a wasp. The body fell to the ground and crunched on impact.

"I'd rather not die at all, but that's going to depend on Trev," Jack replied.

With a few more trigger pulls, Jack emptied the launcher. The threatening cloud reformed, now thinner, but the swarm was darker and closer, and the buzzing was louder. He popped more grenade cartridges into the launcher.

Cassie shot at the cloud again and missed. She squinted. She'd exhaust herself trying to pair precognition with low-range shots. She had to make them count.

A group of emperor wasps headed toward Jack and

Cassie. Jack incinerated half with a well-centered shot. Another portion disappeared with his second shot.

Cassie concentrated and led her next target with her pistol, then held her breath before squeezing the trigger. Her bullet tore through the wasp and sent its body tumbling to the ground.

She whipped her gun to the side and fired again. The wasps' short distance and aggressive charge meant she didn't have to use her power to hit them.

Another wasp went down. Jack was right. They weren't bulletproof.

Three more shots finished off the survivors in the front group. Jack's next batch of grenades added crispy emperor wasp parts to the pile. The swarm changed direction to move perpendicular to the truck.

Cassie smiled but didn't lower her weapon. "We did it. We scared them off. I was worried there for a second."

Jack shook his head and reloaded. "If only it was that easy." He glanced at her. "You're handier with a gun than I expected. You really do have training."

"Come on," Cassie replied. "Did you really think I would come to a rough event like this in a monster-infested desert without being able to protect myself? That'd be stupid."

She'd lost patience with her cover. While she lacked experience in this region and extensive knowledge of the minutiae of the rally event, she had nothing to gain by letting Jack and Trev believe she was a helpless traveler who'd trip and die the first time anyone said boo. Her gun could help save them, so she'd use it.

That didn't mean she could ignore every precaution. Surviving the next few minutes would mean nothing if she didn't complete her mission.

Jack whipped up the launcher and sent his latest demonstration of explosive bug control winging toward the swarm, which changed direction to swoop back toward the truck. His grenades forced them into a spiraling loop. "I figured you paid someone to get here for the excitement. Tons of tourists like that. I'm glad to see I was wrong about you. We were both wrong about you."

"I think we are all hiding something."

Cassie followed the swarm with the gun. They kept their distance, undulating in the air while sweeping back and forth. It was as hypnotic as it was eerie.

"I know they say most monsters aren't more intelligent than they were when they were normal animals before the Big Change," she began, "but it's hard to see a swarm staying at the edge of the effective range of a grenade launcher and not attribute intelligence to it."

She emptied her magazine, taking down more wasps. She pulled out a new mag and reloaded.

"It's the same up north," she added. "Too many of the monsters seem way smarter than animals, but the scientists all say they aren't intelligent."

"You fight many monsters back home?" Jack asked while reloading. "Is that why you're so good with a gun?"

"I've fought more than you'd think," Cassie admitted. She danced on the edge of blowing her cover. She'd prefer that not happen until she had a better handle on her target. "Forget me. Where's Trev?"

Clanging sounded from the back of the truck. The entire vehicle shifted, and something thudded hard on the ground, followed by whirring. The swarm came around for another pass.

"Follow me!" Jack shouted.

He sprinted around the back of the truck. Cassie rushed after him, curious about the secret weapon that was supposed to save their lives from the deadly swarm.

She turned the back corner to spot a wheeled loading platform carrying a walking tank, aka WT, lying on its back. The humanoid-shaped bipedal vehicle bristled with a heavy rotary machine gun topped with a grenade launcher as one arm and a smooth-bore rifle of some sort on the opposite—a directed energy weapon, she assumed, most likely a laser rifle. The armored ammo crate on the back of the WT was almost as big as the body. An eyeless head bristled with short antennae.

Cassie frowned. Its modest size bothered her. This was less a WT than an exoskeleton, not much bigger than Trev, who she presumed was inside. As far as Cassie knew, nobody could make a WT that small, including technology-leading conglomerates like 46P1.

The incessant, loud buzzing reminded Cassie of the wasp danger. Her confusion about the current limits of technology would have to wait until the fight ended.

Jack lifted the grenade launcher and fired projectiles across the front of the swarm. Cassie downed stray survivors. The lift whirred and rolled away from the back of the truck.

"Why is he waiting to activate the WT?" Cassie asked. "If he waits too long, they'll get us."

"He's got his reasons," Jack answered.

Cassie looked between the WT and the swarm, frowning. A soft hum emanated from the WT. The humanoid bent its knees and stood.

She squinted and stared at the WT. "Trev, you in there?"

"Good job buying me time, both of you," he announced through a speaker. "I'll clean up."

Trev lifted the machine gun, and the weapon spun to life without any preamble. The report was deafening. The belt fed the gun a river of high-velocity lead that tore through the swarm and produced a fine mist of wasp guts, coating the other wasps and slowing them. That made them easier to hit.

The swarm spiraled toward Trev, forsaking the intelligence they'd displayed before. He mixed grenade blasts with machine gun fire to fill the sky with explosions and bullets. Wasp chunks splattered all over the desert. A bright, thin purple blast from the smooth-bore rifle cut through a line of wasps, slicing them in half.

Cassie stared at the WT. The weapon both entranced and confused her. The odd shape of the individual shots and their visibility pointed away from it being a standard model combat laser or any of the other few directed energy weapons she'd seen deployed on WTs.

Did Trev's power somehow allow him to modulate laser energy? That'd explain the odd nature of the shots. It also explained why he kept alluding to her seeing his power if the situation got too dangerous.

She'd find out later. For now, the blasts' power and ability to tear through the monsters pushed her remaining fear away. In minutes, they'd shifted from being future victims of the emperor wasps to their Grim Reapers.

A group of wasps broke away from the main swarm. Trev nailed most of them, but a single wasp escaped the onslaught by hugging the ground and zigzagging toward Jack and Cassie.

"Watch out!" Trev shouted.

Cassie couldn't save Jack from Burning End by letting a monster kill him. She called on her power, the final flight path of the wasp slipping into her mind. She gritted her teeth, a small spike of pain in her head as she pushed past her usual precognitive time horizon.

She twisted to avoid the wasp, but it changed direction and tried to jam its stinger into her chest. Without looking, she jerked up her gun and put two rounds through the insect. Her shots ripped it apart.

Jack stared at her, his long tongue hanging out of his mouth. Despite his reptilian appearance, the look reminded Cassie of a confused Golden Retriever.

"That was—" he began.

"Luck," Cassie finished with a smile. She blew on the barrel of her gun. "Sometimes a girl's got to be lucky to survive."

"I'll take luck since it's working for me," Trev declared. He swept his weapons back and forth, shredding and burning giant wasps until nothing was left in the sky but an acrid smell. His attacks spread the remains of the swarm over hundreds of yards. The machine gun spun down with another whir. "None of the pre-race reports said anything about emperor wasp swarms. I knew we should have installed a flamethrower."

Jack rested the grenade launcher on his shoulder, still eying Cassie. "We didn't die. Go, us."

Smoke billowed from Trev's machine gun as he stomped over to the lift. "Get the platform lowered so I can get Hercules back aboard the trailer. As is, we'll get a penalty, but they should give us a nice bonus for taking the swarm down. It's got to count for more than a normal monster."

Despite having burning questions, Cassie hurried back into the truck while Jack and Trev reloaded the WT. She controlled herself for ten minutes, letting them pull away from the cave and get back on course. After they'd reached a smoother patch of ground, her question fell out of her mouth without thought.

"You could afford a walking tank?" she asked. "Or maybe you couldn't. Is that why you're so desperate to win? You borrowed money for an experimental WT, and you have to pay somebody back? Somebody...what did you call me? Somebody sketchy?"

"You *are* sketchy," Trev insisted. "You're just not shady."

His grin hadn't left his face since he'd gotten back behind the wheel. Cassie couldn't say he hadn't earned it. "What makes you think Hercules is an experimental WT?"

"Because it's so tiny." Cassie put up a hand. "I know. It's not the size that matters. It's how you use it."

Trev snickered. "Sometimes it's both."

"What I don't get is how it's so small," Cassie continued.

"I didn't think they could be. Everything I know about WT design says they can't."

"Really?" Trev's gaze flicked up to the rearview mirror. "You're an expert on WTs? You're a secret engineer?" He frowned. "On the other hand, that might explain why you'd come to a race like this. You don't seem like a gearhead, but your Rageful Rabbit shirts seem something like an engineer would like."

"Rage Rabbit, and no, I'm not an engineer," Cassie answered. "I don't need to be an engineer to know WTs aren't small. It has to do with the energy density of the cells and internal muscle polymer configuration." She shrugged. "Look, I'm not an engineer, but I've had a conversation or two with engineers who know what they're doing regarding WTs. Hercules is too small."

She sighed. She was all but screaming her true identity to them.

Trev looked at Jack. The lizardman cupped his chin before nodding to Trev.

"We didn't borrow money from anyone to build it," Trev explained. "It did cost a lot, which is part of the reason we need money. Also, we moved to the Republic from DC. That's not cheap. We needed to get a place. That's not cheap. You get the idea?"

"Where did you even get it?" pressed Cassie. "The Republic restricts WTs, yet you've got one in the back of your truck that you're casually using to kill monsters during a famous race."

"Sure, they restrict them. They do what most old American countries do to restrict them." Trev grinned. "They restrict the buying and selling of WTs. We didn't buy this

WT. Nobody sold it to us, so we're not doing anything illegal according to Republic law. We confirmed that with a government official in Tucson."

Cassie scoffed. "Oh, you got a delivery from the WT fairy because you were a good boy last year? Or did Santa and the Easter Bunny coordinate and bring it together?"

"I built it," Jack interjected.

Cassie stared at him. "You built a WT? By yourself?"

Jack shrugged and looked away. "Yeah." He scratched an eyelid. "Trev helped with the work but not the design. The design's all me."

"I've got the street smarts and people smarts," Trev offered. "He's got the making powerful secret weapon smarts."

"Okay. Cool, I guess." Cassie didn't know what to make of that admission. He might have been a natural genius, or perhaps accomplishing the ridiculous feat was an artifact of brain alteration from the Big Change. She cleared her throat and turned to Trev. "Okay. I believe him."

"You do?" Trev asked.

"Sure."

"That easily?"

"For now, until I have a reason to believe otherwise." Cassie nodded. "I don't know if I would have believed you, but Jack is credible."

Trev winced. "Ouch. That hurts."

Jack shrugged. "It also makes sense."

Cassie rolled her shoulders, trying to process the situation. The shift back from pitched battle that could cost them their lives to the race disconcerted her. She was far more used to deadly battles ending with time to decompress, if only to process after-action reports.

"Why didn't you use Hercules before?" she asked. "If you'd used it against the fire iguanas, Jack wouldn't have needed to get out of the car."

"Because it takes time to deploy." Trev shrugged. "It's cool as hell to use, but all that coolness burns away profit. Bullets and grenades aren't any cheaper in the Republic than in the Confederation. It's a balancing act. Profit vs. cost whenever you kill a monster with Hercules."

Cassie shook her head. "Forget doing stupid races and killing monsters. If Jack can make an energy cell with that much density, he could sell that design to a big company or government for way more than you'd make running around in this truck for a year."

"That's not where we're going with this," Trev replied.

"I don't think you two know what you've stumbled onto through Jack's genius," Cassie shot back, trying not to shout. "I don't understand exactly what that energy weapon is, but I'm sure you could sell that design, too, unless it only works because of your power."

Trev's smile faded. "We have our reasons for keeping Hercules under wraps. We won't be selling him to anyone." He frowned. "That was a close call with that last wasp. You okay?"

"I'm good," Cassie insisted. "It didn't get that close."

She didn't like the sudden change in conversational direction. She'd been so obsessed with the WT that she'd forgotten she'd shown off her power during the fight.

"Yes, I noticed," Trev replied. "You *are* good. Far better than I suspected."

He started whistling, obviously not wanting to continue the conversation.

Cassie chalked up the encounter as a win. They'd all survived, and she'd learned more about Trev. The problem was, he'd also learned more about her before she was ready.

CHAPTER TWENTY-ONE

Their truck rumbled along, free of aerial insect threats or fire-breathing iguanas. They'd passed an abandoned car and a broken-down truck topped by a driver throwing what appeared to be acid balls at cacti for entertainment. They hadn't run into any monsters for a couple of hours.

Despite the dangers of the last battle, Cassie wanted them to fight. She wanted to see Hercules in action again since the WT impressed her, and another battle would give her more insight into the secrets of the machine...and Trev.

Her thoughts alternated between believing Jack built the WT and finding that too ridiculous to accept. While obsessing over the technology, she spotted a cell tower off to the side, protected by turreted machine guns and a single turreted laser. Signs offered warnings in English and Spanish not to approach the tower or risk being fired on by the automated defenses.

A bloated, rotting monster corpse lay a hundred yards from the tower. The advanced state of decomposition and the distance from the truck made it impossible to figure out what had attempted to close on the cell phone tower before being annihilated.

She'd seen warning signs around cell towers before. She'd never seen a cell tower with a computer-guided automatic turret that killed monsters. The world was both the same and vastly different.

Jack ran his finger across his tablet. "Drive east for thirty miles. There should be no major obstructions or natural mazes. The terrain is rough, but with our wheels and size, we shouldn't have much of a problem."

"Yeah," Trev agreed. "Imagine the poor bikers out here. It's amazing that any of them finish with all this rough terrain." He nodded forward. "For us, this is nice. It's almost like a road trip now." He accelerated, and the truck shook in protest before calming down. "I can make up some time here, even if those dumbass wasps screwed us. They better earn us a big bonus for the time they cost us."

For once, the truck offered something approaching a comfortable ride. They'd departed from a rocky and plant-filled mess to the cracked, overgrown remains of an old asphalt road. The road and the armed cell tower sighting filled Cassie with melancholy.

"When I was younger, I had a friend of a friend whose dad went on a scientific expedition to Antarctica," Cassie mentioned. "This was before the Big Change. I was, like, eleven or twelve." She shrugged. "He was an ecologist. I didn't care at the time other than the cool factor of knowing somebody going to Antarctica. It was so different and exotic."

"Okay," Trev replied, tension in his voice. "And?"

"We all went to their place one day for an Antarctic departure party," Cassie continued. "He talked about what he would do down there, but I was barely paying attention. Something about drilling ice cores to study the ancient atmosphere. I remember asking about his phone because I was obsessed with thinking about him staying in touch in the Antarctic. You know what he showed me?"

"I'm guessing a phone," Trev chuckled.

"He showed me a satellite phone," Cassie specified.

Trev's brow lifted. "Oh. I see where you're going with this."

"Think about that. We used to have phones that could bounce off satellites in space. Now, it's nothing but deadly junk up there, making more deadly junk. We might never be able to go into space again. It's just sad when you think about it."

Trev's gaze flicked to the rearview mirror. "You're a weird woman, Cassie."

"Excuse me?" She snorted. "I don't have to take that from a weirdo like you. The only normal one in this truck is Jack."

"Most people would disagree," Jack noted.

"When you were trying your damnedest to flirt your way onto this ride, you acted like you didn't know anything about anything," Trev narrowed his eyes. "You even acted like you barely understood what an MQI detector is. Now, you're all nostalgic for satellite phones, and you mentioned you had conversations with WT engineers about muscle polymers and energy cell density."

"Sue me. I have an inquisitive mind, and I worked around smart people. As for the phone, don't you ever get nostalgic for what we had? We've rebuilt, but we're nowhere near back to where we were. Way fewer people. No satellites, for a start. There's no real plan to retake space. We were talking about going to Mars, and now we're stuck on Earth."

Trev snorted. "I was a kid. I didn't have a satellite phone. Most people didn't back then. It's not something I miss."

Jack nodded. "I didn't even have my own cell phone."

"We had things like GPS and satellite imagery." Cassie sighed and slumped in her seat. "Excuse a girl for getting philosophical after a life-and-death experience. Almost being killed by giant metal-eating bugs can have that effect on normal people. I'm sorry I'm not a desert wasteland badass like you, Trev, though I get now why you're not afraid of Burning End. That WT will shred any bandits who dare get close to you."

"Exactly, and you didn't see how sturdy Hercules is," Trev replied.

Cassie's breath caught. The WT also took a long time to deploy. She couldn't forget that. It was a fundamental weakness.

She stared at Jack until he looked her way and cocked his head to side with a quizzical expression. Despite what she had just said, for all she knew, these might be his last few hours before Burning End killed him. The threat of the vision hung over everything, and her participation in the monster fight had reminded her how dangerous the Sonoran Desert was.

A fight with the bandits might come down to who could react in seconds or even milliseconds. Trev, Jack, and

Cassie would have to be a solid, perfect tactical unit to take down a gang with superior numbers. Nothing she'd read about Burning End suggested he operated solo.

The boys hadn't missed her evident skill. She knew and understood that. Their comments and quick looks confirmed it. They had to know she was more than a simple tourist. It might be time to face that head-on.

Trev snickered. "If you're going to get spun up every time a monster tries to eat you, you won't last long around here. Then again, you're not from here." The mirth vanished from his face. "I never thought to ask you since I didn't care before. What do you do? You know, for a living, when you're not being hot but annoying human ballast."

Cassie's breath caught, and her heart rate kicked up. Trev's question came far too soon after her thoughts about telling them the truth. She licked her lips. She couldn't dismiss the chance that his true power was telepathy. It was time for a test.

I'll give you a reward if you tell me the magic word, she thought. *The magic word is "Hercules." Acknowledge that, and we'll move forward. I'll tell you everything.*

Trev didn't react. He kept his eyes on the road. Nothing changed about his demeanor.

I'm going to bomb this truck. I will take out that WT and turn you over to Burning End.

Cassie grimaced, realizing how hard it was to think a lie yet not also let the plan to lie drift into her thoughts. Again, Trev didn't react. Her thoughts started to drift, and she remembered her training. Most telepaths couldn't dig past surface thoughts. All she needed to do was flood her mind and sprinkle in test thoughts to take Trev off-guard without letting on she was lying.

Snake. Fig. Lightning. Teddy Bear. I'm going to shoot you in the back of the head tonight. NEUS. Pacific Alliance. The Unified Korean Republic. Rage Rabbit is way better than Hercules, which is nothing but you compensating.

Trev's complete lack of reaction convinced her he wasn't a telepath. She refused to believe a man that cocky and happy-go-lucky could suppress a response to a mental threat or her taunting.

"Well?" Trev prodded. "Is what you do for a living a big secret?"

"I'm between jobs right now," Cassie offered, choosing her words carefully. "It's not like most places will let you take a month off to go be a participant in a weird monster-culling race in another country, even one that was part of old America."

"What did you do, then?" Trev asked. "Here I was, thinking you were a spoiled rich girl. Now, I'm not convinced. You don't talk or act like a spoiled rich girl. I doubt the average spoiled rich girl can handle a gun like you."

"You thought I was a rich girl? You said I was a cougar."

"Aren't all cougars rich?" Trev laughed. "Okay, spoiled rich cougar. Anyway, I was chatting with Jack when we were putting Hercules away. You impressed us both during that fight. You're great with your gun, but that's not the big thing."

He shook his head. "Anyone can train with a gun, given enough time. It's more about how you've handled yourself. Everything that's happened with the monsters and the terrain. It has worried you, but it has not made you run away or scream about how you're going to quit the second we get back to camp." He frowned. "The only thing that spun you up was the mention of the bandits. That makes me wonder."

"What do you think I did before I came here?" Cassie asked. Understanding his thought processes would inform her mission progress. This could end up being a good thing.

"I don't know," Trev admitted. "I think you've had formal training. Not the type you get because you pay somebody, but the type that comes with a combat-related job. I think you've had to kill people, but I don't think you liked it. You don't strike me as the ruthless sort."

"I could be pretending."

Trev snorted. "I saw your attempt at acting the sexy seductress when we met. You're not good at pretending to be anything other than who you are."

Cassie was both impressed and annoyed. "You think you know me, Trev?"

"A little." He snickered. "I don't have you all figured out. I get bits and pieces here and there that are starting to form into the picture on the puzzle box." He tapped the side of his head. "You're a complicated chick. Too complicated for my simple mind to grasp easily."

Jack laughed. "That's rare. Humility from Trev."

"Hey, don't make me sound like that."

Cassie considered telling a lie. She could wrap it in the truth.

There was no point. Each hour, she inched closer to having to make the call for her mission. Her visions showed her important things, but they weren't always easy. She could help usher in a better future if she took risks.

"You were close, Trev," Cassie replied.

"Really?" Trev perked up. "I was?"

"Until recently, I worked as a private security agent. Specifically, I was in the personal protection details for researchers at the Des Moines branch of 46P1."

Trev nodded without a hint of surprise on his face, frustrating Cassie more.

"That tracks. I wondered what your connection was with them when you tensed when I mentioned my mom used to work for them." Trev furrowed his brow. "Your power is sensing attacks? Sensing murderous intent? Limited telepathy and empathy? I'm guessing empathy. I don't think those bugs have enough of a mind for telepathy to work against them."

"You're way off." Jack shook his head. "I'd bet it's trajectory tracing. I think she can see the lines with her eyes, or her body automatically moves in response."

Cassie sighed. She was tired of lying. A person couldn't win another's trust without offering their own. She still couldn't be sure about Trev, or if he was the man she'd crossed the continent to find, but if he was, she'd begin with a partial truth.

"My power is limited precognition," Cassie announced. "I have to concentrate to use it. It's not one of those things where if I'm sitting there having lunch and a sniper lines up on me, I'll sense the danger. I've worked hard on learning to control my power over the years."

She shrugged. "It used to be that I couldn't consciously activate my precognition, but now I have enough control for it to be useful in direct combat with millisecond time horizons. Beyond that, not so much without putting incredible stress on my body." She patted her holster. "Plus, it doesn't matter if you can see the future if you can't react to it. Extensive combat training helped me turn it on and off as needed, and I've trained my body to react to the combat visions."

Trev whistled. "Precognition. You're right. I would never have guessed that."

Jack laughed. "That's funny."

"Why?" Cassie frowned.

"Your full name is Cassandra, right?"

"Yeah." Her stomach tightened in anticipation.

"It's like me being named Jack Lizardman."

Cassie groaned and let her head loll back. "Oh. You know."

There was nothing worse than running into an educated man.

Trev frowned. "Know what? Would someone let me in on what I'm missing?"

Cassie nodded to Jack. "You tell him."

Jack grinned. "In the Greek myths, Cassandra was cursed. She offered true prophecies for the future, but no one ever believed her."

"Hey, I believe you after seeing you fight, Cassie," Trev commented. "What about longer-term stuff? None?"

Cassie wasn't ready to tell the complete truth. "Not really."

"Seriously?" Trev whistled. "That's still intense. I can see how that'd be handy and super-annoying at the same time."

Jack swiped on his tablet. "You sure you can't see

anything farther out? Do you know if we will win the race? If we know we won't win, we should concentrate on monster hunting."

Cassie shook her head. "I can't see that with limited precognition."

"Does that mean you can change the future?" Trev asked. "Even if it's just seeing a few seconds ahead."

"Everybody can change the future if you think about it," Cassie replied. "I see one version, and ninety-nine percent of the time, I'm only seeing seconds at most, and it's often fragments of moments."

"Huh. It hurts my head when I think about it. I've heard about people with powers like that, but I've never met one."

"It's rare." Cassie closed her eyes and sighed. "I wasn't trying to be a total bitch by not telling you."

"No problem," Trev replied. "You've got no reason to trust two guys you just met with that information, but now, we've fought together. We've saved each other's butts. That means something." He patted his chest. "I felt it. Jack felt it, and I know you felt it."

He clucked his tongue. "Damn. Don't have that much road left. I'm going to miss the smooth drive, but hey, before I have to concentrate and can't talk, if you don't mind me asking..." He frowned. "Before, when we were talking about the Big Change, it sounded... You don't have to tell me if you don't want to, but did your parents make it out of the Big Change alive?"

Cassie smiled. "Nothing happened in Des Moines that was as bad as Chicago, but we did have uncontrolled fires, banditry, looting, and riots. All the fun like that. I didn't go crazy since my parents were there. Dad's power was both useless and awesome. He stopped needing to sleep. He just never got tired. He'd get tired physically from doing work, but not mentally."

"Lucky man," Jack murmured. "I'd get so much done if I didn't have to sleep."

"He did get a lot done," replied Cassie. "Mom could accelerate plant growth. Not, like, crazy fast, but way faster than normal. It was a good combination for a couple who needed to set up a self-sufficient garden in their backyard when the rest of society fell apart."

"You grew up there after the Change as one cozy little family?" Trev asked.

Cassie frowned. "If it had turned out that way, I might not be here now. I lost my parents." She leaned forward to stare at her hands. "I couldn't get hold of any relatives. I was old enough to take care of myself and stand in ration lines, so people didn't pay much attention or care. You know how it was at the time. Everybody was only looking out for their own."

Trev glanced at Jack. "Not everybody was doing that."

"I didn't even know about my power at first." Cassie tapped her forehead. "I'd get headaches with no obvious cause when my parents were still alive. Every once in a while, I'd get weird déjà vu with awful headaches."

She paused. "Criminals, bandits, looters. Call the assholes whatever you want. One day, they came to my house. Things weren't bad in Des Moines, compared to many places, but they weren't great, either. Too many desperate people, not enough stability and security."

"You don't have to tell me if you don't want to," Trev offered.

"Nah. It's fine. I want you to know. I want you to understand me and where I came from." She laughed bitterly. "My parents were supplying food to the neighborhood, and greedy people caught wind of that. If they were desperate and needed something to eat, my parents would have helped them."

"They wanted it all?"

"Yeah. These men showed up to take everything. My parents were in the way, so they killed them." Cassie shook her head. "They didn't even think about setting up a protection racket. They just killed them without a thought and stole everything."

"You saw it?" Trev asked.

Cassie shook her head. "I wasn't there at the time. When I got home, people from the neighborhood were there. They'd heard the gunshots, so they came over, and my parents told them what happened before they died. A couple of our neighbors had combat powers. They tracked the men down and avenged my parents."

"What happened to you after that? You mentioned you couldn't contact relatives."

"I didn't want to stay in the house where my parents were murdered." Cassie shrugged. "I didn't want to be in the neighborhood. Part of it was unfair. I blamed my neighbors for not saving my parents."

"I might have done the same," Trev admitted.

"I wandered around the city for a while, not sure what to do with myself. I helped out here and there, and I took odd jobs. Nobody cared how old you were back then as long as you were responsible and willing to work hard. I helped out at a shelter for a while, cooking and getting free meals and a place to sleep in exchange.

"I didn't have a purpose in life or a goal. I felt numb, but I was determined to live for my parents." She shivered, the memories rawer than she'd expected. "One day, I woke up from a dead sleep. I'd had a dream about the roof collapsing and most of us being buried. I didn't know what to do, so I pulled the fire alarm, and everyone ran out of the building."

Trev nodded. "You didn't think to tell them about your dream?"

"I got the sense that I had to hurry," Cassie explained. "I didn't think telling them I'd had a premonition in a dream would convince anybody, even after the Big Change. The fire alarm was the quickest way to get everyone to safety."

"What happened?"

She laughed. "Everyone was pissed. Nobody wanted to be outside in the middle of the night in November. People got angry and asked who pulled the alarm. The director promised that if the person responsible stepped forward, they wouldn't be kicked out if they had a good explanation."

"You told them?" Jack asked quietly.

"I did." Cassie smiled. "I worked up my courage and told them about my dream. That made everybody angrier. Nobody believed me. They demanded I be kicked out of the shelter, and at the height of all the screaming and yelling, the roof collapsed, just like in my dream."

Trev snickered. "That shut the assholes up, I bet."

"Yeah, it did." Cassie's smile wavered. "It also made people scared of me. Physical powers were easier to wrap their minds around, especially when people were still adjusting to the Big Change. They were all uncomfortable after that."

"You left?"

"Not right away. After weeks of people acting as if I could see everything they were doing or asking me when and how they were going to die, I left town. As you can imagine, that wasn't the brightest idea. I ended up in a bad situation with a bandit, and a 46P1 security team rescued me. During the fight, I saved one of them from getting shot with the spontaneous help of my power."

"So they recruited you into 46P1," Trev surmised.

"They ran tests and realized my ability could only be controlled for short time horizons," Cassie explained.

"You never had another farther vision like the roof?"

Cassie hesitated and averted her eyes. "Their tests indicated that was an anomaly, but they believed very short time horizons were attainable. They trained me so I could activate it at will, and after spending months with them, I joined the company." She shrugged. "Security was a good fit with my power, and it wasn't like I was interested in going back to school."

Trev nodded. "Despite that, you ended up quitting after working for them for what sounds like a long time."

Cassie shifted in the seat, the belt too confining. "Even when I was working for them, there were rumors that made me worry. Discussions of experiments and that sort of thing."

Trev nodded. "That's why you're between jobs?"

"Basically." Cassie sighed. "I worked for years, but it wasn't the rumors that made me leave. 46P1 just wasn't for me. I felt I could do something better with my power than be a glorified security guard."

Her hands shook. Again, she wasn't lying, although she'd omitted key details. Still, even if Trev had accepted her precognition, that was different than him accepting the far more critical precognitive far future visions that made her leave 46P1.

"You wanted to be on a hero team?" Trev asked. "Why not just join their hero team?"

"I had my reasons. It's more complicated than that."

"46P1 plays at being one of the great saviors of humanity, but they're not?" Trev postulated.

Cassie frowned. "It was time for me to move on."

Trev grinned. "Now that I know you're more than human ballast, you'll help us fight going forward. With your powers, you might even kick my ass on a good day."

Cassie had risked opening up to Trev and Jack. While she knew the slippery Trev wouldn't give her everything she wanted, she'd opened the door of trust, and he needed to walk through.

"Why did it take so long to get your WT up and running?" she asked.

"What?" Trev shot a glance at Jack, who shrugged with a practiced nonchalance. "Where did that come from? Why are we talking about Hercules now?"

"It's a simple question," Cassie noted. "I've been honest with you. I'd like you to be honest with me. I think that's fair."

"Uh, because we needed to power it up and make sure I didn't get swarmed at the same time."

"That doesn't make sense. Moving away from the truck

made the WT more vulnerable to the swarm, not less." Cassie injected stridency into her voice. "By the way, I'm qualified to pilot a WT. I bet I have more experience than you. Maybe next time, you two will shoot the monsters, and I will get in Hercules and shoot."

"It's a custom design." Trev frowned. "It'd take days to train you for basic operation. If you want to help, shoot the monsters while we get it ready."

Cassie wanted to press but wouldn't push her luck. The WT was too small and powerful for its design. That much was clear. The implications were less so.

They'd claimed Jack had built it, but they might have stolen it. That might explain why they had to leave the NEUS. She wanted to believe in Jack and Trev but couldn't trust the irregularities she'd witnessed.

The question of Trev's power remained. Combining power use with tech was common in corporate and government security, military, and hero teams. Understanding Hercules was the key to understanding Trev's power, and that was critical to evaluate Trev and determine if he was the man at the heart of her strongest visions.

"I'll have to concentrate on driving soon," Trev continued. "We can pick this up later."

"Sure thing," Cassie replied. "I won't forget."

Trev chuckled. "That sounds like a threat."

"Not a threat. A promise."

CHAPTER TWENTY-TWO

In camp hours later, after the rise of the first evening stars and seeing flares marking chunks of dead satellites and missile remnants in the sky, Trev yawned and stretched under their canopy. The wasp fight had pushed him more than he wanted, but it confirmed Hercules' effectiveness in real battles.

While Jack was building the WT, they hadn't been sure if it was worth it. They both thought it would be a good way to leverage Trev's abilities despite their limits and his lack of training, but neither had worried about anyone questioning the WT on a tech level. Cassie had reminded them that they still needed to be careful and that their hesitation about using the WT wasn't misplaced.

Despite Lana's warning, they hadn't run into any bandits during the race. That didn't mean they couldn't get a license and hunt them later. The more Trev thought about it, the more the idea appealed to him.

Bandits were scum. They preyed on people who were just trying to make it through the day. Most villains claimed to offer something, however twisted, in exchange for their evil acts. Bandits and looters were parasites in human form, so removing them from the world was everybody's duty.

Trev frowned, remembering the conversation with Cassie. He now understood her far better. The inconsistencies and mysteries that had bothered him had been washed away by the truth of her background.

The problem was, every time they talked, the looks she gave him convinced him that she was still holding something back. She'd admitted working for 46P1, and his parents had warned him to be wary of the company.

Not only that, but she'd described working as a security agent. She was the sword of a dangerous company, not a curious researcher or a secretary. He trusted her more, but not entirely.

Trev looked around before frowning at his phone on the table. "Hey, Jack, did you see where Cassie wandered off to?"

Jack called from under the truck, his back on the roller and a wrench in hand. "She said she was going to get something to eat. She declared, 'I need real food, not food in bar form.'"

"That's the most relatable thing she's said in a while." Trev gestured at the phone. "Our final times are in. We blew our lead, and we dropped to fourth place."

"Not bad with having to stop to fight the swarm and the penalty," Jack replied. "It felt longer when we were fighting them."

"Fights are always like that," Trev agreed. "I thought we were going to drop way farther than fourth, too. We can still salvage this race and end up on the podium." He slid the phone into his pocket. "I screwed up by picking the later starting time. I thought there would be more monsters left over." He frowned. "I have bad news, too."

"There's always some." Jack sat up. "Please tell me. It's not healthy to hold it in."

"They're counting the entire swarm as a single medium threat monster." Trev scoffed. "What a bunch of chintzy assholes. I filed a formal protest, but they made it clear that they won't escalate the protest until the race is over."

"We had to fight the swarm either way." Jack hopped to his feet. "At least we'll get something out of it. I wouldn't worry."

"If you say so. I'm still pissed." Trev waved a hand. "I'll be over it by tomorrow morning. I can hold it in until they respond to my complaint."

Jack rolled his shoulders and flicked his tongue. "If we claw our way up to third place or higher, we'll earn more than enough. I think we should focus on finishing faster and ignore monsters."

Trev groaned. "It feels like we armed up and brought all this gear for nothing."

"You don't have to use weapons just because they're available. It's not worth it. I think we should focus on getting the prize money. It's a better bet and more achievable."

"Fine." Trev threw up his hands. "You win. I'll run from anything that looks dangerous."

"We can always go hunt monsters later."

"It won't be as fun or rewarding." Trev grunted in frustration. "But you're right. We need money more than we need fun. We drew a bad card in that swarm. Shit happens."

"We might get lucky, and there won't even be any monsters to tempt you."

Trev squinted at a shadow near the back of the truck. Someone was coming. He lifted his hand.

Cassie wandered in. She smiled, held up something wrapped in foil, and took a bite. "If you were hoping to get any of the tacos, they're almost out. The vendor said he's done, and he's packing up tonight and just hanging out until the convoy leaves after the last day."

Jack looked her way. "Really?" He waved at Trev and ran off. "I'll be back soon."

Trev laughed. "I always forget how much he likes tacos."

He watched Cassie as she polished off her taco. She'd want to return to their earlier conversation. He'd have more control if he initiated the dialog. He nodded at the cab of the truck. "Got a minute to chat?"

"I'm all full of taco goodness. The tacos here versus the tacos in the Confederation might as well be different foods." Cassie patted her stomach and wadded up the wrapper. She dropped it into the tiny metal garbage can Trev had set near the table. "Perfect time to chat."

Trev and Cassie headed to the truck and slipped into the cab. Trev didn't speak until after he closed his door.

"I wanted to talk about what you told me earlier," Trev noted.

"My life story, in other words?" Cassie asked with a faint smile.

"Yeah, basically." Trev stared at her. Even after days of traveling, he found her gorgeous face dangerous. It was far too easy to get lost in her eyes. "So, you're a former corporate assassin, huh?"

Starting with disapproval would give him the upper hand. He wasn't ready for her to ask deep questions about him. Not until he had proof that he could trust her.

Cassie frowned and looked away. "I wasn't an assassin. I was in security and mostly worked as a bodyguard. Not everyone at 46P1 is an asshole, you know, even if the company has problems. Many of the staff are trying to make the world a better place." Her shoulders slumped. "I'm not trying to defend everything the company does, just the people who work for it."

"I know." Trev smiled. "Remember, my mom worked for 46P1. I told you that. I get that not everyone there is scum. That doesn't mean 46P1 is a trustworthy company."

"I know. I quit, remember?" Cassie nodded. "By the way, you never mentioned what she did for the company."

Something was odd about her expression and the twitch of her mouth. His tone bothered her. It was almost like she knew the answer and was testing him. Trev didn't know what to make of it, so he let it go.

"She was a researcher," Trev explained. "She worked for them before the Big Change."

Cassie smiled. "Oh. I see. I figured it was something like that."

"Oh, and by the way, my dad was a cop in the Capitol Police under the old government. When the Big Change happened, he worked without pay while everything settled down. He told me it was his duty to serve and protect." He grinned. "People were happy to have a cop with superstrength in those crazy times. He built enough of a reputation that just him showing up could calm down trouble."

"What about your mom?" Cassie asked with suspicion in her voice. "Did she stay a researcher like your dad stayed a cop?"

"Mom was always brilliant," Trev replied with a wistful smile. "Dad used to say he never understood how a dumb guy like him ended up with such a smart woman."

"That's sweet."

Trev nodded. "I don't know if she was any smarter after the Big Change, but it gave her the power to fly, and not lame floating around. Class-A flight."

Cassie's brows rose. "Wow. That's a nice power. I don't know how useful it is for a researcher, but at least she could commute easily."

"We should have moved out farther." Trev laughed. He leaned over the steering wheel. "You know, the really weird thing is the hero teams."

"Hero teams?" Cassie's face scrunched. "Are you doing free association right now? I'm not following you."

"Sometimes hero teams are open about their members," Trev continued, ignoring her complaint. "They're supposed to be a source of strength and a symbol of security and hope, so teams with public members are trusted more."

Cassie nodded. "That makes sense. People trust someone they don't feel is hiding something even if they understand why they are."

"Yeah, but sometimes, it's important to keep their identities secret, like they did with the Atlantic Shield and the Sword of Liberty. The families and friends of high-profile teams were threatened, especially back then when everything was barely holding together."

Cassie jerked back, her eyes wide. "Your parents were heroes?"

"Yeah, and they didn't want me to be anywhere near a hero team," Trev replied. "They made that clear early on."

"Now that I think about it, a woman with Class-A flight in DC…" Cassie slapped her forehead. "How could I have not realized it when you told me her power? There weren't many people with Class-A flight back then. She was a member of the Atlantic Shield. I don't understand. If both your parents were heroes, why didn't they want you on a hero team when you got older?"

Trev thought his answer over before speaking. "You worked security for 46P1. You know how dangerous things can get when empowered villains are involved."

"Sure, but it all comes down to matchups and training."

"In many ways, we were sheltered in DC," Trev explained. "We had the old government's resources and forces during the transition to the new order." He shook his head. "The government and the corporations acted like they had things under control despite all the people dying, but then the really dangerous people showed up. The villains who realized the old rules didn't apply anymore. The Dark Empress who could make soldiers kill their friends and families conquered the northeast, and a city went up in a mushroom cloud."

Cassie stared straight ahead as if unwilling to make eye contact with Trev. "I want to be clear. Your mom was a member of the Atlantic Shield. Your dad had a day job as a cop, which means he must have been a member of the

Sword of Liberty. Two hero parents but on different hero teams. That's rare, even today."

"My mom was honest with me when the Atlantic Shield formed." Trev turned to her. "She was one of the first recruited since the company trusted her, and her power was flashy and made for good news stories when she saved the day. She explained that hero teams were less about saving people than being living propaganda symbols. Because of that, they didn't have to operate the same way as normal military and security units. She didn't say it was a bad thing. She liked the idea of being a hero at first. She wanted to be a symbol of hope in a time when people needed it."

"Symbols are important, and people needed hope. They still do." She looked his way. "I'm assuming your serve-and-protect dad in the Sword of Liberty felt the same as your mom."

Trev nodded. "Yep. Having married people in different hero teams made things complicated, but it also paved the way for tons of cooperation between the teams."

"They died about a year ago." Cassie nodded. "Your parents were killed when the Altruist attacked DC."

Trev grunted. "Yeah. The bastard kept bragging that he was indestructible, and he'd use his power to bring paradise through spread-out suffering."

"How's that for arrogant?" Cassie scoffed.

"I never got how killing people left and right would lead to paradise, but I didn't worry even when I heard that both the Atlantic Shield and Sword of Liberty had mobilized against him." Trev's hands tightened into fists. "The hero teams got bruises, but they always won, and they won that day. They proved that the Altruist wasn't indestructible, but he took plenty of heroes with him, including my mom and dad."

Cassie leaned over and patted his arm. "I'm sorry. I really am. There's a lot of respect for the Atlantic Shield and the Sword of Liberty, even in the Confederation. The local 46P1 branch honored the sacrifices of the Atlantic Shield."

A memory of a simple handwritten message flashed in Trev's mind.

If something happens to us, sell the house, take what we saved for you, and move out of the NEUS with Jack. Go somewhere far from here. Don't trust anyone just because they're from the government, any government, and especially don't trust anyone from 46P1. We're sorry we couldn't tell you more, but it's for the best. It'll keep you safer.

Trev reached under his shirt and rubbed his necklace, lost in thought, choking up. "I don't care if the hero teams were more about propaganda than saving people. My parents helped save the city that day, and they died being true heroes."

"What are you going to do after this?" Cassie asked. "Assuming you finish high enough in the standings to get the money you need."

"I don't know." Trev shrugged. "Live my life? Win more races? I didn't have real plans after moving here. I just wanted to get away from DC. I…think my parents wanted me to do that. Well, I know they did."

"To a place that has mutant-hunting races?" Cassie laughed. "Fewer big villains attack the Republic, though it's not what I'd call a safe country."

"Tucson's not so bad. Not sure if we're going to stay there forever, but it's a nice spot to figure things out." Trev forced a smile. "What about you? You going to get a security job in the Republic, or are you just here because of this race?"

Cassie began, "I have ideas. I need to take care of things before I can go on with the rest of my life. That's part of all this. At first, I thought it was a mistake, but now I don't believe that."

"It's been fun," Trev replied, happy that he'd told the truth, though vaguely disappointed that Cassie hadn't told him anything else. He patted the dashboard. "I feel alive again doing this, and all that bandit talk the other day made me worry that you'd quit on me."

"You should drop out of the race," Cassie blurted.

Trev snapped his head toward her. "What?"

"You heard me." Cassie squared her shoulders and lifted her chin. "You should drop out. I can hook you up with other jobs to make money now that I know what you're capable of. I was right the other day. The bandit attack is too great a risk."

"Damn it. I wish I had not brought it up." Trev groaned. "Are you still on about that? A handful of bandits here and there isn't a big deal. Come on. You're this hot 46P1 assassin chick who can use precognition in fights. Bandits are nothing to you. I have Hercules, and Jack can support us with his coilgun and the grenade launcher. Any bandits in the Sonoran Desert will have a very bad time if they run into us. You said it yourself."

"I'm not an assassin," Cassie snapped. "I'm serious. Does Jack feel the same way? Shouldn't he have input? You talk about him standing up for himself, but you act like you're his dad."

"I have his best interests at heart, and Jack knows I'll always have his back." Trev shrugged. "I'll rip a monster apart with my bare hands to protect him." He stared at her. "Come on, Cassie. There's something you're not telling me. If you know something, spit it out. You were fine until I mentioned the bandits."

Cassie swallowed. "You can make money another way. Please, if you race tomorrow, Jack might die. You need to pack up and get far away from anywhere Burning End might show up."

"Huh." Trev nodded, not liking where his suspicions were taking him.

His gaze flicked to the glove box. Her extreme reaction didn't make sense.

Cassie whipped out her gun and pointed it at his head. "I don't want to shoot you, but I will if I have to."

Trev shook his head. "Really? This is the play you're going with?"

CHAPTER TWENTY-THREE

The amused defiance on Trev's face sent Cassie's heart into overdrive. A man didn't look that smug with a gun pointed at his face unless he had a plan that didn't end with his brains splattered all over the inside of his own truck. He wasn't even putting his hands above his head. Her split-second decision to use her precognition had warned her that he was about to go for his gun.

She concentrated until the split stress of the immediate future and the present made her head throb. She could only see him smiling at her in the future and saying something.

"At least put your hands up," Cassie ordered. She didn't plan to shoot him, but she couldn't die there.

It didn't make sense. Even if she was wrong about who Trev was, he didn't seem like someone who'd suddenly betray her.

Trev raised his hands. "Whoa there, Rage Rabbit. Don't do something you'll regret. I know you've been keeping things from me, but I don't think you want to kill me."

"Don't make me do something I'd regret," Cassie spat back. "You were the one who went for your gun."

"You used your power, didn't you?" Trev asked. "What did you see? I guarantee you didn't see me shooting you."

Cassie scoffed. "It doesn't matter what I saw. I'm holding a gun on you and not the other way around, so I have the control."

"If you say so."

"I do."

"Who are you really?" Trev asked, shaking his head. "Just because I've got this handsome face and can't rebuild an engine with two pinecones and a bottle of olive oil like Jack doesn't mean I'm an idiot."

"I told you who I am. I gave you my whole sad, sordid life history." Cassie glared at him. "I don't like thinking about the past. Do you think I like remembering how my decent, hardworking parents were murdered by short-sighted bastards? Do you think I enjoy talking about how people I thought were my friends ran me out of the shelter like I was a witch waiting to poison wells?"

"Yeah, this all tracks, mostly. Ex-46P1 security with limited precog ability." Trev worked his jaw and frowned. "There's something still there. I just know it. I want you to tell me. You've been lying to me, haven't you?"

"*I haven't lied to you!* I mean, I have, but you've lied to me, too. Everybody in this camp lies to everybody."

Trev shrugged. "I believe what you've told me. The problem is my gut. It's screaming that a huge piece of the puzzle is missing, and you can't act like I haven't told you important secrets. I just revealed the secret identities of two heroes."

"Who are both dead." Cassie scoffed. "Okay, fine. What do you think is going on? We can start with that and work our way from there."

Trev laughed. "First, I thought you were sent by 46P1 to kill me."

She narrowed her eyes. "Why would 46P1 want you dead? What makes you so special?"

"That was my question for you." Trev shrugged. "It's not that I think I'm that important, but things my parents told me made me wonder about the company and if they might have it in for me. But that's not what's bothering me most."

"What is it?" Cassie kept the gun pointed at his chest. "Spill it."

"It's that you keep obsessing over the bandits even after seeing Hercules. Do you really think a bargain-basement villain who calls himself Burning End could win against our WT?" Trev shrugged. "I'd lay his gang out in thirty seconds. You didn't see how good the reinforced armor or the defense systems are."

"You think you could single-handedly beat a bounty-bearing Class-A-empowered threat with your toy WT? I'll admit you had me going, but I woke up to reality."

"I think?" Trev kept his arms up but wagged his finger. "No. I know."

Cassie was missing something. Either Trev was the most excellent actor in the world, or he had no reason to fear her gun. She didn't understand why he didn't try to take it if that was true. It was like he wanted her to believe she was in control when he was.

"A WT doesn't make you a god." Cassie waved the gun.

"There are many powers that can take out a WT. You can ambush a WT."

Trev rolled his eyes. "The whole pretending-to-be-a-dumb-chick thing just sat wrong with me. I can understand not wanting to tell us your life story when you first met us, but you had no reason to hide being good with a gun or pretend you barely knew what was happening with power tech. It would have made us more likely to take you on."

Trev leaned over and pressed his forehead against the gun. "Wouldn't you be suspicious if the situation was reversed? If I was acting like I didn't know the things I obviously did?"

"What are you doing?" Cassie demanded. She clenched her jaw and willed her hand not to shake. "Do you *want* to die? This isn't a toy, Trev."

"I'm proving a point." Trev's mocking grin grew wider. "I like easy explanations that fit the evidence. I'm not Jack. My brain doesn't put complicated puzzles together for fun. I'm not a dumbass, but nobody's going to mistake me for a genius."

"What's your easy explanation? You said you believed my story about my past."

"I do believe it." Trev wiggled his eyebrows, his skin moving the gun. "But here's the thing. It's not like you quit 46P1 and teleported over here. There were weeks, maybe months between that and your arrival."

Cassie jerked the gun back. "Don't play games with me. One twitch of my finger and you're dead."

His confidence unsettled her. Had she been wrong the entire time? Her visions pointed her toward him, but what if she'd misunderstood? He'd been ready to hold her at gunpoint before she beat him to the draw.

"See, the easy explanation is, this is a bandit honeytrap with honey that needed more prep time." Trev leaned back and started to lower his hands.

"Keep your hands up!" Cassie yelled.

"No," Trev replied. "It gets annoying after a while. Oh, here." He stuck his hands behind his head and leaned back against the window. "That's more comfortable, and they're technically still up."

Cassie's jaw clenched. "This isn't a joke." She sighed and lowered her gun. "You don't care about the gun, do you?"

"No." Trev shook his head. "If you put it away, I promise I won't go for mine. Then again, you can just concentrate and see the future."

Cassie looked between him and her gun and holstered her weapon. "You think I'm a bandit lure?"

"I think they sent you into the camp to look for guys to set up. It had to be worthwhile for them," Trev explained. "That means they'd need to grab something more than a truck. Somehow, you got wind of our supplies back there, plus Hercules. That makes us a good target for ol' Burning End." He laughed. "I don't care how he justifies it. Your boss' name is terrible."

"I don't work for Burning End," Cassie ground out through gritted teeth. "I don't work for any bandits."

Trev shook his head. "I'm not going to bother explaining that the WT would be nothing but parts to you, and the only reason I haven't got rough is because I feel like you're torn. Jack's a great guy. I'm at least a good guy." He grinned. "I got this pretty smile."

"*I'm not a bandit!* Damn it, listen to me. Bandits killed my parents. Why the hell would I work for scum like that?"

Trev narrowed his eyes. "Why are you so certain that Jack's going to die? Do you have a deal with Burning End? Did you manage to convince him to let me go, or is he one of those people who can't stand to let visible mutants live?"

Cassie sighed and lowered her head. "There's something I haven't told you."

"Obviously. That's why we're having this fun but gun-filled conversation." Trev sighed.

"There's something even 46P1 didn't know about my power. I was grateful for the job, but I heard things about experiments with unwilling participants. They'd done enough to convince me that they'd make me a lab rat if they knew the whole truth."

"What's the whole truth?" Trev asked.

"Remember the shelter roof?" Cassie asked.

Trev nodded. "That proves you can see more than a few seconds into the future. I'm surprised 46P1 gave up on trying to develop things more. Seeing a few minutes into the future would be very useful."

Cassie averted her eyes. "I never told them about the roof. I was afraid of what would happen. I was still raw about people's reactions at the shelter, which made me worry about how 46P1 might want to use me. Their training and experiments pushed my abilities further even without them knowing that."

"There it is." Trev clapped.

Cassie jumped and went for her gun again. His hand snaked out, and he grabbed her wrist.

"I'm not going to attack you unless you attack me." Trev slowly withdrew his arm. "Okay?"

Cassie let go of the gun. "I'm jumpy right now."

"You were talking about your power."

She swallowed and nodded. "My ability isn't limited to immediate combat situations. I can see things farther out. Way farther out. Not just a few minutes but days, months, and sometimes years. I can't control it or actively bring it on except in combat time-horizon situations." She pointed at her forehead. "The visions almost always come in my dreams without sound that sear themselves into my soul. Even then, it's harder to understand when it's not about me."

Trev gave an impressed whistle. "Years?" He laughed. "I know what you told Jack, but you didn't have a vision about us winning the race, did you?"

Cassie shook her head. "Nothing like that."

"You can see when something's happening to you more clearly than when something's happening to someone else?" Trev asked.

Cassie gave a shallow nod. "I believe it has to be a person I'm eventually going to have contact with, but I don't know how that all works. Like if I had a vision about…"

She considered blurting the entirety of her mission but held back. She was walking Trev into believing her despite the misunderstanding. Pushing too early could ruin things since he already suspected her. For now, saving lives was more important.

"Say I have a vision about you," Cassie continued. "That

would imply I would meet you at some point, but what if I went out of my way to avoid you?"

Trev grimaced. "Is this one of those things where the universe conspires to make you fulfill the vision no matter what? It hurts my head to think about it."

Cassie shook her head. "No, it doesn't work that way. I know that much. The future can be changed. I prove it all the time, like when I was able to draw my gun on you before you got yours."

Trev huffed. "I want to point out for the record that doesn't mean you're faster than me since you can legit see into the future."

Cassie managed a quiet chuckle despite the situation. "Duly noted. The upshot is I'm seeing possibilities, not certainties. at the same time, just having a vision pushes me. Do you see how that can get annoying and how it's hard to know what to do when I have a disturbing vision?"

"Now I get it. I should have figured it out before. I figured you were telling the truth about your ability not progressing much from combat precognition." Trev folded his arms. "Spill it. Let's get to it."

"Spill what?"

"What you saw that freaked you out so much that you've been trying to get me to quit the race for two days." Trev patted his chest. "It's about me, right? That's why you're acting so squirrelly. Did you see me dying? Because no damned way will I be taken out by Burning End."

"It's not you." Cassie shook her head. "I saw Jack being murdered. I saw a flaming fist punching through his chest, and the official mentioned the bandit Burning End." She sighed. "I couldn't see his face, but what are the chances of it being somebody else? The problem with visions is that they aren't like a drone feed I can control. They're only bits and pieces, like images with feelings. I get what I get, no more, no less. The only thing I could say for sure is it felt like we weren't in camp. We were standing by the truck. The door was open, and the window was shattered."

Trev folded his arms. "This gets more annoying by the second. You've convinced me you've got limited precognition. That doesn't mean I believe this crazy story. I want to. I really do since it explains everything, but it also could be you using a more advanced version of feminine wiles. I have to keep that possibility in mind. Sometimes, the best way to trick someone is to tell them the truth."

"Why would I make up something like that? And if I were a bandit spy, why would I tell you?" Cassie pleaded. "I just don't want Jack to die."

"Because you fell for me? Or heck, you fell for Jack? He's charming in his own lizard-y way." Trev smiled.

"Why would I make up such an elaborate story instead of telling you the truth if I'm a bandit lure?" Cassie clenched her teeth. "Will you just listen to what I'm saying? I don't want Jack to die, and I know you don't want him to."

Trev turned and leaned back in his seat. "I'll never claim to be as smart as Jack, but I do all right. I listened to you, and weighing all the evidence, I believe you saw Jack get hurt."

Cassie sighed in relief. "Thank you."

"That doesn't mean we're dropping out of the race."

"How the hell can you say that after all this? I've been

around you two enough to understand you're good friends. You care about him."

Trev shot her an annoyed look. "He's not my good friend. He's my *best* friend. He's the last remaining member of my family."

"Then why would you risk him like this? It's too dangerous."

"You said it yourself. The future isn't set." Trev gestured at the glove box. "We know trouble's coming, so we can prepare for it. An ambush you can anticipate is an ambush you can turn around on the other person."

Cassie shook her head. "It's not like that. I don't know the time, the place, or anything other than that image. I don't know any of the circumstances leading up to the murder. It could happen tomorrow, or it could happen a week from now."

"So? It means I don't hold back if I see any bandits." Trev squinted through the windshield like he was looking for Burning End to be hiding in the closest tent. "If Burning End is supposed to kill Jack by punching through his chest, the bandits aren't going to ambush us from long range. That allows us to get Hercules up and me to do my thing. I'll put an end to Burning End." He patted her shoulder. "You said it yourself. The future can be changed."

Cassie groaned and slapped her forehead. "You're going to give me a stroke with your logic, but at least you're taking this seriously. That's a start."

"I've got no reason not to take it seriously after what I've seen and heard." Trev chuckled. "Plenty of people keep their true power close to the chest. I don't hold it against you, and I plan to take advantage of it. The problem is, for all we know, running from the race is what would get Jack killed. The best thing to do is stay the course and blow away any bandits we see without mercy."

Cassie gave a shallow nod. Trev was running through the same issues she had, and by her own admission, she didn't have enough information to offer a way to save Jack. He'd only be safe if Burning End was killed or captured.

"What about you?" Cassie asked. "You still haven't told me your power."

"If you're not lying about this vision, you'll see it when I pulverize Burning End. I need to check with Jack first."

Cassie couldn't keep the surprise off her face. "You're going to tell him what I told you."

"Contrary to what you seem to think, we're equal partners. I'm not the dad who gets to boss the son around." Trev shrugged. "It's his damned life, so he deserves to know. He should make the final call if we're going to risk his life."

"What if he says he wants to drop out?"

"Then we drop out and figure out how to get away from Burning End."

CHAPTER TWENTY-FOUR

March 9, 2036, Sonoran Desert, New Baja Republic
Trev glanced at the speedometer. They'd made great time that morning, and despite being in the middle of the pack's starting order, the only monsters they'd seen were long dead.

There also had been no hint of bandits and no radio warnings from the organizers.

He wasn't sure if he wanted the bandits to show up. Part of him figured it was the most efficient way to end the threat. The other part worried about screwing up and getting Jack killed.

When Trev had explained the situation to Jack, he'd been prepared for his friend to tell him they were dropping out. Trev didn't want to, but he'd never insist Jack risk his life against his will. However, Jack wanted to continue. That made things easy.

Trev couldn't let Burning End get near Jack. He understood why Cassie was so afraid. She thought he'd get roasted in Hercules, and Jack would be murdered.

She didn't understand the full scope of his power. If he could take a precognitive by surprise, he could shock the hell out of a bandit boss.

They drove by a group of giant scorpions that had been cut in half, the wounds clean and cauterized by whatever weapon had killed them. One had been crushed and had truck tire tracks on its back.

Cassie leaned forward. "They're far less exciting than I envisioned. Somehow, I thought they'd be more majestic."

"Big bugs are just big bugs in the end," Trev replied. "I hope all these monsters slowed the other bastards up." He drummed his hands on the steering wheel. He tightened his grip when the truck shimmied hard while passing over the uneven terrain, flinging out a spray of dirt that half-buried a scorpion corpse. "Since it looks like all our bonuses got stolen."

"Why didn't you go with Wave One instead?" asked Cassie. "I'm serious this time. I'm not acting. I don't know the strategies well, but you can switch, even if it's rare."

"The speed demons are in Wave One," explained Jack. "They've already set faster times. We'd have less of a chance of finishing high. We've overloaded with gear because we're a Wave Two team."

Cassie shook her head. "I was thinking about the monsters you could have killed, but it doesn't matter now."

"Yeah, too late, even though we'd have more monsters. They don't give high bonuses in Wave One since they're trying to discourage them from doing anything but concentrating on speed. Otherwise, why have it?"

"Ignoring everything else that is going on, this race is insane, and you two are insane for participating. You both have a screw loose in your brains. Maybe Jack can figure out a way to tighten them down." Cassie laughed.

Jack nodded toward Trev. "If I've got one, he's got three loose."

"Probably. That explains a lot."

Trev guided the truck around a heap of rotting flesh that had been a monster. He couldn't identify it, though he didn't know any land monsters in this part of the Republic that were the size of a semi-truck and trailer. "This insane man with three loose screws is going to get us into the top three."

"Is that before or after I die?" Jack asked. "By the rules, you have to finish with a living co-driver and tourist for your times to be official. Otherwise, you're disqualified."

Trev snorted. "Hey, I gave you the right to veto, man. You said, and I quote, 'Let's go!'"

"I was making fun of you, but I also don't want to drop out." Jack sighed. "I reserve the right to bitch about any plan that ends with me getting punched through the chest by a bandit with a flaming fist, but at least if I die, it'll be cool."

"You just want to be able to say, 'I told you so,' before you die."

"Exactly." Jack's tongue flicked out. "I can go to heaven happy as long as I have that hanging over you."

Trev and Jack chuckled together.

"You two really *are* insane." Cassie glared at them. "I don't get how you can treat this as a big joke. I'm trying not to let it bother me, but in truth, I'm scared."

"We can joke about it because we're not scared." Trev downshifted and eased up on the gas. "It's not going to end with Jack dying. It's going to end with every bandit who dares look at him the wrong way dead. I'll pulp them like I pulped those emperor wasps. Anyone who goes after my friends gets what's coming to them."

"You've killed people before?" Cassie asked. "I wasn't sure if you had or you were just acting like it as part of the cocky, badass image you're desperate to communicate."

"I don't go out of my way to kill people, but, yeah, I have. In my defense, they all had it coming." Trev replied.

"That's what I told myself at 46P1," Cassie shot back.

A hidden hole made the truck lurch, and a cactus arm whipped the windshield, leaving a crack. Jack and Cassie jumped.

Trev growled and pulled the truck to the side. "Not going out of my way to kill people doesn't mean I'm going to let a murderous psycho hurt people I care about. I try to give people a chance, and if they throw it away, that's on them. We reap what we sow."

"Really?" Cassie asked.

"Letting psychos who can't control themselves live isn't justice. It's just setting up more innocent victims in the future." Trev frowned at the crack. "We drive all this time without hitting anything big, and now we do it on Day Three. How's that for luck?"

"Does that mean you'll negotiate with Burning End?" Cassie asked. "What if he agrees to stand down and turn himself in?"

"That's not going to happen." Trev snorted. "If he's willing to turn himself in, fine. I don't want to start a fight that could end with Jack dead. But we know he's coming, and if he does make his move, we'll deploy." He nodded at the trailer.

"The show?" Cassie gasped and snapped her fingers. "I finally figured it out."

"Did you, now?" Trev grinned. "What's the answer, O Hot Princess of Assassins?"

"Again, I'm not an assassin, and for the record, since you'll make a joke if I don't specify it, I'm not a princess."

Trev smirked. "You're not going to deny that you're hot?"

Cassie smirked at him. "I didn't understand why you wasted time deploying Hercules away from the truck."

"Now you know?" Trev asked.

"That means whatever's involved uses your power. You didn't want to trip the detector. I think it has something to do with the energy weapon."

Trev nodded. "Something like that. You are close."

"You're going to give up the race for your friend?" Cassie asked.

"Nope." Trev smirked at Jack. "We're going to have our cake and eat it, too. The official warned us about technopaths and related powers. When I checked Burning End's history, the lack of surveillance footage or images supports that asshole having people like that in his gang. His own people will make it easier for me to deploy Hercules without a problem, so I can cut loose earlier and tear them apart."

"Oh." Cassie returned to gazing out the window. "You've thought this through."

"Why do you sound so disappointed?" Trev asked.

"It's not that." Cassie put her hand on her chest. "I just realized I've underestimated you from the beginning."

"We're going to make a sixty-degree turn to the right at the outcrop after the hill," Jack announced, staring at his tablet. "When you enter the canyon, take a left. It'll be a tight squeeze."

"It's time to concentrate on driving instead of chatting," Trev insisted.

The truck cleared the canyon with only a few new scrapes. That freed the team from the worrisome chance of jutting rock tearing into their tires, but the jagged, cracked ground and uneven terrain jostled the vehicle and the passengers.

Cassie groaned. "I'm glad I didn't have a big breakfast. I'm reminded of my WT aerial deployment training with 46P1. I had to do a drop in a plane while being subjected to anti-aircraft fire."

"In a simulator?" Jack asked.

"No, a real plane they were half-ass trying to shoot down. Turbulence doesn't begin to describe the experience." Cassie grimaced. "46P1 security agent training gets intense."

"*Nah, this is great!*" Trev shouted. "*This is fun!*" He kept a tight grip on the wheel and was forced into quick adjustments to offset individual tires leaving the ground and the truck threatening to tip. "This is what makes rally raid fun. You never know what you're going to get. The drivers are your opponents. The terrain is your opponent. The weather is your opponent. In this one, monsters and bandits are also our opponents."

"We've got a natural rock ramp coming in five hundred yards," Jack reported. "Go around it."

"I see it," Trev confirmed.

He wanted to go around it, but a pile of storm-tossed rocks on the right and a massive decaying fallen cactus on the left gave him little choice but to experiment with the limits of his vehicle. He centered the wheel and accelerated. This would be a challenge even for him.

"This isn't a good idea." Jack ducked his head. "I'm going to make you help me with all the repairs before we return to Tucson."

"I'm not doing this for fun," Trev announced. His protestations might have been more convincing without the huge smile.

The truck hit the sloped hill, rattling briefly before all four wheels left the ground. Jumps were never a good idea in anything as large as their truck. Trev knew that, and Jack told him all the time. That had never stopped him from enjoying them.

A jump at an angle was an even worse idea. They'd been in the air only seconds before he realized his fatal mistake. Their rotational motion would end with them landing on their side and end their race.

Trev didn't have time to think, only react. He snapped his left arm up. A purple rectangular forcefield appeared and extended backward from the front left wheel. The truck jostled hard when it struck the field, the abrupt impact realigning the cab to line it up with the ground.

Trev dropped the field after the correction. The truck

landed with loud grinding and jarring wrenches. His stomach turned over before the shaking stopped, but the vehicle continued rumbling along.

"Let's not do that again," Cassie suggested. "I don't want to throw up in a helmet."

Heart pounding, Trev checked her in the rearview mirror. There was no knowing smirk or any other indication that she'd used her power, and her position in the back seat meant she shouldn't have been able to see anything.

At this point, Trev didn't know why he cared if she knew the full scope of his power since she'd shared so much with him. He did worry about her claim to have seen Jack's death. Everything he'd witnessed supported the idea that she was a precog, and he was banking on knowing the attack was coming to turn the tables on the bandits. He also worried that she'd fooled him and this was all a sophisticated bandit trap to get their hands on a free WT.

He frowned. Something else was wrong. He glanced at a black readout clamped to his dashboard.

Trev hadn't been thinking about the MQI detector when he used his power to stop the crash. It should have gone off. They'd demonstrated how it'd react to power usage during pre-race scrutiny, but somehow, he'd managed to use his ability without being detected.

"Halfway through Day Three," Trev noted. The mystery of the failed detector bothered him, but he had no reason to bring it up. "We're still making good time with the help of the occasional wild jump."

Jack snorted. "Don't do that again. It's a miracle you didn't break something with that one."

"Miracles happen. Thanks, Goddess of Racing. I'm glad I'm back in your good graces."

Jack stared at the side mirror for long enough that Trev asked, "Use the reverse camera on your phone."

"I'm not looking at myself," Jack replied.

"What are you doing?"

"Looking for fluid leaks," Jack replied. "My idiot driver keeps forgetting this is rally raid, not motocross. Even worse, he might think this is a demolition derby."

"I haven't run into a single vehicle." Trev laughed. "Hey, I got this far. We've taken out monsters. We got the ultimate tourist, a gorgeous precog, and we're going to win this race. You've got nothing to complain about."

"What about the part where bandits come and kill me?" Jack asked. "You better not get this truck busted up fighting bandits. If I have to spend days fixing it, I'd rather you just let Burning End punch through my chest."

Cassie's breath caught, and she looked at Jack. She still didn't understand Jack's dark and wry sense of humor. He'd been reserved until he'd gotten to know her better.

Trev replied, "Assuming the attack comes before the end of the race, if we can take all their gear and maybe one high-quality bandit vehicle, it might be worthwhile even if we lose the race. If it happens after, then *boom*. It's a nice bonus. I'd prefer we get it over with, one way or the other. It'll be easier to get parts near a race bivouac than if they jump us halfway back to Tucson."

"I'd really like to get it over with," Jack replied. "Not the part with the flaming fist through my chest. That can wait."

"Yeah, I figure we'd best avoid that. We can save that for your birthday. That's a great time for new experiences."

Cassie sighed, exasperated. "I give up. You people are too insane to keep up with."

While the current part of the course lacked the smoothness of the road they'd encountered on Day Two, a conspicuous lack of large plants and a wide path in less sandy soil that had been created over the days of racing made their ride more comfortable and less prone to launching them into inadvertent aerial stunts that might force Trev into using his power. He chalked up the lack of detection to luck, and he didn't want to push his luck again before the end of the race.

"ETA?" Trev asked with a yawn. "My ass hurts. I feel like I've been driving for a month."

Jack checked his tablet. "Based on our average speed, two and a half hours until we hit the camp."

Trev shook a fist. "We're golden. We're too close for bandits to risk an attack. I wouldn't be surprised if they've got the boost suit and security checking the area."

Jack sighed. "It's fun to have something to look forward to."

"Isn't it, though?"

A truck lay on its side. The driver and co-driver were sitting on the edge playing chess, from what Trev could see. The chess players waved at them.

Trev blew his horn in response. "A top-three finish is as

good as ours." After they passed the truck, he spotted the cause of their accident: a blackened crater. "Huh. That looks fresh, but I don't see any debris, so I assume nobody blew themselves up." He scanned the horizon. "I doubt they'd be sitting there playing chess if someone had shelled them."

"Maybe you're not the only ones walking around with a WT," Cassie suggested.

"I doubt that unless theirs folds up really nice. It's only because of Jack's skills that we can get it to fit. I think someone panicked and used a power to stop a monster and crashed." Trev smiled. "Jack, you're a mechanical wizard. I've been driving this bad boy hard this entire time, but I know you've worked your ass off to keep it running. I appreciate you, man."

Jack looked the opposite way. "I get half the prize money. There's no reason for me not to try hard."

"Sure, but—"

The radio crackled to life. Trev and Jack exchanged looks, surprised. The radios were almost never used for anything other than emergencies during the race.

"Help," a static-filled deep voice that sounded familiar to Trev called. "Again, requesting armed and empowered assistance at the subchannel-listed coordinates. Direct coordinates are as follows." The man read off the numbers. "Repeat, this is Diego Aguirre requesting armed assistance against bandits. Enemy numbers are—"

Static overwhelmed the rest of the message.

"How close are we to those coordinates, Jack?" Trev asked. "It looks like we don't have to wait for your birthday for revenge."

Cassie gasped. "You can't be serious. It was one thing when you were expecting to be attacked. Going after the bandits means they'll be ready for you. It means—"

"Not leaving a man to die who radioed for help," Trev finished. "I can be a cold bastard at times, but I'm not cold enough to hang him out to dry."

Cassie looked at Jack. "It might be too late by the time you get there."

"We have to try," Trev insisted. He glanced at Jack. "If it's okay with you."

"Let's save him," Jack agreed. "I trust you, Trev, and I trust you, Cassie."

She nodded. "Understood. I'm glad I bought extra mags last night."

"We're seven minutes away, based on the coordinates," Jack observed. "We've overshot. U-turn and drive southwest."

Trev yanked on the wheel. "Here we go! Time to take out the trash and beautify the Southwest one bandit at a time."

CHAPTER TWENTY-FIVE

A plume of smoke rising in the distance made Jack's assistance unnecessary after a minute. That allowed Jack time to load the grenade launcher and stock a bandolier with flechettes and grenade cartridges before getting out the coilgun. Cassie rested her gun on her lap and shoved magazines into her jacket.

Trev concentrated on weaving around the occasional cactus, shrub, and rock. Otherwise, he barreled through the area, not caring about branches whipping the truck and tires.

This wasn't a game anymore. It wasn't even about eliminating a future threat to Jack. This was about saving a man's life. Two men's lives, really.

He didn't know Diego Aguirre well, but a polite badass with a sense of humor shouldn't be removed from the world by bandits who didn't do anything but take from the world.

Trev clenched his jaw. He didn't know if the world used to be better like Cassie claimed. He was too young to understand anything important before the Big Change. That didn't matter now. All he needed to know was that bandits, criminals, and villains made this world a worse place. Therefore, removing them made this world a better place.

He was no hero. His parents had pushed him to pursue self-centered choices, though they had sacrificed their lives in defense of others. The least he could do was save one merc from bandit scum. Maybe doing so would also save Jack from the same scum.

Trev and his team closed on a dry lakebed. An overturned flat-faced competition truck with a small trailer lay burning near the center. A ring of pickup trucks and UTVs surrounded the burning vehicle, and gun-toting men pointed their weapons at someone in black clothing lying face-down on the ground.

"Yep." Trev nodded. "Definitely bandits."

"We need to stop and prepare Hercules," Cassie warned.

"We don't have time," Trev replied, flooring it. "They'll kill him before we get there."

Jack turned to Trev. "You have a plan, right?"

"Sure," Trev replied. "I've got a plan. Well, I have a well-developed idea."

Jack pulled the grenade launcher and coilgun against his chest. "I should have known you'd already hit your thinking quota for the day."

Trev jumped the truck into the lakebed, the underside grinding and groaning during the bouncing impact. He understood where Cassie was coming from, but he couldn't set up and be cute about stealth when a man's life was on the line. He slid the truck to the side, almost tipping it over and throwing rocks and dirt everywhere. The truck stopped not far from the bandits and their victims.

He was still working on his well-developed idea, but he'd managed to point the back end of the trailer away from the bandits. Hercules was still in play.

Everyone in the cab ducked, expecting a hail of bullets from the bandits. Trev waited for the first shot to summon a forcefield, but nobody fired.

"I've got an idea," Trev mused.

"I didn't love your last idea," Jack replied.

"This one's better…ish."

After removing spare magazines from the glovebox and stuffing them into his pockets, Trev pulled off his helmet, grabbed his gun, and threw the door open. He tossed his helmet on the ground and kicked a small panel near the bottom that extended an opaque ballistic shield from the bottom of the door.

Either he'd talk his way out of the trouble and not need the helmet, or he'd use his power and not need it. He'd discarded it because it was harder for a man to shoot someone when he looked him in the eye.

"You should have deployed your WT from farther away," Cassie remarked as she crawled into the front seat with her gun.

"Like I said, what's the point of responding to a rescue if the victim is dead?" Trev frowned. "Everybody get ready. I have a feeling this won't go well, but it's worth a try."

Trev stayed close to the open door of the truck. He didn't need the cover, but he didn't want the bandits to know that.

The bandits spread out and aimed their weapons at the

truck without advancing. He admired their discipline. He would already have opened fire on someone who showed up like he had.

"Is this a biker convention without bikers?" Trev asked, stepping clear of the door as he scanned the crowd.

Diego Aguirre lay on the ground in a torn Scorching Dawn uniform. His protective vest had been removed and tossed to the side. He lay face-down, with blood splattered everywhere.

"Everybody's got leather jackets," Trev noted. "Wait, the design is familiar, but I don't recognize the skull and emperor wasp symbol on the back."

A man in the center who was small yet exuded a menacing air cracked his knuckles. "You don't know us, boy?"

"That's associated with Burning End's group," Cassie told him.

"Huh. I guess I should have looked you up, Burning End," Trev replied. "I didn't bother because I figured I'd run into you eventually."

Burning End smirked. "If you expected that, you know my reputation."

"I've heard of you, yeah. You're a big deal."

Jack stayed inside the cab. He laid the coilgun on the floor and kept the grenade launcher in hand.

Gun in hand but pointed down, Trev narrowed his eyes. Whatever else happened, elimination or suppression of the bandit boss was a top priority. "Hey, weird question, Cassie. Anybody you know who might cause trouble have a diamond ring? Our guy here's got a ring."

"Yes." Cassie's shoulders sagged. "That's who I saw."

Trev nodded, not surprised. He preferred certitude before he killed someone.

Cassie slid out of the cab on the driver's side. She crouched behind the door and ballistic shield. "You won't be able to talk your way out of this," she whispered.

"I don't want to," Trev whispered back. "I have to play this smart. They've got a hostage in Diego."

Burning End scoffed. "What are you muttering about back there? Did you get cold feet now that you know who you're dealing with?"

"We're talking about your reputation," Trev called back. "There's being a bandit, and there's being a barbarian."

"Barbarian?" Burning End laughed. "I like that. I'm going to own that title. Barbarians brought down great empires in the past. I'm doing the same thing now."

Trev managed not to roll his eyes. A handful of thugs, vehicles, and weapons did not a barbarian horde make.

"You would have had a chance if you'd shot right away," Burning End continued. "Now you're going to have to convince me I shouldn't kill you and take all your shit. I know this merc trash got out a call for help, but it was a mistake to come to help him. Whether you live or die is now up to me."

Trev surveyed the enemy forces. Most held rifles, indicating limited combat powers.

Three men, including Burning End, weren't carrying firearms. That spoke of their confidence in their abilities.

"Wait." Trev squinted at a man with a black eye and a swollen, reddened nose. "You're kidding." He threw his head back and laughed. "It's Will the Ice Dick. Anyone who screws with my friends screws with me, but I still have a race to win. It's everyone's favorite day: negotiation day."

Burning End folded his beefy arms. "Who the hell are you? I don't think you understand the situation you're in, boy."

"Mr. Burning End, sir," Trev replied, exaggerating his sarcasm. "My name is Trev Leon. I received a distress call from the gentleman at your feet. Is he still alive? If he's not, this was kind of pointless."

"He's alive for now," Burning End answered. "He won't be for much longer."

He walked over and kicked Diego in the side. Diego groaned.

"He thought he could take me down." Burning End kicked him again. "I've got to make an example of him, so he's going to die nice and slow. I'm going to put up his body somewhere easy to find so people understand what happens when you face off against this *barbarian*." He lifted his arms. "Death has come for the Republic. I'll burn it all down."

"I'm asking you to let him go," Trev asked with a smile. "Otherwise, we're going to fight. I see you're a smart guy, so you have to understand what will happen. Even if you win, some of your boys will die. That'd be a big waste just to torture one merc."

"Kill him!" Will shouted. "It's that freak-lover from the camp, boss. The one who thinks he's better than us. Fuck him up."

"My boys tell me you caused them trouble at the camp," Burning End lowered his arms. "They say you treated 'em bad. I might have something to say about that."

Trev laughed. "Nah, they got it backward. They messed with my friend, and I gave them plenty of chances to back down. They overestimated themselves and got punished for it because they didn't know when to stop. The second time, it was three to one, and they still lost."

He left the humor out of his voice. "I'm hoping you see the pattern, Mr. Burning End, *sir*. I've got no beef with your horde, but a man like you has to understand that I can't just back down when I and mine are threatened."

Will glared at Trev. "Bitch. You only won because the boss told us we couldn't kill anybody in the camp because it'd draw too much attention. Otherwise, I would have gutted you and cut your dick off. You better get on your hands and knees and beg him to keep you alive. Otherwise, you're dead. I'll cut you open and show you what you look like from the inside."

Burning End cackled. Trev thought the bandit/wannabe barbarian lord should change his name to Loud Laughter. That sort of casual, fun name was more intimidating than a try-hard villain name like Burning End.

"I respect a man who stands up for his boys," Burning End said. "I'll cut you a deal because I like how low your balls hang. Run along. You get to live today, and you can tell your grandchildren how you survived a run-in with Burning End, the flame that will soon engulf the entire New Baja Republic."

"No damned way," Will shouted. "That bitch is mine, boss. You can't let him go after what he did to me."

He stomped over to Burning End. The bandit leader backhanded Ice Dick with enough force to send him to the ground. A bald man on the other side of Burning End shook his head and snorted.

"You talked back to *me*, Will?" Burning End growled. "You think you run this gang?"

Will lifted his head. "He's mine. It's our way."

Burning End lifted his hand, and flames surrounded it but didn't burn his jacket or shirt. "You don't make the call, Will. You'll never make the call." He grabbed the man by the neck with his non-burning hand and hoisted him into the air. "Maybe I'll cut your balls off and give them to him since it sounds like he already took 'em from you."

Burning End threw Will on the ground and glared at Trev. "I'm in a bad mood. Get the hell out of here before you die, boy. I need to remind my boys why I'm in charge."

"I'll leave if you give me Diego," Trev replied. "Look, I'm trying to be a good guy, so you can even have his stuff, but come on, man! You can't expect me to take off and let him get killed."

Burning End scoffed. "The strong survive. That's nature's way. That's the correct way. The Big Change reminded humanity of the lesson they'd forgotten. We're predators. Top of the food chain, and we need to struggle against one another to prove which of us deserves to sit at the very top."

Trev didn't want to debate moral philosophy and implied cannibalism with a bandit whose artistic sensibility had led to naming himself Burning End. He did need to establish the facts to help the man before he made a move.

"Diego's distress signal died," Trev countered. "You should have had your people lock that down right away.

Otherwise, I would not have known where to go. Just thought I'd throw that out there while you're cleaning up the gang."

"Get the right people with the right powers together, and you can do anything you want," Burning End explained, slicing the air with his flaming hand. "Sometimes it's meant to be, just like you were meant to find me, boy." He slapped the arm of the man next to him. "As he was. He's not my real brother, but he might as well be. Fate brought us together. We're apex predators. Burning End and Stone Fall."

The second man raised his fist. Unsurprisingly, it turned to gray stone. Trev bit down the snark that wanted to come out.

Burning End offered a toothy smile that convinced Trev he filed his teeth. Maybe the bandit wasn't being metaphorical about food chains when it came to people. "I like your attitude, boy."

"I'm glad someone does," Trev replied.

"I'll give you one chance." Burning End pointed at him. "You can join my gang." He gestured at the door. "I saw your woman before she hid. You'll have to give her to me, but I won't even kill your freak. He can be our pet."

"You're asking me to join your bandit gang?" Trev wondered.

Will glared at Burning End before standing and training his hatred on Trev.

"Yeah. Anyone who can take down one of my boys without using his power has what it takes."

"I don't think Will would like that."

Will glared at Trev. "I'm going to kill you."

Burning End snorted. "He already lost to you. That's what it means to be part of my gang. The strong survive. The strong dictate the rules as nature intended." He lifted his burning fist. "I'm the strongest, so I make the rules. If Will doesn't like it, he can try to take you down. I don't care who wins or lives since the strongest will win. Before, I would have let you go. Now I think you should fight Will to join the gang."

"Yeah, boss." Will extended his hand and conjured an ice sword. "I'll show that bitch how weak he really is."

"Oh, we're going there." Trev nodded. "Instead of wasting time with the middleman, how about I just take you down?"

He whipped up his gun and fired at Burning End.

CHAPTER TWENTY-SIX

Dazzling white flames flared around the bullet right before it struck Burning End's chest. It vaporized in a bright flash that left the bandit's jacket untouched and a smirk on his face.

Burning End's nostrils flared, and he wagged a fiery finger. "There's having balls, and there's getting ahead of yourself, boy."

"Okay." Trev pivoted back behind the door. "That sucks. You really are a Class-A threat."

"Can I kill him, boss?" Will snarled. "Or you going to make him suffer first? Let me do it. I'll cut him up real good."

"Wait. I want this to go down differently." Burning End knelt by Diego and yanked the man's hair to lift his bloody face. "This kid, his bitch, and his freak are going to die for you, merc. If you had been a real man and not called for help, they wouldn't have had to. Now you're going to see them die." He shoved Diego's face into the dirt and circled a finger in the air. "We'll torture Diego later. Everybody else, shoot the kid and his friends."

The bandits opened fire. Trev jumped behind the door. They sprayed bullets that left spiderweb cracks in the windows and bounced off the door panels.

"The whole thing's bulletproof," Cassie sounded surprised.

Jack threw open his door and extended the other ballistic shield. "A little warning next time."

Bullets pounded the passenger-side door.

"Yeah. The bulletproofing was Jack's idea." Trev backed behind the door. "Run around the trailer to support Jack so he can open the back."

"I can keep them pinned." Cassie raised her gun and backed up toward Trev. "I guarantee I'm better trained than you when it comes to small arms."

A bandit tried to run wide past the door and line up a shot on Trev. Cassie put a bullet through his head when she had a shot. A second bandit jumped and sprayed a burst that went wide. Cassie shot him before he hit the ground. Sweat beaded her forehead.

"Nice," Trev commented, raising his voice to be heard above the overlapping cracks of gunfire and bullets striking the armored truck. "Don't worry about them. I've got this. You go around. Trust me and back Jack up."

Cassie nodded and sprinted around the back of the truck. He heard her open fire, followed by the faint click of the coilgun and screams until a half-ducking Cassie met up with Jack behind the other door.

The lizardman emerged from behind the passenger door when Cassie laid down covering fire and fired flechettes into the clustered bandits. A round tore through one man's neck. Trev synced his attacks to add pressure.

Despite the superior numbers, the bandits were all out in the open, whereas Trev and his friends had cover. Converging weapons fire forced most bandits back to take cover behind nearby vehicles.

Stray bullets and flechettes vaporized before striking Burning End. A handful tore through Stone Fall's shirt, revealing hardened gray skin, and bounced off.

Two bandits rushed around the truck's left side. Trev couldn't manage Cassie's one-shot, one-kill success. He settled for putting two bullets each into their chests. One of the bandits got off a shot, though he had aimed so high that the bullet didn't come close to hitting Trev.

A pop came from the other side of the truck just before a grenade explosion shredded two bandits hiding behind a UTV. The back of the UTV blew up, flinging their flaming bodies toward their friends.

Trev waited for the next explosion to leave his cover and sweep the area with his Revenger, flanking the wounded and disarrayed thugs. He emptied the magazine, and his bullets ripped through the bandits. With one smooth motion, he ejected the spent magazine and loaded a new one to continue the .50-caliber punishment.

Cassie danced back and forth behind the other armored door, her shots selective. She twisted and ducked, always seeming to know when a man was about to shoot at her, though the limits of her power combined with her skills became clear. A bullet grazed her shoulder, and she hissed in pain.

Another clipped her thigh. She downed the bandit

responsible with a shot through the chest before rolling behind the passenger door.

Jack held the grenade launcher in one hand and the coilgun in the other. He arced grenades over the door, occasionally jumping high and back and firing flechettes into any available bandit except Will, Stone Fall, and Burning End. He landed to repeat the process. Stone Fall's chest continued to bounce bullets off, and Burning End vaporized them, and Will ducked behind the two.

Trev scoffed and ignored him, concentrating on shooting through a UTV's door into a concealed bandit. After finishing the man off, he frowned and swept the area for other non-boss targets.

Panting, Cassie yanked out a new magazine and reloaded. "This isn't on my list of favorite activities."

Jack scrambled back into the truck to reload before rolling out. He stayed low, waiting for his chance.

Trev finished his survey of the bleeding and dead men on the ground. "You see, Burning End? We could have avoided all this. Now, you'll have to find new guys to block signals for you. I was only asking for one merc." He glanced at the overturned truck. "Where are his co-driver and tourist?"

"We only needed one example," Burning End grinned. "No reason to keep the others alive when they were unnecessary."

"You really *are* an evil son of a bitch," Trev commented.

"I'm strong. You're tough, but you're not strong enough to win against me. It's a pity, boy. I could have trained you into a true warrior."

"What about Hercules?" Cassie shouted. "You pin them down, and I'll get him going."

"It won't work, and it's not just about the rifle," Trev replied, not interested in explaining his secrets in front of a bandit boss. "Come on, Burning End. This is over. You can walk away, or you can die. Either way works for me. I'm inching toward the second option for personal reasons."

After the fight had started, he'd changed his mind. He couldn't be sure the fatal blow to Jack wouldn't occur because they didn't let Burning End go rather than because they didn't finish him off. He now understood how frustrating it must be to be Cassie and know the future but not the right course of action.

Trev spared a glance at the passenger-side door. The reinforced window displayed spiderwebbing. It hadn't been shattered like in Cassie's vision.

Burning End sneered. "You expect me to walk away after what you've done?" He pointed a flaming finger at Trev. "I respect your bravery and your strength, but it's obvious that you're weak. You're trying too hard to end this without the total defeat of your enemy."

"How do you figure I'm weak?" Trev asked. "From where I'm standing, we started with three versus a bunch, and now we're down to three versus three. I already know I can beat Will the Ice Dick's ass."

Burning End chuckled. "True power isn't about having a gun." He slammed his fist into his palm. Flames enveloped both hands. "True power comes from within. What's your power? I bet you're a good shot, or you have good reflexes. Those are nice powers but not true strength."

"*Let me kill him, boss,*" Will shouted.

"Says the guy who keeps hiding." Trev rolled his eyes. He jumped to the side and put a bullet into Will's face. The wide-eyed bandit reached toward the new hole in his head before falling to the ground.

"Sorry, not sorry." Trev shrugged. "That asshole had it coming. I think we can both agree he wasn't worthy of your gang."

Burning End glanced at Will, then nodded at Stone Fall. "Don't kill him. I want to play with him before we finish him. If he impresses me, maybe I'll change my mind."

Stone Fall's leer turned Trev's stomach. The gray man advanced toward Trev, arms extended, and motioned with both hands for Trev to come at him. "Show me what you've got. Finish me off like you did Will."

Trev put three rounds into his chest. They bounced off with bright sparks.

Burning End snickered. "Don't you understand? Guns are for weaklings. You've annoyed me, Trev Leon, but you've only reinforced the truth of this world. I'm grateful for that, so before you die, I'll show you what true power is."

Jets of flames fired his feet, and he rose into the air.

"*Oh, come on! He can fly, too?*" Trev shouted.

He fired twice and ran. Burning End's flames vaporized both bullets. Trev darted around the front of the truck and headed toward his friends. Stone Fall intercepted him and threw a rock-fist punch.

Trev jumped out of the way, and Stone Fall's blow smashed the passenger door's window. He yanked out his stone hand and shook off the glass fragments.

"The window!" Cassie shouted.

Burning End spun in the air and flew toward Jack, then dropped and landed behind the door. Jack scrambled back, dropping the grenade launcher but retaining the coilgun. The bandit boss brought back his flaming hand and shot forward, his legs flaring in a combined jet to accelerate him for a rocket punch.

Cassie tackled Jack and pushed him out of the way. Burning End flew past the back of the truck before his descent exploded his fist against a nearby mound to produce a cloud of dirt and smoke.

His fiery aura pushed away the dust, and Burning End stood and dusted off his jacket. "Your woman is fast. I'm impressed."

"She's not my woman," Trev replied, his pulse thundering in his ears and his voice a near-growl. "She's a tourist who just saved my best friend's life."

"What do you want, boss?" Stone Fall asked.

"She's still going to die." Burning End folded his arms. "I'm going to watch my brother beat your ass without killing you, then you will sit there while I kill your friends."

He nodded at Stone Fall, who grinned.

Trev laughed. "I tried very hard to cut you a break even though my instincts told me to kill you. Don't get it backward. I didn't do it because I care about killing trash like you. I just did it to stay out of trouble and protect my friend. From the beginning, your stupid minions wouldn't leave us alone." He tossed his gun away and slammed his fist into his palm. "I'm tired of holding back."

"You can't punch him, idiot!" Cassie shouted. *"He'll burn*

you to death, and you'll break your hand on the other one. Hercules is your only chance. We'll hold him off somehow."

"We already broke the prophecy." Trev glared at the advancing Stone Fall. "So it's my turn, and *I'm pissed.*"

"Don't call them prophecies," Cassie complained.

Trev turned his head back and forth to crack his neck. "You okay, Jack?"

Stone Fall advanced with slow, deliberate steps, slamming his fists together.

"I'm not dead," Jack replied. "So I'm okay." He stood and pointed the coilgun at Stone Fall. "We beat the prophecy, Trev. The future is ours. Win this for us."

"Didn't your lackeys tell you what I could do, Burning End?" Trev asked.

"Oh, the murderous bandits get to know, but I don't." Cassie scoffed. "That's not fair."

Trev crooked a finger at Stone Fall. "You first, asshole. You broke my window and pissed me off. Show me what you've got."

Burning End folded his arms. "Make him cry, Stone Fall, but don't kill him."

CHAPTER TWENTY-SEVEN

Cassie didn't understand what Trev was planning, but he'd held out on her. When they'd been at their most vulnerable against the swarm, his ultimate weapon was Hercules. He'd mentioned the WT more than once when the team had discussed dealing with the bandit.

When he asked her to support Jack, she'd assumed the plan was to get to the WT. However, neither man had gone for the tank. Instead, Trev advanced toward Stone Fall with murder in his eyes.

Cassie knelt by Jack, who'd shifted the coilgun to Burning End. She glanced at the grenade launcher by the truck. "Shouldn't we get Hercules?" she whispered. "There's got to be some way to keep him busy. I'll cover for you. If I concentrate on pure defense, I can avoid getting hit."

"Trev's the only one who can run Hercules," Jack whispered back. "There's no point if he's not going for it."

"Because of his power?" Cassie challenged.

"Something like that."

Burning End clapped. "Entertain me, boy. You owe me for all my people. Try to last at least a minute against my brother."

Stone Fall lifted both rock fists. "I'll let you pick what I break first. Just point to the bone, and I'll shatter it."

Trev chuckled. "For a guy who just watched all his buddies die, you're pretty cocky. Has it never occurred to you that *you* could be about to die?"

"It's like my brother said. The strong survive. The weak feed the strong. They were weak, and you're weak."

"The weak feed the strong?"

Stone Fall nodded. "That's nature's way."

"I'm *really* hungry," Trev replied and lifted his arm. "Come on. Do it. Shatter my arm. Show me how tough you are. I bet you can't even make me scream once."

"I'll make you scream until you pass out."

Stone Fall brought back his fist and swung for Trev's forward shoulder. Purple flashed, and a flat square deflected the punch with such force that Stone Fall stumbled.

Trev snorted. "Come on, you big stone asshole. Aren't you supposed to be one of the ultimate barbarians? True strength?"

"*Finish him, Stone Fall,*" Burning End yelled. "Or I'll finish you. The others were weak. You're supposed to be strong."

Trev scoffed. "Yeah, Stone Fall. Show me what you've got." He spread his arms. "I'll make it easier for you." He slapped his chest. "One shot to the sternum should take me down. Bring it."

Growling, Stone Fall swung his rock-fist punch at

Trev's chest. Another purple square blocked the attack. Stone Fall shook out his rocky fist, which now sported cracks.

Burning End clapped. "You stopped playing games, boy. Stone Fall is like me, with strength in both attack and defense. It's not enough to survive his hits if you can't get through his second skin. All you're doing is waiting to die."

Stone Fall shouted and launched at Trev, throwing a wild series of hooks and jabs. Trev parried the blows, the localized forcefields appearing and disappearing with each strike.

"*I'll beat you until you're a bloody smear,*" Stone Fall yelled.

Cassie watched, hating how helpless she felt. Her gun wouldn't work against either bandit, but there had to be some way she could help Trev. It wouldn't do any good unless he went for Hercules. The WT was their only chance of winning.

Stone Fall continued swinging at Trev. The assault forced Trev back, sweating, though he had no apparent wounds. He met each punch with his arm or elbow covered by a forcefield. Stone Fall kept hammering, and the cracks on his hands grew.

"*I told you, boy! You can't win a fight only by blocking,*" Burning End yelled. "You're nothing more than a turtle waiting to get knocked on its back and ripped open. All this effort only gives you a false sense of hope before you die. It's beyond pathetic."

Trev's jaw clenched. Sweat coated his forehead.

Cassie narrowed her eyes. Something had been troubling her about Stone Fall. For a man who could turn body parts to rock, he had not bothered with anything other than his fists and chest. Even if she couldn't get Trev into Hercules, she could help him win against Stone Fall.

She leaned over to whisper to Jack, "On the count of three, we'll run out and fire at Stone Fall. You go for the legs, and I'll go for the head."

Jack nodded. "I'm with you."

Stone Fall kept pummeling Trev, who was forced to hold up both arms and bounce the punches off forcefields.

"One, two," Cassie began, timing Stone Fall's blows. *"Three."*

Jack and Cassie opened fire. Stone Fall's head hardened into rock and bounced Cassie's bullets off, but he screamed and fell to his knees as flechettes tore through his legs.

Trev jump-kicked him, a purple triangular forcefield appearing at the point of impact. Stone Fall's head snapped back. He swayed before collapsing to the ground face-first, the stone layer vanishing from his head, chest, and hands.

Burning End slowly strolled forward and flared, scorching the ground. "I'm not like him. I'm not like you. I have true control of my power. You said it yourself, boy. I'm a Class-A threat."

Jack and Cassie turned and fired at Burning End, but their flechettes and bullets sizzled into nothing before they reached him. They kept firing at his body until they emptied their weapons.

Burning End chuckled. "Did you really think that would work on me?"

Jack glanced at the grenade launcher lying by the open passenger-side door, and Burning End whipped out a white-hot ball of fire that blasted the weapon. The secondary explosions from the grenade cartridges blew it to pieces and tore into the right front tire with a loud pop. The truck dipped.

Trev stomped toward Burning End. "You tried to kill my best friend, and your buddy smashed my window. Your lackeys shot up my truck, and my tires survived all that damned gunfire, only for you to ruin one with your last trick. You've really pissed me off. Now I get it."

"Get what, boy?" Burning End asked. "That you came here to die?"

"I overthought this." Trev raised his fists. "After the fight started, I worried that she'd been right and I should have been trying to avoid you to save Jack."

"Who the hell is Jack?"

Jack raised his hand. "That'd be me."

"Now I understand," Trev continued. "I should have followed my own advice. When you show up, take the biggest bastard down."

"Don't mistake me for Stone Fall or Will." Burning End grinned. Flames sprouted from his whole body, the heat so intense that the air around him wavered. "I'm a force of nature. Soon, I'll be considered an AA threat. You can't even touch me without losing a hand. You think I didn't hear them talking about a WT?"

He threw his head back and laughed. "That's another toy to melt. Throwing bigger, faster bullets at me won't help you. When you chose to stand up to me, you chose death." He pointed at the ground. "Now, get on your knees and beg for your life. Acknowledge my power. You'll die either way, but if you do, I will consider letting one of them go."

"You really like hearing yourself talk, don't you?" Trev

replied. He lifted his hand and gestured for his opponent to attack. "I'm going to do the Republic a favor even though they will short-change me on the bounty because of bureaucracy." He chuckled. "Now, that's being a hero."

"You want to be a hero? They die glorious deaths."

Burning End sprinted forward, each step scorching the ground, and swung. Trev jumped back with a smirk. Burning End tried to kick him in the shin with a leg wrapped in fire. A long, thin rectangle absorbed the blow, and the bandit boss bellowed in frustration. Burning End tried another kick before spinning into a flaming elbow. Trev summoned two smaller squares simultaneously, then his knees buckled, and he shifted back.

Trev panted and wiped away sweat but kept smirking. "I thought I was supposed to be losing my hands, Burning End, *sir*. You're not living up to your name." He scoffed. "You think you will be an AA threat and a force of nature? Give me a break. I was right all the time. You sound more like a proctology symptom than a big-time bandit."

Burning End roared and flowed into a series of combos, punches, kicks, elbows, and an attempted headbutt that Trev blocked with a tight diamond-shaped forcefield. The imperfections in his defense became evident over time—Trev's clothes scorching and his skin reddening.

"*You can't win*," Burning End shouted. "Don't you get it? Your trick with your friends won't work on me. I'm beyond you. I'm the Demon of Flame, and I will burn you down to your bones."

"Do you sit at home and practice your speeches?" Trev bounced on his feet, though he was still panting. "Because if you're supposed to be scary, I'm not feeling it."

"I'll make you suffer. I'll burn you bad enough to put you down and keep you alive in agony. You will live just long enough to hear the screams from your woman and your pet lizard as I turn them to ash."

Jack looked at Cassie, who shook her head. Their weapons could do nothing against Burning End. It was up to Trev now.

Trev's mouth twitched, and a purple aura suffused his body before vanishing in a flash. "Shut your mouth, you flaming piece of shit. Don't threaten my friends."

"This world belongs to the strong, boy." Burning End reared back, then breathed a jet of fire at Trev, who threw up a circular arm field. The bandit killed his fire breath.

"Get some breath mints, man!" Trev exclaimed.

"The Big Change reset everything," Burning End replied with a sneer, "but the corrupt and weak cling to their false power, pretending everything's the same with different names. It's the beginning of the new age of humanity and the era of true humans like me."

Trev spat at Burning End's feet, but the liquid sizzled and vaporized before it reached the bandit. "I don't care about your philosophical villain rant. I don't care much about you bringing down civilization or whatever stupid idea you need to justify your petty-ass crimes. You're just a glorified thug with a nice weapon. If you'd stayed the hell away from me and my friends, you could have continued ruling your pathetic barbarian horde."

Burning End snarled, "I'm both a sword and a shield, boy. You can't win against me. You've proven it."

"That's the thing." Trev patted his chest. "You were doing okay until you pushed me over the line. It's like I keep telling people. I don't go looking for trouble. I just don't run from it."

Burning End tossed a baseball-sized fireball. Trev whipped up his arm with a circular energy shield. The fireball exploded, and the flames spread out in all directions. *"I'm the greatest power in the Repu—"*

With a circular shield protecting him, Trev flung a sickle-shaped purple energy blast at Burning End. The attack sliced through the bandit's neck.

The flames vanished, and blood sprayed everywhere as Burning End's head and body separated and hit the ground with dull thuds.

"Huh." Trev rotated his arm and winced. "It's been a while since I could pull off that combo." He scoffed at the body. "I told you to shut up, asshole."

CHAPTER TWENTY-EIGHT

Trev dropped to his knees and hissed in pain. He had burns all over his body. His heart pounded, and his muscles hurt.

Burning End had been a genuine Class-A threat. Trev couldn't remember the last time he'd been more than scratched when he used his power in a fight.

"Go check on Diego," Trev requested. "I'd hate to think I looked this uncool just to stop Jack from getting free heart surgery."

Jack jogged over to Diego and knelt by the wounded mercenary. "He's still breathing."

"Good," Trev looked at Burning End's body. "I don't think that guy is."

"Good bet."

Diego groaned and lifted his head. Jack offered him his shoulder and helped him to the side of their truck.

Trev managed to stand and shuffle that way. "To head off the 'I-told-you-sos,' I'll admit that was harder than I planned."

Jack lowered Diego to sit and lean against the side of

the truck and hurried into the cab to pull out a first-aid kit. "You didn't *have* a plan. You only had a well-developed idea, and I think it stretched the meaning of 'well-developed.'"

Cassie shook her head. "It was less a well-developed idea than a barely considered brief thought."

Jack nodded. "That sounds right."

Trev groaned. "Ganging up on a wounded man? Not cool."

Diego clutched a laceration in his chest. Jack opened the first-aid kit and looked at Diego's wounds.

"Thanks for answering my distress call." Diego winced. "Thanks more for not running when you saw who it was." He looked at Cassie and Trev. "Who took him down?"

Trev raised his hand. "You didn't see it happen?"

"I see his decapitated body," Diego replied. "That's good enough for me."

Trev looked up and pointed at a circling drone. "The bandit jammer's power wore off." He squinted into the distance when he heard a rhythmic thump. "I'm sure a helicopter's coming, too."

Jack fished out bandages and a topical analgesic. "They weren't going to get involved when a large bandit force was here, let alone someone like Burning End. He could have brought the helicopter down."

"I got arrogant, and I underestimated him," Diego explained. He grimaced as Jack applied salve and bandages, then pointed at Burning End. "I was sure I could take him out, but they ambushed me." He bowed his head. "They killed my co-driver and my tourist before I even got a shot off. Pathetic for the leader of the Scorching Dawn."

Trev knelt by the popped tire. "We killed our time as well as the bandits." He winced when a burn on his leg touched the ground. "At least he'll never hurt anyone again."

"Finish the race," Diego insisted. "If you don't finish, you won't get your monster bounties."

Cassie walked over to Diego and Jack and knelt. "I'll finish treating him. You can slap burn gel on Trev, and he can help you with the tire."

Jack sorted through the first-aid kit and found burn spray and liquid bandages. He handed them to Trev before jogging to the back of the truck and opening the door.

"You care about us finishing the race, Cassie?" Trev asked as he stood.

"I didn't ride with you for three days to quit right before the end." She retrieved more bandages. "You never know. It's a war of attrition, right? You might be the only truck left. You might get first just for crossing the finish line."

Trev laughed. "You've been paying attention. It's not like we'll get as much as we deserve since we're not licensed by the Republic."

"I'll talk to people I know in the Republic's government," Diego said. "I'll make sure you get the bounties on Burning End and his gang without you having to stick around here to collect anything. It's the least I can do for you saving my life. That should help offset your prize money loss."

Jack rolled a mammoth tire out of the trailer and pushed it to the ground with a thump. "Weren't we planning to look through the bandits' gear?"

"We'll go look for a grenade launcher or two real quick," Trev announced, holding his side and clenching his jaw. "After we get the tire fixed. Diego's right. I want the monster bounties, and more than anything, I want to be recorded as a finishing driver in the Sonoran Baja Hunter-Tourist Rally." He coated a chest burn with spray. "I'm not going to let Burning End stop me."

CHAPTER TWENTY-NINE

<u>March 9, 2036, Sonoran Baja Hunter-Tourist Rally Bivouac, Sonoran Desert, New Baja Republic</u>

Lying on the top of his trailer, Trev stared at the stars. Satellite fragment fall was heavy that night, a veritable artificial meteor shower. He smiled before an unfortunate turn put pressure on a bandaged burn on his side, making him hiss in pain.

A slathering of burn ointment and creams and a dangerous number of minor painkillers had lessened the pain. The camp's medical tent had given him several doses of serious painkillers, but he didn't want to take anything that'd mess with his mind until he was home in Tucson.

When all was said and done, they'd finished ninth in their division, which qualified them for a small prize in addition to their monster bounties. It wasn't the epic disaster Trev had suspected, nor was it the glorious podium finish he'd believed was coming.

As suggested by Cassie, despite his superior driving, finishing in the top ten after a major battle and having to swap out his tire reflected the high attrition rate of the rally. He hadn't proven his ability as a driver, only as a fighter. He'd have to come back next year and try again.

A pre-hunt race for bandits might also be in order. He had not realized how frustrating it was not to finish the race without trouble until the official results came in.

"You're lucky you're already dead, Burning End," Trev muttered.

"Trev!" called Jack. "There's a scary woman here who wants to talk to you."

"You mean Cassie?"

"No, she's still getting dinner."

Trev carefully rolled onto his stomach and crawled to the edge of the trailer to look down. A tall, scarred woman who wore a dark uniform bearing the symbol of the Scorching Dawn stood beside Jack.

"Are you Trevor Leon?" she asked, narrowing her eyes.

"My friends call me Trev. I've learned these last few days that my enemies call me 'boy.'" He laughed and jumped to the ground, landing in a crouch and immediately regretting it when his wounds throbbed. "What can I do for you? It'll have to wait a few days if it's anything physical. A pyromaniac messed me up."

The woman walked over and extended her hand. "I'm Skylar Kimison. I'm second-in-command of the Scorching Dawn."

Trev shook her hand. "Is Diego okay? They messed him up bad."

"He's recovering in the hospital. He's stable and should be back to normal soon." She glanced at Jack. "That's thanks to you and your friends risking your lives to take out a dangerous group of bandits. I wanted to personally thank you, and Diego asked me to pass on a message about the distribution of the forfeited property."

Trev stared at her. "Huh?"

"She's talking about the bandits' stuff," Jack clarified.

Trev laughed. "Other than the grenade launcher we took?"

Skylar didn't smile. "Diego made it clear that he wanted us to handle the processing for you. We know people if you want to sell everything. That would be easiest. However, we do ask for a ten percent commission since we'll have to do a ton of paperwork. We can get better prices for you in San Diego than you can in Tucson."

"Sounds fair," Trev replied. "It saves us a bunch of trouble. I've got no problem giving you ten percent to do all the work."

Skylar pulled out her phone. "I'll need your UCID."

Trev got his phone and tapped until it chimed and Skylar's buzzed. "There you go. Pleasure doing business with you."

He'd had trouble getting used to replacing phone numbers with universal communication identifiers until Jack pointed out that UCIDs also had letters in them. When Jack flowed into a tedious discussion about their relative advantages, Trev tuned him out.

Skylar tapped her phone. "Check your message and confirm the bounty amount. We'll forward that to your account, and we'll accept the payment from the government directly. It'll be quicker and far easier unless you want formal acknowledgment from them. That'll complicate things, given that you aren't licensed for bounty work in the Republic. This was the best solution Diego could devise on short notice."

Trev checked the amount and stared at it, slack-jawed. "Nah. I'm good with the money more than the praise. It's hard to spend acknowledgment and praise at stores." He held up his phone. "The bandit bounties were *that* high? This is more than we would have gotten for first place and a dozen medium monster bounties."

Skylar nodded. "Burning End's gang killed a lot of people and got bolder with each passing month. They'd even moved on Republic vehicles and cargo."

"The guy had a high opinion of himself."

"His kind always does." She motioned at the surrounding tents. "Thinking his gang could come so close to this race and mess with it is proof of that. You did this area a service by clearing out that scum. The survivors, including Stone Fall, can help rebuild the Republic instead of tearing it down as part of their sentencing." She clapped him on the shoulder. "Diego messed up. He was the first to admit that."

Trev shrugged. "He already did."

"You and your friends impressed him. If you're ever interested in merc work, look us up. We might not be a hero team, but we help keep the scum under control."

"Thanks," Trev replied. "I'm good for now, but I'll keep that in mind for the future."

"I'll remember your name, Trev Leon. I hope I never have to call you 'boy.'" Skylar waved and walked away.

Jack watched her leave, tongue flicking. "You heard what she said, right? Survivors?"

Trev nodded. "Yeah. It's not like we cut everybody's

throats. I hear the Republic is big on hard labor. Not enough people, too much work and reconstruction."

"That means not just Cassie saw what you can do," Jack cautioned.

Trev shrugged. "Maybe. I doubt guys bleeding out on the ground were watching my play-by-play."

"Stone Fall survived," Jack noted.

"My power was bound to get out eventually." Trev sighed. "That doesn't mean we need to announce it to the world and get 46P1 sniffing around."

"You sure?"

"I don't even know why my parents were obsessed with me keeping it hidden," Trev replied. "Until I can answer that, I won't know how to move forward other than to train my power and not flash it around unless it's a Burning End-level threat." He shook his phone. "The race was fun, but bounty hunting's where it's at for money. A merc company is too much control and overhead."

Jack gestured at a bandage. "Bounties won't always be that easy. This wasn't that easy."

"Good. That means they'll be worth more."

CHAPTER THIRTY

Cassie set her cards on the welded metal table with a grin. "Four of a kind. Read 'em and weep, boys. I am the queen of poker. Fear me!"

"What level villain threat is that?" Trev asked. "Do you have AA-ranked ability to manipulate cards?"

"Maybe I do." Cassie winked. "There's no hero team to stop me from taking it all."

Trev leaned over to check her cards, then groaned and scrubbed a hand over his face. Jack lifted his goggles and stared at the cards.

Cassie scooped up the combined pot of cookie, cracker, and pretzel snack bags. The food tent had offered a discount on the event's last day, and everyone decided it'd be more fun to gamble for food than money.

"How do I know you're not cheating?" Trev asked. He pointed at his eyes. "You can see the future. That's kind of unfair when it comes to card games."

She laughed. "That's too long a time horizon for me."

Trev scoffed. "Likely story, Queen of Poker."

"You'll just have to take my word for it," Cassie replied. "In the interests of disclosure, visualizing cards was part of my 46P1 training."

"They wanted you to learn to cheat at cards?" Jack asked.

Cassie shook her head. "It's easy to set up physical randomization experiments using cards. It's also easy to interpret the visions."

"See! I knew it!" Trev threw his hands up. "It's a cookie, cracker, and pretzel scandal. The Wicked Poker Witch used her power to see into the future and loot our precious snack bags. We need every hero team on the continent to descend on this camp and put her in her place."

Cassie laughed harder. "I swear I'm not cheating right now. I only told you that in the interests of disclosure. Sometimes, a woman can just be lucky."

"I believe you," Jack stated.

"Thanks." Cassie made a face at Trev. "At least one of you is a gentleman."

"Gentlemen don't win brawls with guys named Burning End," Trev protested.

With the race over and Burning End dead, Cassie couldn't cling to her tension despite her primary mission being incomplete. The final battle against the bandit had convinced her that Trev *was* her target, so she was working up the courage to tell him the rest of her secrets. For now, she wanted to enjoy the relief of not having to see Jack die before her eyes.

"Oh, by the way," Trev added, snatching a bag of chocolate chip cookies from her pile. "I talked it over with Jack. We both agree you should get part of the reward money.

You helped with the wasps. You helped with the bandits." He smiled. "You saved Jack's life. We're willing to give you a third of everything."

Cassie shook her head. "I don't need your money. I only mentioned it to get you to leave the race because I was worried about Jack. I honestly don't need it."

Trev made an exaggerated face of offense. "Oh, Miss 46P1 Super Assassin Card Shark Cheater is too rich for us. She can retire and buy her own private island with all the money she's won playing cards worldwide."

Cassie opened her mouth, and her hand snaked out to snatch an oatmeal raisin cookie bag from Trev's betting pile. That treasure had almost escaped her notice.

"Hey, I didn't bet that," Trev complained.

"I didn't notice earlier," she replied. "I'll trade you for two bags of something else."

"Huh?" Trev looked at Jack, who shrugged.

Cassie held up the cookie bag and pointed at the cartoon rabbit decorating the front. "It's a limited-edition bag featuring Rage Rabbit. See? I knew you just weren't cool. Rage Rabbit's in the Republic."

"Technically." Trev picked up a bag and looked at it. "The cookies were imported from the Pacific Alliance. It says they were packaged in Tumwater, Washington."

"They're in the Republic now. That means people here want that brand of cookie enough to import it, so the company thinks using Rage Rabbit as a mascot is a good idea." Cassie nodded as if this were the most crucial point she'd made in the last week.

Trev snickered. "I'm not cool because I don't worship a cartoon goth rabbit from Seattle?"

"Basically, yes. I'm glad you've accepted the truth." Cassie looked away, her cheeks heating. She put her hand to her mouth and coughed. "I'd like to talk to you, Trev." She looked around. "It might be better to do it in the truck. It's important. I owe you answers."

Trev nodded. "Hold down the fort, Jack. Make sure you don't eat any rabbit cookies by mistake. Cassie will murder you in your sleep."

She rolled her eyes and followed Trev to the cab. They climbed inside, and she waited for him to close the door before she spoke.

"I take it there's something you don't want other people to hear?" Trev asked. "I looked around before I made the joke about your powers if you're mad about that."

"My power isn't all that secret," Cassie replied. "Not in the way you're trying to keep your secret. 46P1 already has a file on me and my power. They don't know the full extent of my capabilities, but it's not a secret that I'm a precog." She shook her head. "I'm more interested in *your* power."

Trev nodded. "Yeah, I figured this was coming."

"I also took the opportunity to inspect Hercules earlier, and now I'm more confused. I've never seen an energy cell that compact, and I used to work for 46P1. It's not just cutting-edge tech. It's impossible tech."

Trev grinned. "Jack's a smart guy. He's taking lizard brain in a different direction, moving the edge of engineering reality."

"Come on, Trev." Cassie put her hand on his arm. "Aren't we past the lies? Like I said, there are things I want to tell you and answers you deserve, but I need to know you trust me first. It's pointless to tell you unless you trust me."

"I trust anyone who puts their life on the line to protect Jack," Trev replied. "My power isn't the big deal you think it is." He sighed and rubbed the back of his neck. "My parents told me my power was hard-light manipulation. They also discouraged me from practicing and training with it and told me to keep it to myself. I mostly hung out with Jack after the Big Change, so it wasn't hard to keep people from learning much about it. For the first few years after the Big Change, many people acted like their powers were big privacy issues, at least where I lived."

"Why did they want to keep it secret and not explore it?"

"To be honest, I'm not certain. At first, I did what they said because they were my parents and I was a kid. As I got older, I questioned them, and they implied that if I got better with my power, I'd end up a hero, which was too dangerous. I pushed back, but it was hard to care while I was getting into racing."

Cassie frowned. "Do you think they did that to distract you?"

"Distract me, or reward me for listening to them? A bit of both. It's not like I ignore my power, but it wasn't as much a part of me as their powers were." Trev shook his head. "Part of their concern had to do with 46P1. I think they were afraid of the same thing you were, experiments, though I don't know why my power would be worthy of special attention."

"I see." Cassie looked disturbed by the suggestion.

"You know, when you have a power, you want to play

with it even when you're busy trying to master driving. Over the years, I experimented, and Jack was always building, and we were messing around. He was good at coming up with ideas."

Trev lifted his hand and summoned a circular forcefield. The forcefield undulated between a circle, a triangle, and a diamond.

"What's with the shapes?" Cassie asked.

"It's easier to summon the forcefields or the blades when they are specific shapes," Trev explained. "Jack helped me figure that out, too. I can summon a forcefield over my whole body, but it exhausts me fast. The shapes take less energy. We've learned it's about how I redirect the energy flow from the attacks at the moment and point of impact. It's not as simple as always using the same shape for the same attack."

"They don't have to be attached to your body," Cassie noted. "You can throw them."

Trev nodded. "I can do a lot. We didn't crash once during the race because I used a forcefield to help." He frowned. "That's weird. I'd almost forgotten, what with everything else that happened."

"What?" Cassie leaned forward, her eyes full of interest.

"I used my power in the truck, but the detector didn't register it," Trev explained.

Cassie blushed and looked away. "I meant to tell you. I wanted to encourage you to use your power during the race, so I sabotaged the detector. I kept trying to think of ways to goad you into using it, but I had no idea what your power was, so it was hard to do that."

"You sabotaged the detector, and they didn't realize it?" Trev laughed.

"I used to work security for the company that built it. I know a thing or two about how to mess with the operating system. I wasn't trying to be evil or, uh, sketchy. I wasn't even trying to cheat. I just was hoping to see your power."

"You saw it." Trev lifted his palm and summoned a flat purple line. "Here it is again."

"Hard light makes sense," Cassie agreed. "Then again, it doesn't." She put her hand up to stop him when he opened his mouth to object. "I'm not talking about the physics. I don't understand the science or theory, and plenty of powers are making scientists relearn everything they used to think they knew. When I saw you fight, I saw you block the attacks and cut people. That's consistent with the hard-light idea."

"What's the problem?" Trev asked.

Cassie nodded toward the back of the truck. "Hercules. I figured out that you had to move away from the truck to activate it because you didn't want the MQI detector picking up your power."

"Which was totally unnecessary because you sabotaged the detector," Trev noted wryly.

"Sure, but it's not like I was trying to mess with you or help you," Cassie replied. "In the confusion of the fight with the wasps, I forgot." She gestured at him. "Seeing your power in action, I don't get the connection between hard light and a WT. Is it just about the energy rifle? It's a bit much to build a prototype WT just to cover up your power."

"It's beyond that and because my parents were wrong

about my power," explained Trev. "Or maybe they understood and didn't want to tell me the truth. I'll never know." He sighed and leaned against the headrest. "They weren't around, and I was hurting. I wanted to understand who I was better, so I experimented beyond the hard light. Jack helped me."

Cassie leaned forward, leaving her hand on his arm.

"Jack figured that I wasn't a hard-light controller. One day, he was working on something and babbled about energy, power, and mass." Trev waved a hand. "Anyway, he had me concentrate to try to charge one of his energy cells, and it worked. We figured my power is less hard-light manipulation than a special type of energy-field manipulation.

"I've been experimenting and trying to grow my capabilities, and it's stressful and hard to handle too much at the same time. We know I can make more than hard-light shields and blades. Supercharging energy cells and batteries is just the start. That's why the WT won't work without me. You need my power to keep the energy cell charged."

Cassie looked away, trying to understand what his parents had been hiding. "Do you think your parents were concerned about a specific threat, or they just didn't want you to be a hero and figured you couldn't if your power wasn't well-developed?"

"I don't know. Everything I told you was the truth. They were happy to be on hero teams at first, even with the compromises, but after a while, they got..." Trev gritted his teeth. "Disgusted is the only word. They didn't have a problem with hero teams as symbols and propaganda, but they didn't like they'd become tools of corrupt government officials and corporations."

Cassie frowned. "Like 46P1?"

Trev nodded. "They helped people. At the same time, they might be sent somewhere to help with a twisted version of what somebody high up called peacekeeping but was really oppression. When I went through their things after they died, I found a message warning me to move and telling me to avoid the government in general and 46P1 in particular. I assumed they meant the NEUS government, but I'm not ready to cozy up with any government yet."

"Do you think they were set up?" Cassie asked.

"I don't know. The fight with the Altruist was recorded by tons of people from different angles. It's hard to see how." Trev's hands tightened into fists. "I wish I knew. I can't seek revenge if there's nothing to avenge. All I'm left with are questions I might never have the answer to and a power I'm just beginning to understand."

He punched the dashboard. "I've got Jack, and I need to make sure we both survive. My power's the way to do that, but I'm nervous. I can't help but look over my shoulder and wonder if an assassin cougar is coming for me."

Cassie smiled. "I'm seriously not an assassin, okay?"

"So, you admit you're a cougar?"

"Again, I'm only twenty-five." Cassie rolled her eyes. "Be serious for a second."

"I know you aren't an assassin, but what about the next 46P1 security agent I run into?" Trev looked at her, his gaze haunted. "I'm not afraid to die. I *am* afraid to leave Jack alone. He needs me, and I'll be the first to admit I'm still processing all this and everything that happened with my parents. I've made mistakes, and I'll make more."

"Why are you telling me?" Cassie asked. "I know I asked, but why do you trust me so much now? We've only known each other for a few days, and not long ago, you thought I was working for the bandits."

"Because you asked, and you saved Jack's life when I got cocky and pushed too hard." Trev shook his head. "I keep telling myself that confronting Burning End was the right idea. Now I don't know. If you hadn't been there, Jack would have died."

He smiled. "I want to trust you, and you've told me a lot about yourself, good and bad. I'm also telling you because I think you have something else you want me to know. I figure if I spill my guts, you will spill yours. That's fair, and we end up on a level playing field."

Cassie swallowed. Her heart pounded. Her doubts about her self-appointed mission and the man sitting across from her melted.

"I didn't end up your tourist by accident," Cassie began. "I came to this race looking for you from the beginning."

CHAPTER THIRTY-ONE

Trev let the smirk out. "I do have that effect on women."

"Don't make me shoot you." Cassie glared at him. "We're trying to be serious, remember?"

"Okay, I'll be a good boy." Trev chuckled. "How did you end up assigned to me? Was it a precog trick?"

Cassie shook her head. "Conventional systems intrusion."

"In other words, hacking. They teach you that in 46P1 agent school?"

"Yes." Cassie shrugged. "Remember, I worked for them for a long time. I'm trained for infiltration and target neutralization."

"Along with fighting and WT piloting," Trev listed. "I won't use the A word, but just saying…"

"I was trained to be useful," Cassie admitted. "I was with 46P1 for nine years, so I had a lot of time to learn to be a good little soldier. I spent most of my time on elite bodyguard duties. Also, I was sent on missions in the Northern Confederation and the Pacific Alliance, including providing hero team support or dealing with bandit and monster sweeps." She let out a quiet chuckle. "It's only your freaky Southwestern monsters I don't know how to deal with."

Trev glanced at the glovebox. "And here I felt like a badass for picking up good moves on the streets. My parents even had me go back to school. I've got a diploma and everything."

"Did Jack go?"

Trev shook his head. "He tried for a while, but people kept messing with him, and I kept beating their asses. My parents refused to come down on me for protecting Jack since they didn't like that people were looking the other way when he was picked on."

He frowned. "To be honest—and he wouldn't admit it if you asked—he stopped going mainly because he thought he was holding me back. I thought about dropping out too, but he convinced me not to, and it turned out he could do better with independent study anyway, especially given that my parents were more than happy to fund his projects."

Cassie smiled. "All's well that ends well."

"Something like that." Trev shook his head. "Back to your 46P1 cyber-ninja assassin honeypot stuff."

"The best tools are sometimes the most straightforward," Cassie explained. "Some of the race organization staff's systems are sophisticated and well-protected, but many aren't. They weren't as worried about protecting the security of tourist assignments. It was harder for me to sabotage the detector than become your tourist."

"Sure." Trev nodded. "I kind of suspected something

like that. I care more about why you were so hellbent on being my tourist and getting close to me."

"Like I told you, my precognitive ability normally has a short time horizon," Cassie noted. "It's stressful but controllable for combat. It's all but random after that. It's hard to explain, but I know when I've had a vision versus a dream."

Trev shrugged. "Your vision saved Jack. I'm not going to question them. I now understand why you acted the way you did when you arrived. I wouldn't have believed you if you just showed up and laid all that on me."

"I figured." Cassie took a deep breath. "This all goes back to my power and my old job. Although I was disenchanted with 46P1, it was misleading of me to imply I left because of that. In truth, a vision pushed me over the edge shortly before I quit. After I had the vision, I knew I had a mission. I had to find the man at the center of it."

Trev searched her face for twitches or signs that she was joking. He found nothing but a serious woman who was desperate to be believed.

"I'm the man in your vision," Trev guessed. "I'm guessing this vision was about something more important than a hunter-tourist rally."

"Yes. You're in the vision but older, and technically, it was a series of visions, which is beyond rare for me." She shivered. "Even thinking about it freaks me out."

"Take your time. The race is over. We don't have to get up early tomorrow."

"My vision involved an older version of you leading a powerful hero team." Cassie looked down and furrowed her brow. "I don't know how to explain what I'm about to say since it's not like my visions come with sound, just images and sensations. Fleeting bits of understanding."

She looked out the side window into the darkness. "The hero team you lead isn't working for a government or a corporation. They aren't used to oppress people or make the elites look good. They aren't just about convincing people their government cares. They are independent and dedicated to protecting the world."

Trev chuckled. "Come on. I'm a cocky guy with a big ego, but I'm supposed to become the leader of the ultimate hero team? I won't leave a man to die, but I'm no hero."

"Only because your parents didn't want you to be one," Cassie challenged. "Now you have to ask yourself if they did that for the right reasons."

"It goes beyond that." Trev gestured at the window, frowning at the cracks. "I came here to run an exciting race and make money. I got in a bunch of fights along the way. The idea of me leading a hero team?" He laughed. "It gets funnier the more I think of it."

"Laugh if you want," Cassie replied. "That was what I saw in the first of three linked visions. I saw two more after that one. In the first, you were fighting a small army, but…" She sighed. "This is going to sound insane."

"We crossed that bridge a long time ago, Little Miss Sees-the-Future-While-Cheating-At-Cards-During-Assassinations. You can't go back to pretending this is all normal."

"In that vision, Jonathan Tallmere is there. I'm sure he's in charge of the army you're fighting. The vision isn't one hundred percent clear about why he's there, though he didn't seem happy."

Trev jerked back and smacked his head on the door. He winced and rubbed it. "Jonathan Tallmere, as in the CEO and founder of 46P1?"

Cassie nodded slowly. "I can't be certain if he was just there or leading the army, but the army wasn't just empowered security. There were conventional 46P1 security and WTs."

"Assuming we trust your vision, that could mean everything from Jonathan Tallmere being a bad guy to somebody's controlling him," Trev suggested. "Or maybe he was unhappy because of the army. He might have been on my side, trying to regain control of the army."

"I just don't know."

"If I was evil and an AA-level mind controller, taking control of him would make sense. Being super-obvious like the Dark Empress of Bangor will get you targeted and taken down." Trev folded his arms. "There are all those stories about 46P1, but those might just be rumors."

Cassie nodded.

"You do understand that I'm not ready to declare war on 46P1 based on an unclear vision, right?" Trev asked. "Even with my parents telling me not to trust the company."

"I'm just trying to tell you everything I know so you can make an informed decision."

"You had another vision?"

"Yes, and the last vision was even further out."

"Weirder than Tallmere?" Trev frowned.

"No, I meant I believe it took place farther in the future."

"Further in the future than the one where I'm running a hero team?"

Cassie nodded. "Yes." She stared at her hands. "I tried to convince myself it wasn't real at first."

Trev frowned. "Why?"

"Because it scared me. In it, the hero team was fighting a villain made of pure purple light. The rubble of a city lay beneath him, half-blasted away. This is the part I really can't explain. Somehow, I knew the man of light was linked to the truth behind the Big Change."

She shivered. "If that's real, he could be the most dangerous man on the planet. Far more dangerous than Ground Zero or the Empress of Bangor. The Big Change was the greatest mass casualty event in human history."

"You believe all that?" Trev asked, searching her eyes and face for hints that she was lying or joking. "Purple Light Guy does seem suspicious, given my power."

"I do believe it. I wish I didn't since my life would be much simpler, but I do." Cassie smiled wistfully. "When I had the visions, I looked through the 46P1 files I had access to and some I needed to poke around to get. I thought that if Tallmere was involved in something dangerous, maybe I'd find evidence of the mysterious hero from my first vision in the company's systems."

Trev smirked. "You mean the mysterious me?"

Cassie rolled her eyes. "I didn't know who the hero was then. During my research, I stumbled upon a file about your parents. It didn't have information about them being heroes, but when I saw your picture, I recognized you as the younger version of…"

"Me?"

"Exactly. Right then and there, I decided I needed to track you down. That eventually brought me here, where my seduction failed, so I hacked the race systems to become your tourist."

Trev chuckled. "When I think about it, that's the least disturbing thing about this entire conversation."

Cassie laughed back. "Yeah, I suppose it is." She spread her hands. "There it is. The reason I'm so obsessed with you. I've told you everything I know for certain and held nothing back. What do you think?"

"I don't know. I really don't." Trev shook his head. "It's hard to wrap my head around what you're saying. I know you believe what you saw, and I don't doubt you saw it, but that doesn't mean I'm this future ultimate superhero like you're saying."

He rubbed his temples. "On the other hand, Tallmere and 46P1 are sketchy, and it'd make sense if my parents knew something so bad that they wanted me to keep my distance from doing hero work for either the 46P1 or the NEUS, which is under 46P1's influence."

A hopeful look crossed Cassie's face. "The only real question is, where do we go from here?"

"I'm not ready to believe I'm a fated superhero of prophecy." Trev grinned at her. "You really are Cassandra."

"I can shoot you and end the prophecy right now," she replied with a mock glare. "The future can always be changed."

"I also liked taking down those bandits and saving Diego," Trev admitted. "I don't think it'd hurt to help people occasionally while we figure things out. Jack always tells me I need a goal other than what I eat for dinner, so he won't object after I tell him all the crazy stuff you said. We can figure out if I'm who you think I am. If it's all wrong, then whatever. At least we had a few laughs along the way."

Cassie sighed with relief. "You don't know how glad I am to hear that. I thought that after I told you everything, you'd tell me to go back to Des Moines and never talk to you again."

"In the meantime, I'm going to get something out of it. Whatever I might be in the future, I'm still a cocky guy who likes his rewards." Trev pointed at her.

Cassie's brow lifted. "You want me as a reward?"

Trev laughed. "Not exactly. I can shoot a gun and throw a punch, but not as well as an elite ex-security agent for 46P1. More training wouldn't hurt. We don't only have Hercules to hide my powers. Right now, I'm more powerful in the WT than without it, but if what you're saying is true and I train with you, that won't be true. You could make me stronger in every way."

Cassie put her hand on his shoulder. "I'm more than happy to train you. We can improve our abilities together. I know you don't accept it yet, but you're fated to be the greatest hero of your generation."

"When a beautiful woman asks you to do something, it's hard to say no."

Cassie scoffed. "I wish you believed that a few days ago."

Trev liked her hand on his shoulder more than he should. He reached up and tugged it off before his inherent feminine wiles defense failed. "To be clear, if I become convinced that this is more trouble than it's worth, we'll be done. Okay?"

"I understand," Cassie answered. "I don't believe it'll come to that, but I understand."

Trev pulled out his phone. "The bounty money the mercs sent our way means I didn't have to win the race, though I want to come back next year and prove something."

"What do you have to prove?" Cassie asked.

"I want to prove we would have been the fastest. Those bandit bastards screwed our time." Trev shook his head.

Cassie stared at him in disbelief. "I tell you that you might be the ultimate legendary hero and that you'll be taking on the CEO of one of the most powerful corporations on the planet, and you're more concerned about proving you can take first place in a desert race."

"What's the problem?"

Cassie groaned. "We've got a lot of work to do to get you ready, hero."

THE STORY CONTINUES

The story continues in book two, *Bounties and Changes,* coming soon to Amazon and Kindle Unlimited.

Claim Your Copy Here

MICHAEL'S NOTES

AUGUST 19, 2024

Thank you for reading all the way through the book, and then reading these author notes as well!

I never wanted to be in the race...

As I sit here, reflecting on the story you've just read, I'm reminded of an experience that partly inspired this tale - my encounter with the 'real' Baja 1000 a few years ago.

For those unfamiliar, the Baja 1000 is an annual Mexican off-road motorsport race held on the Baja California Peninsula. It's renowned as one of the most prestigious off-road races in the world, attracting daredevils and adrenaline junkies from across the globe.

In our story, you've followed our protagonist and his friend as they tackle a "Mad Max" version of this grueling race. Their motivation? Cold, hard cash. No heroic saves or world-changing quests here - just the raw pursuit of fortune in a high-stakes, high-octane environment.

You might have noticed a new character in the mix - a

particularly loquacious young woman whose constant chatter grates on our hero's nerves. Her addition to the team adds a layer of interpersonal tension to an already stressful situation, mirroring the way unexpected challenges can arise in the midst of carefully laid plans.

While crafting this narrative, I drew upon a personal experience that, while not as dramatic as our fictional race, certainly left an impression.

During a move, my wife and I found ourselves navigating regular roads in our SUV, surrounded by the chaos of the Baja 1000.

The competition trucks, in their frenzy to gain an edge, would tear past us on public roads, leaving trails of oil, shredded tires, and debris in their wake (usually just dust, rocks and close maneuvers I didn't want to be a part of).

It felt as though we had inadvertently stumbled onto the race course itself - a surreal and somewhat terrifying experience that blurred the lines between spectator and unwilling participant.

There was even a 'pop up' gasoline stop where you got your gas out of 55 gallon drums. I know that wasn't safe.

This brush with the raw, unfiltered energy of the Baja 1000 sparked my imagination.

What if the race was even more extreme? What if the stakes were higher, the dangers more acute? These questions led to the story you've just read - a tale that pushes the boundaries of the real-life race into a realm where the line between competition and survival becomes increasingly blurred.

In crafting this narrative, I aimed to capture the gritty realism of off-road racing while injecting it with a dose of speculative fiction (superhero, post-apocalyptic and unwilling hero). The result is a story that I hope resonates with the thrill-seekers among you, while also providing food for thought about the lengths we go to for financial gain and the unexpected alliances formed under extreme circumstances.

Thank you for joining me on this dust-covered, adrenaline-fueled journey. Whether you're a long-time fan of motorsports or simply enjoy a tale of high-stakes adventure, I hope this story has provided you with a few hours of entertainment and perhaps a new perspective on the world of off-road racing and a desire to join our characters in book 02!

Ad Aeternitatem,
    Michael Anderle

BOOKS BY MICHAEL ANDERLE

Sign up for the LMBPN email list to be notified of new releases and special deals!

https://lmbpn.com/email/

For a complete list of books by Michael Anderle, please visit:

www.lmbpn.com/ma-books/

CONNECT WITH THE AUTHORS

Connect with Michael Anderle

Website: http://lmbpn.com

Email List: https://michael.beehiiv.com/

https://www.facebook.com/LMBPNPublishing

https://twitter.com/MichaelAnderle

https://www.instagram.com/lmbpn_publishing/

https://www.bookbub.com/authors/michael-anderle

www.ingramcontent.com/pod-product-compliance
Lightning Source LLC
LaVergne TN
LVHW091711070526
838199LV00050B/2352